BROKEN TRAIL

BROKEN TRAIL

AMANDA CASILE

Content Warning: This novel touches upon sensitive subjects including body horror, disturbing imagery, death of a loved one, and children in peril and may be disturbing to some readers.

CamCat Books
2810 Coliseum Centre Drive, Suite 300
Charlotte, NC 28217-4574

This is a work of fiction. Names, characters, places, and incidents are either products of the author's imagination or are used fictitiously.

Hardcover ISBN 9780744312065
Paperback ISBN 9780744312089
eBook ISBN 9780744312102

Library of Congress Control Number: 2025940123

Book and cover design by Maryann Appel
Interior artwork by George Peters

5 3 1 2 4

To my loves, E, M, and D

Thank you for always exploring the wilderness with me

And to all the bitches still being burned as witches

May we leave all our pyres empty

AUTHOR'S NOTE

WHILE BROKEN TRAIL and the mountain on which it is set are purely fictional, its general location outside Vancouver would place it on the unceded traditional territories of the xʷməθkʷəy̓əm (Musqueam), Sḵwx̱wú7mesh (Squamish), and səlilwətaɬ (Tsleil-Waututh) Nations. My book intentionally does not attempt to tell the stories of these peoples as I do not feel they are my stories to tell. However, if you'd like more of their stories, there are many amazing Indigenous Canadian authors for you to check out, including but not at all limited to:

Lance Chalmers
Richard Wagamese
Christopher Dinsdale
Janet Romain
Drew Hayden Taylor
Joanne Arnott

There are also many excellent horror and horror-adjacent works written by Indigenous authors that you should absolutely go find and read. I have included my favorites below, but there are many more:

Never Whistle at Night by Shane Hawk
Bad Cree by Jessica Johns
My Heart Is a Chainsaw by Stephen Graham Jones
Moon of the Crusted Snow by Waubgeshig Rice
Beast by Richard Van Camp
Indian Burial Ground by Nick Medina
And Then She Fell by Alicia Elliott
The Unfinished by Cheryl Isaacs

I hope you enjoy,
Amanda Casile

CHAPTER ONE

BLOOD POOLED IN the corners of his mouth and dripped from the slashes across his arms and cheeks. His heartbeat pounded in his ears as he ran, branches tearing at him as he sprinted further, further, further from the trail. He wanted to look back, to check on her, but he couldn't stop or even slow to get his bearings because *it* was right behind him, the beast of the thing. With every audible exhale close behind him—too close—he imagined its putrid breath caressing his neck, humid and hungry. The beast was closing in.

His stomach pitched as he stumbled forward over a root, chin cracking against the ground, mud mixing with the blood on his tongue. He coughed and retched and raised himself up, but not fast enough. Something sharp wrenched into his side, and a jaw closed around his throat, tightening, tightening, tightening.

The last thing he heard before the world went black was his fiancée's bloodcurdling scream.

CHAPTER TWO

"I HOPE YOU'RE not thinking this will be a survival story. Most of the characters didn't survive. And those of us who did, well, you know . . ."

Juliana leaned away from Clara and gestured to herself—slight frame draped in gray, hospital-issue sweats—and then to the small room.

Clara laid a recorder on the arm of her chair and poised her pen over her clipboard. "You're thinking of your life as a story? And yourself as a character." She filed this away—coping mechanism? Delusion?

"Isn't it? Aren't I? Apparently I'm all over the papers as far as Seattle."

"I need to establish that you know the difference between what's real and what's a story."

"Do *you* know, Clara?" Juliana stood and filled two plastic cups with water at the small sink tucked into the corner. "Sorry, I'm not allowed anything stronger than water in here."

Clara took a sip, trying to swallow down her doubts. "Yes, I know what's real. What's real is that you're stuck in this hospital and you shouldn't be. I want to help you with that."

"This is what they do with people like me." Juliana's gaze drifted up the wall to her left, to the empty space there. She shook her head nearly imperceptibly before returning her gaze to Clara's. "I'm sorry, but I don't think you can help me. It doesn't matter now, does it? The judge gave his sentence. I know what they all think of me. You should give up."

Juliana pulled her long hair into a messy bun on top of her head, securing it with an elastic from her slender wrist. The gesture was one Clara's own daughter Tilly did several times a day, and the similarity left her a bit off kilter. Juliana stood, crossed her arms—a fragile barrier—and leaned against the bars of the window.

Juliana wasn't much older than Tilly really, but dark purple valleys hovered beneath her eyes and in the hollows of her cheeks. Her gaze held no fire, no spark for life that Clara still hoped Tilly would get back someday. Whatever happened to Juliana on that trail, it killed something vital within her.

"I won't give up," Clara said. She may have failed with Emilio. With Tilly—more than a few times. She wouldn't, *couldn't* fail with Juliana.

But you're so good at failing, her inner voice taunted, sounding suspiciously like her mother.

"What happened to Gavin, Juliana?" Clara pressed, not for the first time. "If you just give me a few more details, I can help you."

Juliana's eyes were flat, a black contrast to the sunset blazing through the barred window behind her, as she ran them up and down over Clara's body and shrugged. "You *are* determined." It was a word so rarely applied to Clara that she startled a bit. *Determined.* She'd been called a push-over, unmotivated, indecisive. Never determined.

"I *am* determined. Determined to get you out of here. Since when do we institutionalize people just because they've lost someone they love?"

"I didn't just lose him," Juliana whispered, and Clara thought of the images she'd seen in the file. Too many of Gavin's insides visible. Too few of his outsides. There was no way—*no way* Juliana could have done that to him.

And yet, the judge had convicted her. There had been a lot of pressure to wrap up the case, both from the public and from the organizers of Broken Trail's triumphant opening. A new trail, set to revitalize the hiking industry in the area. It was bad publicity if an aggressive cougar or bear were making it its home and hunting grounds. But, fish and wildlife apparently hadn't seen any signs of wild animal involvement.

Apart from the teeth marks on Gavin's throat.

"We are going to appeal. If you'll help me. So, I need to know what happened to Gavin. Who do you keep saying didn't survive—are you talking about him?"

A tremor flashed across Juliana's face, her lips peeled back to reveal shiny white teeth. "Not *Gavin*. He was nothing. Gavin was useless."

Clara swallowed hard and reached forward to erase a few seconds of recording. "I'm going to remind you that I'm recording this as evidence in my case."

"Your case?" Juliana arched an eyebrow.

"Of course I meant our ca—*your* case. So, if not Gavin, then—"

"*Them*," Juliana hissed. "The ones who never leave me alone. The ones waiting, waiting, always waiting."

A nurse peeked in through the door at that moment, making Clara jump. She tapped her long purple fingernails against the edge of the door.

"I'm closing up for the evening shift, Mrs. Gomez. Will you be much longer?"

"Err . . . just a few more minutes, Leah. I'll make sure to lock up and sign out with—Is it Dani on nights this week?"

Leah nodded. "Don't forget to go home yourself, Dr. Gomez. Remember your girls."

Clara bristled at the familiarity. Leah had only been the lead nurse on Clara's shift for a few weeks and, while yes, they had chatted over lunch breaks, she wasn't ready to take best-friend-level advice from her nurse on duty.

Except, as the door clicked shut behind her, Clara realized she did need the reminder. A glance at her watch showed it was already almost seven. How had so much time passed already? Her younger daughter Maddy was at a sleepover, but Tilly would be at home waiting for her. They were meant to have a mother-daughter bonding night.

"Shit," she muttered, returning her eyes to her clipboard. She needed to get to the bottom of Juliana's trauma before it was too late. This institution was eating away at Juliana. She was a victim, not a murderer. Clara just needed to prove she hadn't committed a crime out of insanity but rather was now *appearing* insane due to the trauma of watching her boyfriend be mauled by a bear or a cougar or whatever wild animal left him in the horrific state he was found in.

She re-crossed her legs in the lumpy armchair squeezed into Juliana's tiny hospital room. She decided to take another tack. "You said you and Gavin used to hike quite a bit?"

Juliana gave a nod and gazed out the window. "My grandmother always told me nature was a balm."

Clara leaned forward. "But you hadn't hiked Broken Trail before."

Her patient's eyes snapped up to hers, quick and impatient. "I'm sure you know that trail had only just opened."

"Yes, of course. So this was your first time?"

"My grandmother was right. Nature has always been a balm. You should take care of your daughters." Juliana leaned forward and took Clara's hand between her own. Clara startled, static electricity lighting up her arm. "What are their names again?"

"Madison and Matilda," Clara said automatically. "Eleven and seventeen."

"Beautiful," Juliana whispered. "So nice that you can be there for them. I never knew my mother. It's tragic when those you love are taken from you too soon." Light glistened off the tears in Juliana's eyes.

"I know, and I'm so sorry for your loss," Clara said, lamely. People always assumed, because of her training, that Clara would know the right things to say in moments like this, but the truth was, she was a shitty psychologist. That's the real reason she went into criminal psychology—she figured she wouldn't have to listen to and dissect other people's feelings as much. It was more profiling, determining "yes this person has an underlying mental health disorder" or "no they're actually evil."

Tears fell over Juliana's cheeks in slow, silent rivers, and Clara wanted desperately to pull her hand out of the woman's grasp.

"I'm—I'm really sorry for all that happened to you." Clara looked at her their linked hands and swallowed back the lump that swelled unexpectedly in her throat. She couldn't even handle her own feelings, much less someone else's.

"*Sorry?*" Juliana's voice slithered from her throat like a dry rasp, so jarring Clara finally did pull her hand away. "I lost everything and you're *sorry?*" The sun slid down below the top of the mountain outside, the shadows engulfing Juliana's small frame as though she were slipping below the opaque surface of water. Loss surrounded her like a tangible entity, its tendrils flooding their barriers and reaching toward Clara like liquid fiddleheads unfurling in fast motion.

Juliana's hospital issued shirt slid to the side, revealing a tattoo inked along her collarbone—an owl with wings outstretched, beak open in a silent cry, one of its eyes nothing more than a pitted hole. The woman straightened and loomed over Clara, her presence suddenly larger than before, thin lips pulled back in a teeth-exposing snarl. Now there was fire in those black eyes, but not the youthful spark Clara had been looking for earlier. It was a cold fire, a fire in which something grew, feral and meaty, ready to devour all in its path.

"I—I didn't mean. I meant I'm so—I meant all the things that happened to you shouldn't have happened. You're a . . . a victim. It's not fair. But if you let me help you . . ." Clara stammered, pressing herself further back into her chair, her clipboard sliding from her hand onto the floor with a harsh clatter.

Juliana grabbed Clara's arms above the elbow, digging her nails in. Her breath moved the tiny hairs along Clara's forehead. "You want to help me? Let's see you try."

Clara froze a moment transfixed, too stricken to pull away. Any resemblance to Tilly was gone. Juliana was all teeth and eyes and skin. And that terrifying owl tattoo that hovered just at eye level as Juliana dipped her head and licked Clara's cheek, chin to temple. Her tongue was warm and rough and sent a shiver of nausea through Clara.

A streetlight outside switched on then, banishing the darkness beyond the window, and Juliana pulled back, seeming to shrink again. She sagged onto the bed, a low whimper escaping her chapped and purpled lips.

Clara bent to retrieve her clipboard with a shaking hand and pulled herself into the chair once more before her knees gave out. She wiped a forearm across her cheek, but it came away dry, rather than slimy with saliva as she'd anticipated. She looked at her arms where Juliana's nails had dug in, but there were no red marks.

Her thoughts flailed, trying to make sense of what just happened as she searched for the right words to say. Juliana sobbed into her hands on the bed across from Clara. Had any of that really happened? In Juliana's file, there wasn't a single mention of mental health issues or therapy in her adult life. As a child, she'd had a few difficult times in school, and eventually they'd brought in a psychologist, but after age twelve, any mention of mental health issues stopped. She'd graduated from high school at an alternative school near her grandmother's house and had been accepted to the University of Washington's English program two years ago, which is where she'd met Gavin. On paper, Juliana appeared to be a well-adjusted, motivated college student. She got decent grades, had a group of friends, and none of them reported odd or aberrant behavior.

So, why did she just lick Clara?

Or . . . did she really?

Clara swallowed. "Shh-shh," she whispered, and placed a hand on Juliana's bony back, shoulder blades poking up like fragile wings. The tension in her chest receded like a tide and she found herself gasping for breath.

She thought of all the times she'd comforted Tilly over the years, over a scraped knee or a lost soccer game or a broken heart. She wished Tilly would come to her now, as easily as she used to, instead of keeping her feelings so bottled up inside her, always behind closed doors until she exploded like an atom bomb. Tilly felt lost, distant, but Juliana was right here, beneath Clara's palm. She could help her.

"Nothing can help me," Juliana said, rising up and wiping a hand across her puffy eyes. "They won't leave me alone." Some of her dark, frizzy hairs came loose and hung in front of her face.

Clara blinked, confused. "Who won't leave you alone? The nurses? I can talk to them, maybe? I—I want to help."

"Okay," Juliana whispered. "Okay you can try to help. But first, I need a favor."

"If I'm able to, I will do it," Clara whispered, wanting nothing more than to save this girl.

CHAPTER THREE

DR. BENTON'S OFFICE smelled inexplicably of mint and Pine Sol, despite every surface in the cramped space being coated in a layer of dust at least a centimeter thick. Dr. Benton was squeezed into a vintage vinyl chair in classic hospital teal, which squeaked when he turned toward the door. He rested his elbows on one of the stacks of files lining his desk and took Clara in.

Clara looked around a few moments before lifting another stack of files off the chair opposite Dr. Benton and moving them to the floor. She sat and let out a slow exhale, an attempt to release the tension that had been plaguing her ever since she arrived home the night before to find the house empty, Tilly nowhere to be found. But that was a problem for home Clara. Right now, she needed to focus on work. And Juliana. Something she could fix.

"Thank you for coming in, Clara," Dr. Benton said, a slight wheeze trailing his words.

"Thanks for seeing me, sir. I had a few questions for you."

He nodded. "And I you, but please, ladies first."

Clara crossed and uncrossed her legs before finally planting both her feet firmly on the floor and trying to sit up straight in the uncomfortable chair. "I'd like to request a short leave for Juliana Crawford, patient 1832. I have reason to—"

"Ms. Gomez," Dr. Benton interrupted, his voice patronizingly patient. "I had a feeling you might come to me with a request regarding that particular patient. And that's precisely what I wanted to speak to you about."

Clara's fingers went to the edge of her blazer, plucking at the tiny threads there that held the whole hem together. "Okay?" she responded.

"The nurses tell me you've been spending quite a bit of time with Ms. Crawford."

"Sir, I assure you—"

"While I admit she is an interesting case, I must remind you that you have a substantial caseload of other inmates who are also deserving of your intervention, some of who are still awaiting trial. You have an obligation, Ms. Gomez, to serve each and every one of your patients equally."

Clara's muscles tensed, a familiar ringing building in her ear. What he was saying was true. It filled her with the same sickly shame she felt when her mother pointed out all the times Clara had embarrassed her in front of her "society" friends.

She gave a nod. "It won't happen again, sir. But if I could just take patient 1832 on a short, therapeutic outing? I feel we are quite close to a breakthrough. I'm happy to submit the paperwork, but I wanted to speak with you first." Her words stumbled over each other. It wasn't the way she'd intended to pitch the idea, but he left her no choice.

"There is no need. Ms. Crawford has demonstrated that she is not safe outside the confines of this hospital. It would be a disservice to the public, to Ms. Crawford, and to *you* Ms. Gomez to allow such a thing. I cannot give my approval for this. Now, please, ensure you meet your other patient quotas this week, yes?" He picked up a file and began shuffling papers around, indicating that their meeting was complete.

Clara burned with frustration. The reason Juliana appeared unfit to go about in public was because she was trapped in a tiny room with barred windows. Her only socialization time was spent with other inmates—who consisted of murderers and worse—or her psychologists and nurses. That would drive anyone insane.

Hell—Clara thought, remembering her episode with Juliana—it was even driving her a little bit insane. Juliana was right. She needed to be in nature. To feel its balm.

"I'm helping Juliana create a case for an appeal, and I think the key to having her open up is to get her out of this, frankly, *stifling* hospital. I think if I can just do that, we'll be able to see the real Juliana, not this traumatized inmate we've created."

Dr. Benton steepled his hands under his chin. "*We've* created? Ms. Crawford came to us exactly as she is now. We didn't do this. That is all Juliana. And it's my professional opinion that she's going to be here a long, *long* time. Now, Clara, if you can't maintain objectivity on this case, you may need to be placed on leave." His face softened momentarily. "I know you are going through a lot right now. So please, if you need support, don't hesitate to ask. In the meantime, back to work with you." His serious scowl returned as he made a shooing motion with his hands and spun his chair around to a stack of files in the back of his office. Clara showed herself out, hands shaking with unexpected rage.

CHAPTER FOUR

CLARA'S KNUCKLES WERE white against the charcoal of her steering wheel, lip pressed between her teeth. She ran the encounter over and over in her mind, wondering if she'd made the right choice. Adrenaline coursed through her veins, the rush almost a relief after the numbness and exhaustion she'd been walking around with for the four months since her divorce. She hadn't even cried when Emilio left, simply jumped back into life like nothing had changed, just one less plate at the dinner table, one less pair of shoes clogging up the entry. It was a skill she'd learned from her mother. So what if she and Emilio had been married almost twenty years? Clara had a job, a family to support, didn't have time to delve any deeper than that.

The car chimed and Emilio's name popped up on the dash screen. Clara checked the clock. "Shit."

Juliana cleared her throat in the passenger seat. "Everything okay?" her voice rasped, but otherwise that was the only evidence she'd been crying less than an hour before. When Clara broke the news to her that Dr. Benton had refused her outing request, Juliana sobbed and something inside Clara had shattered.

Now she sat, ramrod straight, in the passenger seat, hair pulled into a tidy ponytail, eyes tracking the trees shooting past outside the window.

Blood pounded in Clara's ears. *What have I done? What have I done?* "Uh. Yes. I mean, not really. That's my ex." She glanced beside her, guilty, apologetic. Her problems were minuscule compared to what Juliana was going through. "Shit," she hissed again through her teeth. She couldn't bring Juliana home, could she? She hadn't thought beyond pulling the car around to the back parking lot where Juliana said she would meet her. They hadn't discussed where they would go.

Juliana's eyes sparkled, otherworldly in the headlights from an oncoming vehicle. "Oh no. Do you need to take it?"

"Absolutely not," Clara responded. Emilio didn't need any more ammunition to push for full custody. If he caught wind that she'd helped an inmate escape, there would be no hope for her at all. Eventually someone *would* catch wind of it, though. There were cameras in the facility. They were probably checking them now.

Another chime interrupted her thoughts. She held her breath and glanced at the name on the dash screen. "Message from Dr. Benton," the green letters glared at her.

Clara swallowed past the low hum building in the back of her throat. The familiar beginnings of a panic attack. The enormity of what she'd done. She clamped her teeth down and breathed slowly through her nose. All she'd done was provide a vehicle and wait in the back parking lot for a few extra minutes until Juliana came out the back door, looking as calm as a summer day. She wasn't even running.

But why should she? She was harmless, hurting, grieving. And they were keeping her in there like some kind of prisoner. Clara had done the right thing. The right thing for this girl. Clara glanced over again. Sweat trickled down her back beneath her blouse and she turned up the A/C.

"So, where should I take you?" she asked, wondering what Tilly and Maddy would say if Clara brought home a guest for the night. Juliana's file indicated that she had no living family.

"Don't worry," Juliana said, "we're almost there." In her lap, her fingers twisted in and out of a hole in her sweatpants.

A sign passed in Clara's peripheral vision—Route 10. Juliana froze, motionless.

Here. A whisper slid through the Subaru's interior like a circling raptor. Clara noticed her hand hovering over the turn signal. Had Juliana said that? She glanced beside her. Juliana's head turned slowly toward her, eyes wide. "Do you want to go for a hike?" Her voice was mechanical, flat. Clara's breath quickened.

It was the road to Broken Trail. She'd past the exit every day on her way to and from work, and each time she wondered what it was like. What kind of trees bordered the entrance to the trail? How grueling was the climb? Which wildflowers were in bloom when Juliana was there, unaware that the love of her life would be torn apart in mere hours? She had never had a desire to go there herself, though. There was always some kind of invisible barrier, almost like a revulsion, that kept her from ever entertaining the thought of flicking her turn signal and sliding off to the right. No, it wasn't revulsion. It was fear, she realized. Fear of the wilderness. Fear of the unknown.

But now . . .

The lane markers split, the exit ramp widening out to her right. Juliana continued to stare at her, silent and motionless. Now the urge swelled inside her like a wave pulling her car off onto the tributary of the exit, almost as though she weren't even in control of it. Tilly and Maddy were both busy, the sitter lined up to take them to their evening swim class. Clara had time. There was nothing there for her but the empty house and echoes of her old life.

"I think . . . maybe we should—" Clara trailed off.

Juliana gave a barely perceptible nod. Clara flicked her turn signal and exited the highway onto the smaller two-lane road that snaked its way through suburbs before quickly ascending into the mountains.

They rode in silence for a while, Clara's insides spinning like an out of control carousel. She wanted to help Juliana, really she did, but as she tried to focus on the road, images of Juliana tearing her hospital garb, her slick tongue sliding up Clara's cheek, her matte black eyes gazing out the window—images that reminded her perhaps she was wrong about Juliana—muddled her thoughts.

Sirens blared in her skull. This was the wrong choice. She had made a terrible mistake. She was sure of it. How had she even ended up in this situation? Trying to help someone—Clara should know better. She could barely even help herself. Did it count as abduction, even if Juliana wanted it?

Had Clara committed a crime? Juliana had no known next of kin, but what about friends? Friends who would come searching for her if she went missing from the institution. Not to mention Dr. Benton. Clara slowed, nausea gnawing at her insides, looking for a place to turn around.

"Tell me about your girls." Juliana's voice made her jump.

"They're . . . well, they're doing okay. You know?"

Juliana nodded and leaned forward. A "keep going" gesture. "Still into sports?"

Clara started babbling, on autopilot. "They both love swimming, although Tilly's been missing a lot lately, since the . . . since Emilio left. Maddy's my artist. Tilly loves music. They're good. Really good," Clara said, her eyes still frantically searching the edges of the road for a pull out. Was the road here always so narrow, or had it been washed out with the rain a few weeks ago? "Sometimes I just wish there were like, an instruction manual though. I mean like, for parenting. I wish someone would just tell me what to do. You know?"

Juliana's hand clamped over Clara's forearm. "You don't always have to do what the voices tell you to."

Clara gasped. "What?"

Juliana's vice grip released. "You don't have to do what people tell you to. That's all. Trust your gut."

"Okay," Clara said, though she was beginning to think nothing about this was okay. Her gut had gotten her into this mess. She swallowed and darted a glance over to Juliana who sat, perfectly relaxed in the passenger seat, twirling a lock of dark hair. Had she imagined it? But her arm still stung from where the woman's anemic fingers had dug in.

As the road curved, the foliage grew denser, tightly packed trees leaning over as if to welcome them with a hug. Or rip them from the vehicle. Clara shuddered in the darkness.

The Subaru bounced and swayed over the rocks and potholes. Just then, something ghostly white bolted across the double beam of her headlights, flashing once, twice before disappearing into the night beyond. Clara stomped on the brakes, and the weighty rear of the car swung right and then left before steadying itself again. She came to an abrupt halt, her ears pounding with wingbeats. Or was it heartbeats? She couldn't tell the difference. She gently withdrew her right arm from across Juliana's midriff, where she'd flung it in some misguided maternal instinct.

"Sorry," she whispered. Her breath came in short bursts as she eased the Subaru back into a slow roll forward. The headlights caught another flash of white, in a tree beside the road.

"It's just an owl," Juliana said, but a shiver ran through Clara. She turned the heat up in the car. The creature's black eyes were empty, as though all the shadows of the night stared at her through a mask.

Clara tore her gaze away—*just an owl*—and pressed the Subaru into a faster stumble. Her back arched forward, away from the seat, a pointless fear response.

Heat rose in her cheeks, embarrassment at her inability to experience awe at the sight of such a thing. Instead, a growing sense of dread crawled up from the depths of her gut. The shadowy trees pressed in further, making her wonder—not for the first time—what the hell she was doing out here in the middle of the wilderness as the sun slid further and further below the horizon.

"I think I should take you back."

"No." The single syllable was firm and solid, a gavel sliding down between them. Clara flinched and Juliana's face softened.

"I can't go back there. You don't know what it was like. This is good for me. Exposure therapy, like you said." She turned to gaze out the passenger side window again at the trees sliding past in blurs of dark green and black. Her hand pressed against the glass, fingers splayed wide.

The road opened up into a clearing on the right, just big enough for three or four cars to park. Clara eased into one of the parking spots. A fresh signpost hung straight ahead, bright white paint marking the start of Broken Trail. She took a steadying breath, reminding herself the owl sighting was a beautiful experience, not a creepy one. Since when did she become so jumpy? *Maybe since you broke someone out of a mental institution?*

She swallowed back the bile that rose in her throat. Out here, they were entirely alone. The loneliness she'd felt inside for the past four months now surrounded her on all sides. Something real, solid, that would never leave her.

A voice swirled through the car, nothing more than a whispered promise, a memory. *Forever*. He'd said it to her so many times, their fingers, bodies, lives intertwined. And now he was gone, leaving nothing but a cold, dark hole in the space he'd filled for decades.

The mechanical clunk of Juliana's door opening brought Clara back to the present. A chill filled the car as Juliana stepped out into the forest. She turned back with a sad smile before inhaling deeply. "Feels like just yesterday I was here with Gavin. Starting our hike. Come on," she said as though mirroring Clara's thoughts of loss, "I'll show you the trail."

Clara gazed down the path in front of her; only about eight feet of it was illuminated by her headlights before it turned to the left and disappeared into the shadows. "Isn't it a bit late?" she asked. "It's already getting dark." Again, she felt startled by the quick passage of time.

"We came all this way," Juliana said. "Come on."

Come come come.

The word echoed around Clara like dry leaves in the wind. Slowly, haltingly, as though learning a new dance, she unbuckled her seatbelt, pulled the lever, and swung the door open. She stumble-stepped out into the cold, her skin instantly tightening around her, breath catching. It was unseasonably cold, or maybe it was just the altitude.

It's the chill of fear, she thought. But fear probably wasn't necessary here, she reminded herself, the bear that attacked Gavin would probably be hibernating. There was nothing here but harmless trees and darkness. Beautiful owls, silent nights. Solace.

"What happened to me wasn't just wildlife." Juliana's voice floated back to her from up the trail where the woman stood like a specter, illuminated by the headlights Clara had left on so they could see. "It was . . ."

Clara hurried behind her, hoping to catch the words lost in the wind. "It was what? I didn't hear you." Frozen mud crunched underfoot, and she slipped on the frosty tree roots and rocks. Her feet urged her forward, moving on their own accord, while her toes curled away from the cold. She wore simple flats, not having planned to go fucking hiking up a mountain at night. The insistent *ding ding ding* of her open-door warning faded behind her as she scampered up the lighted section of trail.

The wind blew, and a susurration made its way across the forest. Branch to branch, whispers and creaks moved closer, corporeal, insistent. It crescendoed, echoing like a hundred discordant voices in Clara's head. She covered her ears with her stiff-frozen hands and turned back toward the car, but the trail behind was dark. Hadn't she left the headlights on? When she spun back around, Juliana had vanished from view.

"Juliana?" she called. Her voice sounded painfully quiet, as though the forest swallowed it whole. "Juliana?"

No answer. Clara reached for her phone to use its flashlight, but she must have left it in the car. "Fuck," she hissed and continued further up the earthy-smelling path, her impractical shoes slipping across the cold ground, near-frozen mud flowing over the low edges and leaking in to slick the area under the sole of her foot.

Her toe caught on the edge of a rock and she tumbled, something sharp hammering into her knee. "Ow! Juliana. Where are you? We need to go. This was a bad idea!" She stood again, slowly, gingerly, her pulse beating a rhythm in the fresh wound, the beginnings of a trickle down her shin.

The space around her was black as pitch. How much time had passed? She could barely see her hand in front of her face. Where was Juliana? She couldn't just leave her in the middle of nowhere. But she couldn't stay in the freezing, dark woods all night either. She turned in what she hoped was the right direction and stumbled down the trail.

The whispers of the woods grew louder, nipping at her heels, a pack of wolves. They began to coalesce, like scattered puzzle pieces forming a picture of their own volition, and their collective yell pierced her mind. *Come.* She ran faster. *Come come come*

A cloud cleared from in front of the sliver of moon, and in the faint silver light she saw her Subaru sitting there, almost translucent, unreal. The door hung open but the interior was black. She tumbled into the driver's seat and slammed the door shut, grasping for the keys in the ignition but coming away with only air. "What?" she whined, her breath catching. She patted down all the surfaces, reaching down to her footwell, poking into her pockets. As her frantic search for the keys continued, something pelted her driver's side window. Then another banged against the windshield. Suddenly the car was surrounded by objects hammering into it, the sound of it like the most extreme hail storm.

"What the *fuck*?" Clara paused in her search only to see hundreds of wings beating against the windows, windshield, sunroof. "Jesus," she whispered, momentarily stunned into inaction. Her heart hammered in her chest, mouth going dry. She had to get out of here.

She laid on the horn, hoping the blare of it would scare away the ravens, but they continued to batter against the car. There was a louder, cracking bang beside her head as a beak hit the window there, then another. Her throat tightened in terror. She had to go. She couldn't wait here. Clara let out a sob and pressed the horn again. Maybe Juliana would hear it and come. Clara couldn't leave her here, where Gavin had died, abandoned in the cold of night. The thought of it turned Clara's stomach. No, she couldn't leave Juliana here. But where had she gone? Another crack on the windshield, and Clara saw a small chink in the glass, as though a pebble had been thrown against it at great speed. Another crack resounded against her driver's side window again.

"Fuck," she hissed, reaching again with frantic fingers into and under everything in search of her keys, until she noticed the jab at the back of her thigh. They were smashed underneath her the whole time. She retrieved them with shaking fingers. She knew she'd left them in the ignition. Knew the headlights had been on. Hadn't they? Clara shook her head. She was really losing it now. She had to keep it together.

Could it be Juliana doing this? Maybe she'd removed the keys to save the car's battery and hid in the backseat out of fear? Maybe being where her boyfriend had died was just too much. Shit. Clara had known it would be too much. She couldn't even imagine what led her to bring Juliana out here. Clara cast a glance into the dark depths of the seat behind her, fully expecting to find a huddled, terrified Juliana there. But her gaze landed on nothing but crumpled papers and snack wrappers. The beating against the windows intensified, setting off a high-pitched whine in the back of Clara's throat.

She shoved the keys in the ignition, turned over the engine, and sped back toward the highway, tires squealing as she tried to outrun her mind's image of Juliana's dark form on the trail, a flurry of owls and ravens surrounding her, eyes black as winter.

CHAPTER FIVE

CLARA'S DASH LIT up with an incoming call as soon as she turned back onto the highway. She barely remembered the fevered sprint out of the woods, the one lane road passing by like a surreal blur. Her mouth tasted of blood and she forced herself to release her teeth from where they clung to the inside of her cheek, a nervous habit she'd started in college and never managed to shake. Her stomach was wrapped up in knots, and she exhaled deeply, trying to release it.

She tapped a finger against Emilio's name on the screen, imagining he were a bug she could simply crush with the pad of her finger, a problem so easy to force away.

"Clara?" His voice echoing in the empty car ignited a host of visceral memories. Family road trips, the day he proposed, the fight over where to spend Thanksgiving, whispered predawn nothings. She shuddered. "Clare?"

"Yeah. I'm here. Sorry I'm just . . . I'm just in the car. Work ran over."

A scoff on the other end of the line. "Ya think? It's almost nine p.m. Tilly's here."

"There? Wait, you mean *your* house? She's meant to be getting home from swimming now."

"Yes. Here. And swimming ended an hour ago, not that she went, though."

"Maddy—" Clara swallowed. How had it grown so late? She was sure she'd be home before eight. Bile rose in her throat.

"Maddy is fine. I mean, all things considered. The sitter drove her here too. They were both a little . . . confused when they got home from swimming and the house was dark. Where were you?"

"I told you. Work ran over."

"Clara." She knew Emilio so well, she could see him pinching the bridge of his nose, squeezing his eyes shut. This was going to be bad. "The cops brought Matilda here."

The Subaru swerved to the right, Clara's surprise jerking her so violently. "Cops? What—why?" Her teeth found the familiar grooves they'd worn on the inside of her mouth. Was it possible the cops had been notified about Juliana already? No. That was too fast; it wasn't possible.

Tears pricked the edges of her eyes. She blinked them away, the knot in her stomach returning with a vengeance. She inhaled and let it out slowly. "The girls know that if I'm not home when they get dropped off they can just have screen time and I'll make them dinner when I get there," she said, trying to keep her voice as even as possible.

"Jesus, Clara. This happens often?"

"This? No . . . this—I'm always home by eight. Okay?" She inhaled through her nose again, willing away the urge to puke.

"You weren't tonight."

"Why are the cops involved?" *I can fix this*, she thought. *I have to fix this.*

"Maybe I should wait until we're in person."

"I'm on my way to pick them up. Should be there in like a half hour."

"I didn't say tonight. They're going to stay with me tonight. But we do need to talk."

"No. Monday nights are mine."

"You aren't even *home*, Clare."

She could hear the strain in his voice. Emilio rarely, if ever, yelled.

But she knew when he was holding back.

"I have a very stressful job!" She ran a hand over her face, wiping away the image of Juliana tearing at her sweatpants.

"Your *job* is to be a mother to your children."

"Fuck off. Do not come at me with this again. We agreed long ago that I would have a career. End of discussion. We are not discussing this right now. Or ever."

"Clara, plenty of women have careers and still manage to prioritize their families. I have never understood why this is so difficult for you." Again, the sigh, the pinched forehead and squeezed eyes. "Listen. It doesn't matter. What matters is that Matilda was almost arrested tonight. She was caught stealing beer from the Giddy Mart. The owner there decided not to press charges."

"Okay," Clara said slowly, feeling like she'd been dropped from a great height, hit the surface of water wrong after a jump off the high-dive. "Okay . . . so . . ."

"They want to live with me for a while, Clare. And I think it's a good idea. The cops brought her to your house first—it's Monday after all, like you said. Your day. But the house was dark, so Tills asked them to bring her here."

"I'm coming to get them."

"They're already in pajamas."

"They don't have their toothbrushes."

"You don't think they have toothbrushes here? Beds? A home? They have everything here, Clara. We're all worried about you. It's not forever, just till you sort out whatever's happening at work."

Clara gritted her teeth together until her jaw squeaked, images of Juliana's ghostly white face dancing through her mind. "I'm not letting you take the kids. You've taken everything else."

"I'm not taking the kids. I'm *giving* you a break. Some time. Isn't that what you always asked for? Time to focus on your career."

"Dammit! Do not spin this like it's something I fucking want!"

"I gotta go. Maddy wants to read together. Maybe let's talk tomorrow? I can swing by over lunch. When they're at school."

"You are a *fucking asshole,*" Clara yelled, but he had already hung up. So only the night outside was there to listen.

The floodgates opened finally, the sob she'd been holding in through their whole phone call exploding out of her like a waterfall. She forced it back inside, pressing the heel of her hand against her forehead, and redialed the number, but he didn't answer. Fucking Emilio.

She wanted so badly to drive over to his house right this minute, but a voice inside her head told her that would make everything worse. They all needed time to cool off.

And besides, she *did* need to sort herself out. When Emilio mentioned cops, Clara was sure it was related to what she'd done, not a simple teen theft at a liquor store. A weird feeling of relief washed over her when she realized the cops were after Tills and not her. But it was only a matter of time before they realized Juliana was gone. Her teeth dug into the tender skin of her cheek again. She needed to fix this.

A text came in, the chime nearly making her jump out of her skin. An unknown number.

She clicked on the screen and the disembodied voice of Siri read out the words:

Thanks for the ride. Sorry I had to split. I didn't want you to get in trouble. Taking an Uber back now and will explain everything. Leaving your name out of it. You're in the clear, friend. Talk soon.

Clara looked at the number again, as though she could make sense of the digits there. She shook her head. Who else would thank her for a ride, tell her she was in the clear? But how would Juliana have a phone or money for an Uber?

Clara's mind swirled. She was certain Juliana hadn't had a phone on her when they'd left Solara. She pressed her fingers into her forehead and pulled into her driveway. This was too much to process at the moment.

She dropped her keys in the bowl beside her front door and flicked on the kitchen light. The house was quiet, cold. Like a tomb. And indeed, something dead did linger here, the wisps of her relationship with Emilio.

She saw it in the painting hung above the fireplace. They'd picked that one out together at some thrift store and then laughed as they stuck it in a fancy frame, joking that all their friends would probably think it was "high end art." She saw it in the coffee maker she had to dredge up from the basement when Emilio took their good espresso machine with him.

But it wasn't just that relationship that had died. She saw Tilly's hastily dropped backpack, the wet bathing suit probably still balled up inside it.

Saw Maddy's latest sculpture on the kitchen table with the blue ribbon taped onto it from her school art show.

Clara leaned against the counter with a sigh. Emilio was an asshole for sure, but there was at least one thing he was right about. Clara should have been here.

She pulled out her phone, intending to text her friend Naomi for sage advice—it was helpful having a best friend who was both a lawyer and just plain good at everything—but she nearly dropped the phone.

Instead of her home screen which normally sported a picture from five years ago of her girls in a candy store, she was greeted with a close-up photo of an owl.

An owl with only one eye.

CHAPTER SIX

JULIANA. THE NAME rode in on the October sunshine streaming through the window, burnt orange like the trees outside. Thoughts of a dark forest and flapping wings shimmered and shifted in her sleep-addled mind, like fish under ice. She'd lain awake most of the night, huddled under her blankets, muscles tense. But she must have drifted off sometime around dawn because a scent of coffee pulled her from the depths of a nightmare. Briefly, she thought of Emilio in the kitchen burning toast and fighting with the espresso machine.

She reached a hand out of her duvet cocoon to the other side of the bed. A slight depression dented the mattress from years of forming around his body. Her fingers felt around for a whisper of his warmth, but the bed was cold, of course. She brought her hand back to her chest to quell the wrenching stab. A depression there too, from years of forming around him.

This was going to kill her.

No.

She folded Emilio up, her origami wound, and shoved him back into the deepest part of her. A splinter beneath the skin of her heart. Easily ignored until she breathed the wrong way.

Juliana, her inner voice thrummed. The memories grew stronger, the ice around them melting. She snapped her eyes open and leaped off the bed, pulling on a pair of sweats from the nearby chair, heart pounding in her ears. She checked her phone—no calls from Solara, the police, or otherwise. And no more owl pictures; her lock screen sported the usual photo of her girls. She must have imagined the whole thing. It wouldn't be all that surprising, considering all the stress and exhaustion of yesterday. A sigh of relief strangled halfway out of her throat when she stopped.

Who was making coffee?

If the kids were at Emilio's, she thought, raking a brush through her tangled, mousy locks, then why did the house smell like coffee?

At the top of the stairs, Clara took a deep breath. Whoever was downstairs had easy access to her house. Clara and Emilio had never been free with keys to their place—they hadn't even given copies to old Mrs. Dougal next door. Maybe it was Emilio. She pressed down the little hopeful flutter inside her. It wouldn't be Emilio. He was surely at his house, "protecting" the kids from their mother. Clara clenched her teeth. Emilio had been a wonderful husband on many levels, and he was an even better father. But these four months without him let her see that, lonely or not, she was better off out from under him.

But if not Emilio, then who? An intruder who brewed coffee? Her heart pounded in her ears. Who knew what kind of strange people invaded homes? She had heard so many stories from her colleagues and her own clients, it was impossible to discount any scenario as unbelievable. She suddenly felt very vulnerable, alone in this big empty house, with nothing to protect her soft flesh other than the old, threadbare sweats she wore as pajamas. Clara fished her phone from her pocket, finger hovering over the emergency call button. She took another breath and descended the stairs as silently as she could, barely breathing.

The coffee had just finished percolating by the time her toes touched the cold tile floor. A woman with straight black hair that cascaded past her shoulders leaned against the counter, an empty mug between her two hands, eyes staring intently at the coffee maker. She looked up when she heard Clara enter.

"Morning," she said.

"Naomi?" Clara's breath released in a *whoosh*.

"I heard the news. How are you holding up?" Naomi's voice was staccato, to the point, as usual, but her eyes belied her concern.

Clara pulled up short, still trying to shake off her panic. "I'm . . . okay?" Which news? Had she heard through the grape vine that the girls were staying with Emilio now? It couldn't be the news about Juliana. Naomi worked in conjunction with Solara, frequently representing the inmates there, but Clara doubted she was on the top priority call list for an already-convicted inmate going missing.

"I've been worried sick about you ever since Dr. Benton called."

Clara gritted her teeth. Scratch the theory that Naomi wouldn't be called first. Naomi pulled the carafe from the coffee maker and poured a steaming mugful. She added a dollop of milk, and Clara watched it swirl around like a cloud of smoke.

"Dr. Benton?" she croaked. So they were talking about her behind her back now? Naomi passed the mug to her before pouring one for herself. Clara clutched it for dear life in her shaking hands.

"He was very worried. He knew how close you and Juliana were."

Clara nodded dumbly. This is not the way she thought this conversation would go, once people found out she'd helped Juliana disappear. For one, she thought there would be more handcuffs.

Unless the mysterious text last night *had* been from Juliana. Perhaps she did go back and clear Clara's name. Clara tried to rationalize how something like that would even be possible. Even if Juliana had claimed to have left on her own, surely there were cameras in the hospital. Someone must have seen her drive away with Juliana.

She took a quick sip of coffee. It was too hot, but the burn down her esophagus meant she was alive. For the time being. "We were—are—close. As close as my professionalism allows, of course."

"Honey." Naomi's face softened, and she covered the distance to Clara in a few swift strides, her pristine white Lululemon's swishing almost soundlessly. She wrapped her arms around Clara's shoulders. "Want to talk about it?"

The room spun. "Are you . . . punking me? What is going on?"

"I know it's hard she's gone, Clare. I know you saw Tilly in her."

"Gone . . . how? So . . . you know?" Clara pulled back, swallowing back the barb of Tilly and focusing on the small pieces she could hold onto.

Naomi put her hands on Clara's cheeks. "I can tell you're still in shock. That poor, poor unfortunate soul. You did your best for her, like you always do," she whispered. "Don't be so hard on yourself." Clara nodded dumbly. "Now, drink this coffee before it goes tepid. Come on, let's sit on the porch."

Clara followed the knife slice of her best friend out onto the covered porch she and Emilio had built together the year before Tilly was born. She'd told Naomi one day, mid-construction, "If our marriage can survive this, it can survive anything!" But she'd been wrong.

They sat in the gaudy rattan furniture his mother gifted them, and Naomi curled her legs beneath her. "Where are the girls? Shouldn't they be up?" she asked, looking around like she'd only just noticed the empty house.

Clara's hackles rose. She was still reeling from the unfinished conversation about Juliana, and the fact that the cops hadn't busted down the door yet. "They're at Emilio's. He wants them to stay there for a bit. I got home a little late yesterday and—well, he's going to use it in his case for custody, it sounds like."

She hated the way her voice sounded. Out of control, whiny. Naomi never had a hair or tone of voice out of place. She was always impeccable, and Clara hated to admit to herself the amount of energy she'd spent over the years trying to emulate Naomi's effortless ease. Now, with her divorce scrawled across her face like a neon sign and her job turning into a massive question mark, the gulf between Clara and her best friend had never felt larger.

Naomi's eyes went wide. "Oh honey. On top of everything—Although maybe that's for the best. With them away and your leave from work, it will give you some time for self-care." She turned a palm over in her lap and admired her manicure.

"My leave?"

"Dr. Benton told me all about it. I think it's a great idea. That's what stress leave is for, after all. This is a lot to process."

"I'll say," Clara mumbled into her coffee mug. She let her gaze wander across the yard, to the small bit of forest on the far side of the road. Her phone buzzed in her pocket.

"Sorry?" Naomi asked.

Clara glanced at her phone. A text had come in from that same unknown number: a square of thick foliage, drooping conifers, all of it imbued with an almost hypnotic vibrant green. Clara sighed, wishing she could dive right through the screen into the picture. Just looking at it ignited a sense of calm within her. *Nature is a balm.*

"Clara?" Naomi snapped her out of her daydream, and Clara quickly shoved her phone into her pocket.

"Nothing. Just, yep, stress leave." She nodded.

"Exactly." Naomi leaned forward. "I was thinking, Clare. You need a project. Something to take your mind off everything at Solara and to help you and the girls—I don't know—renew your bonds or something. What do you think?"

Clara swallowed back the strangled feeling that took hold of her throat. Naomi always had ideas about what Clara needed.

"Actually—" Clara started, ready to head Naomi off at the pass. She took a breath to give the idea time to form in her head and then turned back to Naomi. "I did have a thought. You know how you've been trying to get me and the girls to go on a hike with you? Well, I think we finally should. You know, with my . . . leave? And, self-care or whatever?"

Naomi's eyes lit up. "Girl, I think you are *on* to something! A trek through the woods is exactly what you need."

Clara let out a nervous chuckle, the type that always wormed its way out of her when she was about to make a bad decision. "Exactly. I think it will really help me process whatever . . . whatever happened."

"Of course it would. Nature cures all that ails you."

Clara froze momentarily, hearing the echo of what Juliana had said, what she herself had thought only moments earlier. She fingered the phone in her pocket as she geared up for the next thing she was about to say.

"And I think—I think the hike we do should be Broken Trail."

CHAPTER SEVEN

Vancouver, BC
May 2, 1974

Three crows on the windowsill this morning. The birth of a daughter. My mother taught me how to count crows, and I haven't forgotten.

I'm pregnant, which is something I never expected. But I guess that isn't saying much. For quite a time, I found it astounding that I was even alive. I didn't think about what would come of my life beyond just surviving.

But even when I did start to think of it, a real life with a future, babies were never a part of it. I've always been a solitary person. I'm okay with that. It's hard to make friends when you land suddenly in the middle of civilization at eleven years old, knowing no one, no family to speak of. It's hard to make friends when you're so visibly different from everyone else. But I've long gotten used to the stares by now.

It is my bark, these uneven lines that run across my face and forehead, weaving in and out of each other and changing the shape of my hairline. The ridges and hollows that striate my neck, my arms, my legs. It makes me tree-like: strong, silent, stoic. Trees see death all around them and still they soldier on, ever upward, to the white light of the sun. I don't much mind being like a tree.

Trees stand solid on their own. But more and more of late, I see my life straying from that solitary path. First, it was Donald—what that man sees in me, I have yet to figure out. Clearly, it's not my looks. I've always been a good person. I know this, good and kind and honest. But "lovable" is new to me. And yet, there's Donald. Always looking at me as though I shine on him like the warm sun above.

And now, this baby in me. A little girl, if the crows are to be trusted, and they always are.

Marie. I will call her Marie after my sister.

CHAPTER EIGHT

THE WOODS WERE never far.

Clara lived a city life, always had, but her city was surrounded by the sort of wilderness not known by most other urban centers. On more than one occasion, Emilio had to chase coyotes from the backyard. They had special garbage cans to keep the bears from rummaging. She'd even been camping a couple times as a child in the mountains nearby, when her father tried to act the rustic outdoorsman for a while. Back before the accident.

She remembered hair glued to her cheek with marshmallow, smoke in her eyes, limbs goose-bumped with mosquito bites. It lasted one summer before her parents mercifully called it quits and gave in to their city dispositions.

Clara had never achieved the sort of oneness with nature that she observed in her friends and neighbors. Where Clara was content to have drinks on a patio and stroll the busy streets, her friends all planned ski trips and trail runs and multi-day camping adventures. They possessed a kind of yearning for the outdoors, along with a seemingly innate knowledge of how to survive there, that she just couldn't muster. Why would you willfully subject yourself to that kind of discomfort?

If she was honest, it wasn't just the discomfort that kept her from immersing herself in nature's beauty, because she *could* see that it was beautiful sometimes; it was fear. There were too many unknowns in the woods, too many shadows, hollows, holes. Too many places for danger to lurk unnoticed. And no one out there to tell you what to do. Those few times she had camped with her parents, the flickering campfire didn't spell peace for her, instead it intensified the blackness beyond and made her skin crawl with the feeling of being watched. She shivered in her mother's arms, not from the cold, but from terror. The walls of the tent were too thin to keep the shadows out.

And yet, here she was driving headlong into the very wilderness that gave her nightmares. Not for the first time, she wondered what had possessed her to suggest this trip to Naomi. She'd thought about backing out numerous times over the past few weeks. But each time, a text from Juliana would remind her how good it would be for the girls. It took a few days before Clara had finally built up the courage to ask the mystery texter if she was, in fact, Juliana. She'd responded with a hysterical laughing emoji.

Of course it's me! Who else would it be?

And ever since, they'd been texting almost daily. At first, Clara tried to be covert, in case someone might use her text history as evidence of her involvement in Juliana's escape attempt. She asked Juliana if she got in trouble for leaving.

Yes, but Dr. Benton was so proud of me for realizing my mistake and coming home that he made my punishment quick and painless!

And Clara asked what people were saying about her stress leave.

Not much. But your replacement has some big shoes to fill.

It didn't take long before their conversations turned more casual. Juliana often talked about how much she missed Clara and how she couldn't wait to see her again soon. Juliana fully supported Clara's hiking idea. Clara was afraid she would be upset that they were going to Broken Trail, but instead she'd texted *Not at all! If you hadn't told me that, I would have suggested it anyway!* and sent her recommendations for viewpoints and spots her kids might like.

Clara knew it was unprofessional to keep in contact with her while on leave, but she was so grateful to have a friend she could count on, especially since Naomi had become hot-and-cold these days.

Sometimes she was overly solicitous and supportive, constantly asking how Clara was feeling, which was very unlike Naomi's usual distant personality and made Clara exceedingly uncomfortable. But other times, she would stare at Clara with her brows creased—a face that reminded Clara entirely too much of her disapproving mother. Clara thought she knew why: Naomi was not at all pleased with their choice of hiking location, but had reluctantly agreed.

"Isn't there any other trail you've been interested in? Jay has such a great list of local trails, even ones not open to the public."

"It's going to be perfectly fine," Clara had said. "The case is closed—you should know, since you were on the team that closed it. There are no dangers in those woods."

"Still, Clara. It's only been reopened a few weeks."

Clara tongued the grooves in her cheek and inhaled. "Listen. I really think it will help me feel closer to Juliana. And, I know I'm just on leave, but I really do miss her." Clara's emotion wasn't feigned. A thin sheen of tears blurred out Naomi's face.

Naomi softened then and wrapped her arms around Clara. "Okay, hon," she said, patting Clara's back. "Okay. Let's do it. It'll be good for you. And the girls, too."

With Tilly disappearing for days at a time and Maddy's constant sulking, Clara knew this was her last chance to bring this family back together. Juliana was right, she couldn't back out now.

THE SUBARU RATTLED over the wet ruts and exposed rocks of the dirt road. Clara swore under her breath as she tried to keep up with Naomi's Tesla, which was always disappearing one bend ahead of her. She squinted her eyes to blur out the chinks in the windshield, not wanting to recall the swarm of ravens she encountered her last time here. *It wasn't that bad*, she thought. Maybe she'd imagined the whole thing—maybe the divots in her windshield had been made by a stray pebble thrown by a truck on the highway. Maybe even by the damned Tesla she couldn't manage to keep up with.

"Mom, could you try not to steer directly *into* every pothole?" Tilly sat in the passenger seat braiding and unbraiding her long auburn hair, her bare feet on the dash, phone propped on her knee playing TikTok videos about god knows what.

"How the hell is Naomi's *Tesla* navigating this road better than our SUV?" Clara wondered aloud.

"My teeth are rattling," Maddy called from the back seat. Her hair, redder than Tilly's, was pulled back in a smart ponytail. She wore the new gear Clara had splurged on: Gortex cargo pants, wicking layers, microfleece, hiking boots. Almost everything Naomi had listed for them. "But I don't mind," she amended after glancing at Clara's exasperated face in the mirror.

"I don't remember the road being quite so rough when I was out here last."

Tilly glanced up momentarily from a TikTok that sounded like someone catching an alligator in a garbage can. Or maybe a lion biting through a cake plate. "You've been here before?"

Clara felt the tension thicken, and she wasn't sure why. Surely Tilly kept thousands of things from her, and it's not like this was a secret.

She swallowed, the sound of wingbeats filling her ears. Memories of her panicked rush back down the trail to the darkened car so many weeks ago. Juliana's ghostly face. Clara's hands tightened on the steering wheel. She forced a relaxed eye roll toward Tilly. "Of course. A couple weeks ago. I wanted to make sure it was safe." The lie felt heavy on her tongue.

"I still can't believe you're dragging us with you on your midlife crisis journey or whatever. And to the murder trail even!"

"Matilda! No one was murdered." *As far as I know.* "I don't know what made you think that anyway."

"It's all over TikTok. That crazy lady who butchered her boyfriend. He probably deserved it anyway. They always fucking do."

"*Matilda*."

"Don't Matilda me. You're dragging your helpless kids into these unsafe woods, Clara. But of course, do whatever feels good to you." Her voice dripped with venom.

Clara bristled at the use of her name. "It's going to be perfectly safe. We're just going to have a perfectly fun time! Don't believe everything you see on the internet."

Tilly snorted and turned back to her TikTok. Clara heard snippets of it over the Olivia Rodrigo songs Maddy had loaded onto their car playlist. Something about an animal, people yelling. Clara focused on the rear bumper of Naomi's car in front of her, and tried to make more of an effort to avoid the potholes.

"I wouldn't bring you to a trail I hadn't sussed out first," Clara lied.

The road stretched out between the two cars, tires crunching over a muddy mix of rotted leaves and wet gravel. Trees passed by in a blaze of green fading to orange and brown, autumn having fully descended on this area by now. Luckily, the weather was on their side, but Clara wondered—not for the first time—if they might have timed this trip a bit too late in the season. A four-day backpacking trip in the wilds of BC in early November? It seemed ambitious at best, dangerous at worst.

Unfortunately, all the earlier time slots had been reserved in the system already. And, as Naomi had said when Clara had voiced her concern over falling temperatures, at least they may not need to worry about bears. As luck would have it, after a cold snap at the beginning of fall, things had heated up to warmer than typical for their trip. Clara tried to relax her jaw.

"This will be fine. Naomi wouldn't lead us astray," Clara said, reassuring both herself and Tilly. When not selling bikes at his shop, her husband worked for Search and Rescue on these very mountains for goodness' sake. They'd be fine.

"Sure. I *totally* trust you, Mom."

Tilly pulled out another braid and started over again while her phone volume seemed to increase of its own volition. A girl's scream rattled out of the old iPhone and then—

Clara's eyes shot over to Tilly's lap. A white owl crossed the screen. Another bloodcurdling scream and the owl's face flashed up close, a single black eye—the other a blank white. Clara's breath stopped.

"Mom!" Maddy screamed, and Clara looked up just in time to see a huge, hulking shape in the middle of the road. She swerved, the back tire catching the edge of a rock and sending the car sliding left. She fought to regain control, the steering wheel shaking under her hands.

"What was it?" she asked, her voice shrill. "A bear?"

Tilly sighed, lowering her feet from the dash one at a time and retrieving her now silent phone from the floor. "A dead deer. Just roadkill, Mom."

Clara's breath came in bursts, throat tight. She glanced at Tilly, checked Maddy in the rearview, eased the car to a slow roll. She forced herself to let out a long exhale and then take in another long breath.

"We're okay," Maddy said.

Clara ran a hand through her hair. "I hope Naomi and the kids are all right. What if they hit it?"

Tilly's bored voice broke her reverie. "If they hit it, they'd still be there, crushed. But they're not. Naomi was probably watching the road"—she gave Clara a pointed look—"and drove right around it without almost killing everyone. Tell me why we're on this stupid trip again?"

Clara ground her teeth. "It's hard to watch the road when you've got some kind of horror movie going on your phone right next to my face. What are you looking at on there anyway?" She reached over.

Tilly snatched her phone away. "I was just texting. God, you're intense. And anyway, I'm out of cell range now so it doesn't really matter anymore."

"We're on this trip, Matilda, because we need to regain some fucking semblance of family time and respect around here!" Clara didn't realize she was yelling until she reached the last word. Her whole body shook. *Breathe. In. Out.* She tried, but it was no use.

Tilly turned her face to the window. "Well, I'd say we're off to a smashing start."

CHAPTER NINE

NAOMI STOOD STRAIGHT as a compass needle, studying the map at the trailhead. A large purple rucksack clung to her back like it was a part of her, a shell grown from her own flesh. Aiden and Thea stood near the rear hatch of their car, strapping lightweight sleeping pads to the bottom of their packs.

Clara wondered again what possessed her to suggest this trip. She pulled her keys from the ignition and secured them in the inside zipper pocket of her new Gortex jacket. No messing around with lost keys again.

"All right, everybody out. Packs are in the back," she said, swinging open her car door. Their footsteps squelched in the mud as they made their way to the trunk and shouldered their burdens. Clara bent her knees a few times, testing the weight of it, much heavier than it had felt when she'd loaded it back at the house. How was she supposed to carry this thing for four days, uphill? She clicked the waist strap shut.

She was its prisoner now.

Naomi approached, smile blooming brighter than the late morning sunshine. "This is wonderful! We've got the perfect weather to start. I'm so glad we're doing this." She patted Clara on the shoulder. "A hike was a good idea."

"Did you see that deer?" Clara asked, adjusting her shoulder straps for the third time.

"Deer?" Naomi looked around at the edge of the woods.

"Yeah, the giant one? On the road? Dead?"

Naomi cocked her head to the side and gave Clara a funny look. "I must have missed it."

"You couldn't have missed it. It was—What are you doing?"

Naomi started on Clara's straps, loosening everywhere she had tightened and tightening everywhere she'd loosened.

"How's that? Better, right? You'll get used to the weight of it soon enough. The first kilometer is a bit of a climb, but then it levels off for a good long while before we approach the first peak. And there's a waterfall to keep us motivated."

Clara raised her face skyward and breathed in. She had to admit, the weather *was* perfect. The sweet scent of freshly fallen leaves was earthy and comforting. The sky was the kind of blue that went on forever, unbroken and electric, and the deciduous trees leaped like flames between the conifer's greens. She could enjoy this. Clara shifted her pack one last time. She *would* enjoy this.

Thea and Maddy separated off from the group to compare hiking boots and admire each other's packs. They looked like distorted mirror images of each other, Thea dark with waves of long black hair like her mother, Maddy all pale freckles and red curls, but both the same height, wearing matching backpacks, and full of giggles. Back before Emilio left, they used to joke that Thea looked more like him than his own kids.

"Hey, Tilly." Aiden stepped up next to the back of the Subaru. He flicked a curl of sandy hair from in front of his eyes. While Thea and Naomi had hair black as fire pokers, Aiden's hair was a mop of unruly light brown, the same color as his eyes. He blended in with the porridge of leaves and pine needles and muck at their feet. Emilio always used to joke that Aiden looked more like Clara than Naomi, with his light hair and eyes. "Need some help getting your pack on? It can be a bit—"

"I got it," Tilly said, hefting the pack onto her shoulders, wrinkling the pattern of her Royal Blood T-shirt. She'd refused the new hiking clothes Clara had shelled out for, all except the hiking boots and jacket Naomi insisted on, the latter of which was dangling unused from the side loop of her backpack. Tilly stomped away from Aiden to go study the trail map.

"All right, team, listen up. Step one, safety check. Because," Naomi glanced at Clara, "we've already all inventoried our bags, right? Tents, fire starter, water filter, emergency tarps?"

Clara nodded obediently, patting the water filtration system dangling in a bag off the left side of her pack. She'd packed her own things, but hadn't really run a secondary check of the kids' bags after they were packed. It was only four days, right? What could go wrong?

"Great," Naomi continued. "Then safety next. Everyone's wearing boots. Car keys secured. Packs tightened and not chafing anywhere?" Everyone's heads bobbed except Tilly who still stood staring at the map as though her eyes could burn holes through it and maybe through this whole trip. Clara reached up to massage her forehead. Four days to break through that shell.

A high-pitched sound assaulted Clara's ears, and she snapped her eyes open again to see an emergency whistle between Naomi's lips. She let it drop to the string around her neck. "If you get lost, blow your whistle in three sharp bursts. Don't wander far from the group without ensuring you have water, food, and an emergency shelter with you."

Clara looked at Thea and Maddy. "Or, how about just don't venture far from the group at all?"

"Good thinking," Naomi said. "All right, gang, let's go." She passed Tilly and headed up the steep, narrow path, lithe and agile as a cat.

The kids filed in behind her, with Tilly and Clara coming last. Tilly scowled at Clara but said nothing.

THE HIKE WAS grueling, as Naomi had warned. The first hour was a steady steep climb, more than the promised kilometer. Apart from the candy blue of the sky, the rest of the world was a faded, rustling yellowish-brown, as though they strode through old parchment.

The crisp air and smell of earth filled her lungs. She raised her gaze, following the bobbing rainbow of backpacks in front of her. The happy jingle of bear bells—though Clara kept trying to convince herself the bears would be asleep—and laughter-like rattle of the leaves filled the air. For the first time since Emilio left—well, since much longer than that if she was honest—Clara was beginning to feel alive.

She ran her fingers along the papery leaves and jagged branches that lined the trail. Not even Tilly complained, despite the climb. Clara's chest swelled. She'd made the right choice, coming here. As Juliana said, nature was a balm.

Maddy stopped suddenly, making Thea knock into her back. She pointed skyward. "Look!" Five sets of eyes joined hers and Clara let out a gasp. A swarm of birds circled overhead. Birds of prey for sure, massive wings outstretched as they swirled in circles that were as gentle as they were ominous.

"Bald eagles," Aiden said. "They must be here for the salmon run."

"There's so many!" Tilly said. A smile twitched at Clara's lips at the sound of true awe in her surly daughter's voice. She was right, though, there had to be at least twenty of them, probably more.

Clara lowered her eyes to watch her older daughter. Tilly reached an arm back to pull a water bottle from the pocket on the side of her pack, her fingers grazing it but not gaining purchase. Clara pulled the bottle out and passed it to Tilly with a smile. One that was miraculously returned.

"Let's make it to the first crest of this hill. Then we can break for lunch," Naomi called from the front of their little parade. Obediently, they filed back into line and trudged upward once more. Clara's smile hadn't faded. The mud squelching at their boots below felt like a cozy call home; the eagles watching their progress from above were their guides.

A breeze kicked up, and two large ravens took off from a branch in front of Naomi, disappearing into the Douglas firs on the other side of the path, making Clara jump. Her heart pounded against her ribs. Ravens, just like the ones that had mobbed her car last time she was here.

Clara glanced up at the swirling eagles above, trying to regain her sense of peace and awe. Nature was a balm, after all. But the birds had grown shadowy, their wings moving strangely, tail feathers split in a V, and she realized they weren't eagles at all, but ravens. And there were more now. Thirty. Maybe fifty. All circling overhead, clustering closer and closer.

"Hey!" she started to call out to the group, but they were too far ahead.

Come.

Clara spun, the quick movement throwing her balance off. The word was a whisper, a chill that hung in the air only for her, a thought inside her head. The voice was familiar, but not her own. She swallowed and turned back to the trail ahead. Her eyes found

Tilly's red backpack again, bouncing along the trail in front of her, bells jangling merrily. An anchor. She had to get ahold of herself.

COME.

It thundered in Clara's head this time, so loud she jumped. Her hands instinctively went to her ears and she crumpled forward, bracing for another thunderous blow. But none came. After a moment, she lowered her hands and started up the trail again, hurrying to catch up.

"What's with those ravens?" Clara asked, breathless, as she came parallel with Tilly.

"Ravens?" Aiden asked from up ahead.

"The birds, circling? They were all black and—"

Tilly eyed her, the skin between her brows pinched together. "I'm pretty sure they were eagles, Mom."

"They do that this time of year," Aiden said, smiling. "It's pretty amazing."

Clara shook her head. "They looked all black to me." She thought of the shadowy birds caked like a coating on the outside of her car, banging to be let in.

"Okay, Mom. They were ravens. Whatever. Come on." Tilly rolled her eyes and turned away, picking up the pace. Clara fell into line behind her.

CHAPTER TEN

THE FIRST CREST of the hill turned out to have one hell of a view. Gazing out over the forest, the snake of river winding below her, the tension over the swirling birds earlier faded, and Clara almost had to rethink her stance on hiking.

The feelings that welled up in her as she looked into the valley far below were almost akin to what she felt when she gazed on her daughters' faces for the first time. How in the world could anything so beautiful exist? She stared for what felt like an eternity while the others behind her busied themselves with setting up a picnic. Her thoughts were interrupted by the unexpected buzz in her cargo pants pocket.

Clara pulled out her phone and squinted against the glare. She was pretty sure Naomi had said there would be no service for the whole trip, but maybe up here on the edge of the mountain she caught some lingering thread of 5G.

A message popped up.

It was Juliana on her new number.

Have a great hike, Clare! You made the right choice. See you soon.

Clara smiled. If there was one person she could count on supporting her unconditionally, it was Juliana. Clara filed off a quick "thanks!" before putting her phone on airplane mode and sliding it back into her pocket. It was unlikely she'd connect to the grid again any time soon, so best to save battery life.

She turned around to see Tilly waving her phone around over the edge of the cliff. "You've got service up here?"

Clara shook her head. She hadn't told any of them about her continued relationship with Juliana of course, not even Naomi. "Nope," she said. "Just . . . taking notes. And pictures. Isn't this beautiful up here? I had no idea views like this existed so close to our house."

Tilly put her own phone away and crossed her arms, but stayed beside Clara, gazing outward. "It *is* pretty beautiful. I'll give you that. Wish we didn't have to torture ourselves to get here though. Like maybe we could just look at a virtual tour from the comfort of our own fucking couch?"

"Language, miss," Clara said, but without any force behind it. She quirked a half smile. "Do you *really* prefer the couch to this?"

"Ask me on day four when my feet are more blister than flesh," Tilly responded, mirroring her half smile. Then she turned and walked to where Maddy and Thea munched on sandwiches, avoiding Aiden who sat alone a few feet away.

Naomi wandered up and handed Clara a hummus and cheese sandwich on homemade bread.

"Enjoy the day-one luxury," she said, grinning widely. "After this, it's all jerky and freeze-dried meals."

Clara took a nibble. Naomi had insisted that, though they divided up the food for the rest of the trip between families, she wanted to pack a special, fortifying day-one lunch for everyone. Clara tongued the seeds caught in her teeth and tried to appear grateful. "So good," she mumbled.

"I know, right? Thea and I found a new hummus recipe that we absolutely love. Want to know the secret?"

"Sure?"

"You have to peel the chickpeas."

"You're joking." Clara looked at her best friend—the sun glinting off her Barbie-pink jacket that looked like it had been freshly ironed, even though she was pretty sure you can't iron Gortex—and realized she could absolutely imagine her spending hours squeezing tiny garbanzo beans between her fingers until their peels slid off.

Naomi shrugged. "It makes much creamier hummus. So worth it. We also added a dash of peanut butter. Secret ingredient!"

"Oh yeah," Clara said, chewing hard. "I'm definitely getting nutty hints."

"This is great, isn't it? Nothing but us and nature. I'm so glad you suggested a hike. Aiden's been so stressed about college applications. We needed this break."

"Oh . . . yeah. Right. College." Shit. She'd meant to check with Emilio what the status was on that. As far as she knew, Tilly hadn't sent out a single application yet, but Emilio had been taking the lead on the college planning anyway, at least before the split. Clara didn't even know Tilly's short list. Or if she even had one. She'd started spending longer days at work since taking Juliana on as a patient, and the past year slid by so fast, she hadn't even realized it was application season.

"Where has Tilly applied? Aiden's got his fingers crossed for early decision at U-Dub." She put a hand beside her mouth and hissed in a conspiratorial whisper, "Don't tell anyone, but I've got a friend there who said he's basically a shoe-in! But if he doesn't get in there, it would be nice to have him at UBC, keep him close."

Clara nodded dumbly and let her gaze wander around the camp. Something just beyond the tree line caught her eye. Mammalian movement was distinct from that of plants or bugs or even birds, the smoothness of it, joints bending and skin stretching in oddly human ways.

Clara's eyes refocused, homing in on the shadows while Naomi continued chattering beside her about the benefits of UBC's medical program over U of T. Shadows shifted beyond the tree line. The muscles of Clara's arms and legs twitched taut. Her mind hummed. *Bear? Deer?*

But as her vision adjusted, Clara could make out a mop of unruly hair and, beneath it, a patch of furless skin, vaguely human skin.

Her own skin prickled, an itch she was too terrified to scratch. Was someone watching them? From the shadows?

"Clara?"

Clara blinked a moment and turned back to Naomi.

"Has Tilly picked a major?"

"Oh, um, I think so? She's still just settling on . . . something. Talking with her advisers." Clara was rambling, she knew, but she didn't really care about Tilly's college prospects right now. Her eyes scanned the edges of the tree line, searching for that unmistakable patch of skin, unruly hair. But all she saw were branches and shadows. "Did you—"

Naomi put a hand on her arm, making her jump. "I know application season can be stressful. Tilly will take care of things in her own way and her own time, though. I know you're doing a great job supporting her."

Clara nodded dumbly. Were these meant to be words of wisdom? Reassurance? Clara wasn't sure. She felt so removed from Tilly's life these days, she almost felt like she was talking about someone else's kid. Clara made a mental note to ask Tilly more about college.

"All right, folks!" Naomi announced, clapping her hands. "Let's get a move on. If we don't start back up now, we won't reach camp before sundown, and nobody wants to pitch a tent in the dark."

Tilly groaned but pulled herself to her feet. When Aiden handed her pack to her, she stared daggers at him before sliding it on gruffly and starting back toward the trail. Clara scanned the edges of the clearing one last time, the feeling of being watched sticking to her like cobwebs.

⟶⟵

THEY REACHED THE first camp just as the sun began to slant low through the trees, bathing everything in an ethereal, orange light. The hike had sort of leveled off, but never as much as Naomi had promised. That, coupled with the fact that Clara peered over her shoulder every few steps, settled an exhaustion over her by the time the sunlight began to fade.

She couldn't wait to get the pack off and examine the raw bits of her shoulders where it seemed to chafe no matter how she adjusted the straps. Camp consisted of a few fire rings scattered among the trees, with gravel squares plotted out near each one. Shadows stretched long across the moss and leaf litter at their feet as they set up their tents in two of the squares.

"We're the only ones here," Clara said. She'd been dreading sharing space with sleeping strangers, but now confronted with the vastness of the forest, she found herself wishing for more people about.

She tried to keep her movements confined to the pockets of remaining sunlight, feeling a cold chill creeping up her spine.

Naomi hammered a stake into the ground with a rock, the echoes ricocheting off the trees like gunshots. "We're late in the season," she said, breathless. She shrugged. "I didn't expect to see many others. Still, someone might show up. Thea, can you help me with the other stakes?"

Thea and Maddy had dropped their packs in a heap and were frolicking through the trees with the magical, bottomless energy of youth. Clara's whole body ached, her feet were blistered. She could hardly stand to set up the tent. Thea flitted over to where Naomi was working and took over the hammering at an even quicker tempo.

Maddy hovered near Clara and the heap of green tent fabric in front of her. "Can I help, too?" Clara smiled and passed her one of the tentpoles, showing her where to insert it.

"Will we have a fire soon?" Tilly asked from where she'd flopped herself on a makeshift bench hewn from a log. She rubbed her arms for warmth and leaned back against her big red backpack, which she hadn't bothered to remove yet. Aiden stood near the opposite bench, digging through his pack while side-eyeing her.

Naomi stretched and surveyed the camp. "There should be some firewood left near the bear box. We aren't meant to use found wood, since we're in a park. Maybe you and Aiden could go up and check? The bear box should be nearby."

Aiden's head snapped up at his name. He glanced at Tilly. "Come on, I'll help you find it."

"*Or* you could just go find it yourself," Tilly said, staring at the trees in front of her.

"You'll warm up quicker if you come," he responded. Tilly shrugged, zipping her fleece higher.

"Tills," Clara said, "go help with the wood. Everyone else is doing something useful."

To her surprise, Tilly untangled her arms from her pack and stood with a huff. She trudged up a nearby slope with Aiden to where Naomi said the bear box should be. Aiden tried awkwardly to start a conversation by asking how school was going for her before they finally trailed out of earshot.

"Speaking of the bear box," Clara said to Naomi, "should we be moving our food stores up there at some point?"

Her friend nodded. "Not so much for bears at this time of year, but there are squirrels and other small creatures that will chew right through your tent to get to a granola bar. So, yeah, we'll move everything up there in a bit." She bent again to toss her sleeping mat and bag into their maroon tent. Thea did the same.

"So, the bears are hibernating?" she asked, trying to keep her voice level. "There's nothing else up here that could bother us?"

Naomi brushed her hands against the Barbie-pink jacket and let out a laugh. "Nope. There's some bobcats sure, and maybe a cougar or two, but they won't mess with us."

"That . . . doesn't put me at ease."

But the truth was that it wasn't cougars or bears or bobcats making the hair on the back of Clara's neck stand on end. It was that person, watching from the shadows. The more she ran the memory reel back in her mind's eye, the more certain she was that it was a person standing there.

She swallowed back bile as the memory of Juliana's last words to her flitted through her mind: *What happened to me wasn't just wildlife.*

What *had* happened to Juliana and Gavin up here, she wondered. And for the first time, the question came with a shiver of fear.

Clara stood back and eyed their little green tent. Lopsided, but set up. She couldn't believe the three of them would all fit in there, but she wasn't about to give her kids another reason to complain, so she kept the thought to herself, just like she did the image of the person watching them.

As soon as she saw the tent was fully up, Maddy busied herself inside laying out the sleeping mats. Clara ran her hands up and down her arms, trying to stave off goosebumps, then went to check out the closest fire ring.

The sun ducked further below the horizon, turning the forest to a dull purple. Their tent glowed green in the gloom, Maddy having taken in the lantern.

Clara worried about Aiden and Tilly coming back down the slope in the quickly falling light, but she saw two bouncing headlamps making their way cautiously back down the hill. Of course Aiden was prepared.

Hollow cracks rang through the woods as the teens deposited the wood near the fire ring. Aiden pulled a small hatchet from a loop on his pack and began to split off some kindling. He stopped after a few splits and stretched his arms above his head, his back cracking. Clara attempted to divine the look her daughter gave him. Aiden passed Tilly a small piece of wood and something else, something that flashed in the dim, purplish glow of twilight.

A knife. For a moment Clara was about to protest, but stopped herself. “Can you make some shavings?” Aiden asked her. “I can show you how.” After glaring a moment, Tilly took the knife and confidently began raking away at the wood, creating a tiny tendril nest. Clara relaxed and grabbed her pack to dig out the freeze-dried dinners.

Camp was coming together.

Giggles emanated from the green tent, where Maddy and Thea told ghost stories. Aiden and Tilly had gotten the fire going and appeared to be on almost speaking terms, if Tilly glowering and sighing every time Aiden said something counted as speaking. And Clara stood over their Primus stoves stirring pots of spagbol and fried rice.

“We did it, you guys,” Naomi said to no one in particular. “We hiked almost ten miles today. Everyone should be pretty proud.”

Clara smiled, the fears of earlier in the day now seeming irrational. She was really doing this, she could take her family camping. She could be a good mom.

"I brought a bottle of something special," Naomi said with a wink. "Tiny, because pack weight, you know. Should we crack it now or save it for our last night?"

Clara was about to respond, when a sound came from down the trail. She turned, the trees flashing grayscale in the swinging beam of her headlamp.

CHAPTER ELEVEN

FIRST IT WAS only footsteps, the snap of a branch, crunch of dirt underfoot. Clara's pulse quickened. Her mind flashed back to the figure she saw watching them. But then she heard a man laugh and the distinct sound of multiple footsteps. Just another group of hikers.

"Looks like we've got company," Naomi sighed, taking her sweet-smelling bag of fried rice off the top-heavy burner.

The footsteps grew closer and Clara could make out three people, their faces invisible behind the bobbing headlamps. "H'llo there," a man's voice called.

"Hey," Tilly and Naomi responded simultaneously into the gloom. Clara squinted past the headlamp's glare as she turned off the Primus and portioned the gloppy freeze-dried meal into three bowls.

At that moment, Aiden dropped a match onto the nest of filaments and the fire sprang to life, turning the towering trees around them into an orange stage on which black shadows writhed and danced around. Clara almost preferred the darkness.

Two boys and a girl, college age, strode into view at the orange circle's edge, dropping their packs onto a tent platform a few yards away. Clara eyed them warily. She watched as they dumped out a tent from one of the packs and began assembling it in the faint fire glow. The sound of a can opening echoed through the trees and one headlamp's beam arced up toward the sky, like a beacon, as someone took a sip.

One of the boys laughed that grating, almost metallic laugh she associated with drunk college boys. Loud, too loud, taking up all the space in the room. Clara turned away.

The younger girls emerged from the tent, toques pulled over their ears, and darted over. "The fire's lit!" Thea called. They filed onto the bench across from Clara, both balancing their camp bowls on their knees.

Aiden leaned back on his haunches, admiring the fire before settling next to Tilly, who nibbled disgustedly at the glop as she watched the newcomers set up camp. Naomi passed a stainless steel mug to Clara, the sharp scent of peat and fermentation wafting through the air. "Here," she said, also eyeing the new trio, "we'll probably need this."

Clara took a sip, letting the sweet, earthy taste burn over her tongue and warm her belly. The sparks from the fire flew skyward, crackling and then extinguishing in the black like fairies' last breaths.

"Mind if we join your fire?" The trio stood behind Tilly, headlamps off and a small cooler in one of their hands.

"Sure!" Tilly twisted to meet their gaze.

"Sweet," said the guy with the cooler, settling in next to Tilly. "We got up here a little later than planned, thanks to *someone*." He jostled the other boy, who raised his hands in a gesture of innocence and plopped down beside Naomi.

The girl slid in next to him.

"Anyway, it's a little dark to get a fire going now, so we appreciate it." The boy with the cooler passed a beer to each of his companions and offered one around the circle.

"We're good," Naomi said, raising her mug.

"And the rest of them are underage," Clara added.

Tilly shot her a withering look.

"I'm Rocky." The boy cracked his beer. "And over there are the lovebirds Sonia and Brian."

Introductions were made. Then Rocky said, "You guys staying one night or going the whole way?"

Naomi scoffed. "The whole way, of course. Why come only halfway?"

"You guys are pretty brave, doing it with kids and all. We're only doing one night, heading back to the city tomorrow."

Naomi sat up straighter. "It's not like they're strangers to hiking. They've practically been doing it since birth. I did the West Coast Trail when I was pregnant with Aiden." She gestured across the fire to her son.

Clara took a larger swig of her whiskey, and noticed Tilly rolling her eyes. They smirked at each other. Naomi wore that pregnant hike like a badge and whipped it out at any opportunity.

"That's pretty impressive," Sonia said, coaxing another eye roll from Tilly.

"It's not the hike itself, but what's in the woods." Brian spoke up for the first time, and Clara was surprised to hear an accent tilting his vowels.

"What's in the woods?" Tilly asked, turning her eyes to the shadows behind her sister's head.

Rocky let out that laugh again, like thunderclouds gathering overhead. "You might want to scoot a little closer before we tell you."

Clara cleared her throat—the audacity!—but didn't speak up for fear of embarrassing Tilly again. Their shared eye roll felt like a soothing balm on their relationship, and Clara was reluctant to pick at it too much. It was all harmless, anyway. They were in a big group. Still, it was enough to make Rocky lean slightly away, with a penitent glance her way. The knot in her stomach relaxed.

But only briefly.

"Rumor has it," Brian continued in his lilting voice, "these woods were a haven for witches escaping burning at the stake."

Naomi sighed. "No witches were *burned* in British Columbia."

"Witchcraft is just a thinly veiled excuse to persecute women and First Nations people," Tilly mumbled, staring at the fire. She met Naomi's gaze then, her face hard. "Look it up. Men are still burning bitches for being witches. Just the fires look a bit different these days."

"Even so," Brian continued, undaunted. "Some say ghosts wander not far off the trail. *Some* say there are still witches out here living in these woods. A girl and a woman. They thirst for blood and naught more."

"Dude," Rocky snorted.

"Take care to not wander far or they'll take you. Remember, the black river runs deep. They will swallow you whole."

Silence descended on the group, nothing but the crackling fire and the gentle rustling of leaves far above. Clara swallowed, her breath shallow. She knew it was just a silly campfire story, but she couldn't escape the icy chill tickling her spine.

Maddy and Thea leaned forward. "Who are they?" Thea asked. "Tell us more!"

"It's all just made-up shit," Tilly said.

"Sure you're not scared?" Rocky rested a hand on Tilly's knee, sending a furious jolt through Clara. But just as she opened her mouth to put an end to it, a massive shadow swooped low over the fire, arcing from high in one of the Douglas firs. "Jesus!" she shrieked, and the kids—even Aiden—screamed. Naomi leapt to her feet, arms out like she could protect the whole group from an aerial attack. Rocky fell backward, half off the low bench, overturning his beer.

Naomi let out a great guffaw then. "It's an owl," she said breathlessly. "Nothing but an owl."

The rest of the group relaxed, but Naomi's words drove a sliver of fear into Clara's ribs.

It was indeed an owl, now perched just within the light of the fire, its single black eye locked only on Clara.

THE SCARE SEEMED to have united the group, all except Clara. Naomi now joked as much as Rocky, and Sonia and Brian seemed to have no end to their ghost stories, though thankfully no more about this trail. At least Clara had taken the opportunity to sit between Tilly and Rocky as everyone regrouped.

Still, Clara couldn't shake the frozen fear that had wormed itself under her skin. Long after the owl had flown away, she still sat silent, listening to nothing but her heartbeat. The owl had only one eye.

When the marshmallows had been roasted and Rocky's cooler ran out of cans, Maddy made her way around the fire to curl up next to Clara's legs, resting her head on her knee. It was getting late, Clara realized.

Reaching the same conclusion, Naomi spoke up. "We should get an early start tomorrow, to reach the waterfall by lunch." She stood and stretched. "Time to tuck in, troops."

Following her lead, the group began to find their feet, fumbling around by the light of the fading flames. As Thea and Naomi tossed water on the fire, Rocky leaned in to whisper something in Tilly's ear. Aiden stepped forward, placing himself between them and asking her a question Clara couldn't hear. Clara held her breath. Tilly hissed something back at him, but by the time he headed for his side of camp, Rocky had already turned away, stumbling back the way Sonia and Brian had gone.

"I'll take the food up to the bear box," Clara offered. She patted Maddy's head. "Go ahead and get cozy in the tent. I'll be right back."

Naomi helped her gather the food together into a bag that Clara shouldered. She trudged up the slope to where Naomi pointed out the box. It was a large, metal affair with bear-proof handles. Her hands were so cold in the November evening air, the box almost proved human-proof too. But she managed to wriggle it open and toss the food inside, slamming the door securely shut.

She straightened, preparing to march back down the hill, but her headlamp caught on a face directly in front of her. Pale, ghostly. Her heart leapt into her throat as she staggered back. Her headlamp cast a wider glow.

The owl again. Perched on the bear box.

White as bone, expressionless, glowing in the ray of the headlamp. Its good eye, inky black and unmoving, stared at Clara. But somehow she felt like the other eye, just a sunken socket, was seeing her too. Boring into her.

She forced a shaken exhale.

"Hi, owl," Clara whispered, her pulse pounding in her ears. "Just . . . making my way to my tent. Friendly owl." Her voice shook as she edged around the large creature. Its head swiveled to follow her.

Then it took flight. Wings as wide as Clara was tall beat nearly soundlessly against the air. The wind whipped against her face twice, three times, then it was gone. Clara raced back to the tent and yanked the zipper shut behind her.

CHAPTER TWELVE

A DARK RIVER carved its way down the mountainside, sliding between the trees, flowing over jutting rock faces, seeking. Where the sun hit it, it glowed a sanguine red, shapes undulating just below the surface. It spoke in whispers, screams, they reached out to Clara like arms, hands, claws.

Clara was there, at the water's edge. She leaned over—there was something in the water calling to her. She reached forward with one hand, ripples as her pale fingers brushed the surface. Something grew nearer, hovering just below the dark surface of the water, a form just deep enough that she couldn't make out the details.

A moment before it breached the surface a noise behind Clara made her turn. She spun to see Juliana, naked and pale, with lips drawn and teeth bared. She lunged from the tree line and dug her nails into Clara's soft flesh as if it were the dough her daughters used to play with. Blood ran in rivulets down her arm, gathering on the tip of her finger in bulbous red drops before falling to the muddy riverbank. Clara struggled, but Juliana's grip was vice-like.

Juliana's mouth made no motion, yet her voice filled Clara's head. *Come!*

Clara lurched, finally breaking free of Juliana's claws. She teetered and then fell backward into the river's depths, her scream swallowed as the water shoved into her nose and mouth, stopping her breath.

Clara snapped her eyes open, clutching her neck and inhaling great gasps of air. Her sleeping bag felt soggy, a viscous fluid coating her arms and legs. Sweat from the nightmare. The scent of iron and flesh filled the cramped tent. She massaged her sore shoulder and tried to slow her breathing. *In, out. It was only a dream.* But panic still stood on her chest.

She sat up to get more air. And screamed.

It wasn't sweat that coated her limbs, her sleeping bag, the inside of the tent. It was blood. She'd woken into a massacre. The tent walls were coated in crimson spatters, the floor a pool of thick red. She covered her mouth with shaking hands, spreading the red liquid to her cheeks, tasting the iron tang on her tongue. She didn't want to look, but she had to. Whimpering, she took in the bodies of her two daughters, eyes closed and breath stilled. Something snapped inside her, a hollow crack of a twig. She screamed again.

"*Mom!*" Someone had her by the shoulders, shaking her. The world was black. "Mom!"

She opened her eyes to see Tilly's face in front of hers, her brow knitted more in irritation than concern. Maddy sat beside her, bleary-eyed. Both very much alive. Relief flowed through her so suddenly and forcefully she felt nauseous. "Tilly?" Tears stung her eyes. She wrapped her arms around the two girls, who pulled away from her embrace, confused and maybe a little repulsed by the sudden show of emotion. Great sobs erupted from Clara, lopsided and noisy, like something chunky pouring out of her. Tears burst forth, clotted and fleshy.

"Jesus, Mom, what is your deal," Tilly said. "The tent is flooded, by the way."

Clara gathered herself and looked down. Her daughter was right. The sleeping bags, pads, everything was soaked. The walls oozed moisture where the fly rested against them.

"I think we should have staked out the fly," Maddy said, shrugging.

"Duh, genius," Tilly responded, thwacking her sister on the shoulder. Clara pressed the heels of her hands against her eyes, and pushed away the last of the nightmare. Only water. Rain. A leak. Not blood. Inhale, exhale. She could deal with this. No one was dead.

But water was a problem, too. How could they make the rest of the trip with soaking gear? Tears threatened again, but Maddy was staring at her with big, helpless eyes, and even worse, Tilly was shooting her death glares from the other side of the tent as she pulled dripping socks and T-shirts from her backpack.

Clara exhaled. "Okay. Okay, we can get through this. We're not abandoning this hike." She tried to shrug off the blood-soaked haze of her dream, tried to muster some energy after the mostly sleepless night. She had to mother through this. "Let's—We'll build a fire. We probably have a little bit of time before we need to hit the trail again."

"Mom, it's still pouring," Tilly pointed out.

"Tilly, would you just . . . bear with me, please? Maybe if you had just *helped* for once in your life. If you'd helped with the tent set up this—"

"I built the fire, remember? It's not like I sat around doing nothing. I cannot believe you're going to make this whole thing my fucking fault. Typical."

"I should have known to stake out the sides," Maddy said. "Dad—" she hesitated. "Well, Dad showed me how before. Because otherwise you get condensation. Obviously." She shrugged again, running her finger against the water seeping in through the nylon wall.

"Just stop *talking*. Both of you, for god's sake." Rain battered against the tiny, too-porous shell surrounding them and Clara couldn't escape the feeling that she was still underwater. Drowning, being pushed down into the humid depths. Her throat tightened again, and she felt the walls closing in. Couldn't get enough air, it was all tainted by the salty, metallic scent of too many bodies too close together. Sweat and blood and dampness. She leaned across the soaked bedding and ripped the zipper open, emerging like a snake from an egg, head and torso first, into the wet dirt, then slithering her feet out. She needed to breathe.

"Mom, wait."

She ignored it, not even sure which of them had spoken.

Boots on, she stood and reached back in to grab her rain jacket. Not that it mattered. In the thirty seconds she was out from under the protective shield of the tent, her hair and everything else on her was soaked.

Naomi's maroon tent squatted solid on its gravel square a few steps away from theirs. The rain beaded off it like it was a goddamned camping commercial. She was sure everyone inside was dry and sleeping soundly.

She glanced at the fire pit. A few unused logs from the night before leaned around the outside of the rusted metal ring, useless now, soaked through. The rain dripped off her eyelashes and ran down her upper lip into her mouth, bringing with it the taste of salt. Streams of it ran over her nose. She was drowning standing up. She tightened her hood and began to trek up to the bear box where she hoped some dry wood waited.

"Mom." Footsteps crunched on the gravel behind her. "It's no use. You can't get the fire going in this deluge." Clara turned to find Tilly, no jacket, her auburn curls matted to her wet forehead, T-shirt with the name of some unknown rock band stuck slick to her torso. She slurped at the rainwater that danced on her upper lip, like a sniffle. Tilly raised her arms and dropped them to her sides again, helpless. "We just . . . we just have to turn back."

A hopeful look crossed her green eyes then. Suddenly she was no longer the avoidant teen Clara had been dealing with in the days leading up to this trip. She was just a child, and she needed Clara. "We could just head back," she said again, in that small voice Clara rarely heard her use anymore.

Clara reached out a hand to the girl's soaked shoulder and gave it a squeeze. Bonding on a fun trip was one thing, but Clara knew that bonding over shared problem solving was much stronger. Maybe overcoming a shared, negative experience was just what they needed. "We'll get through this, Tills," Clara said. "Help me break camp."

Tilly nodded and made her way back to the soaked tent. She glanced up the narrow trail, shrouded in rain and fog. She would show Tilly they were capable of besting their obstacles, that they didn't need to give up as long as they were together. They could do this. The only way out would be through this storm.

MADDY AND TILLY had wrung out the sleeping bags as best as they could and packed them away in their sacks. The mats would be strapped to the outside of the backpacks and would dry while they walked, assuming the rain ever let up, which really was their only hope of getting through this. They'd separated their clothes, dry from wet so the dry clothes would stay dry. Fortunately, they each had at least one pair of mostly dry socks. Otherwise they'd be covered in blisters by the next campsite. All they had to do now was pack up the tent and grab their food.

Voices came from outside the tent as the others—Naomi's family as well as Rocky's gang—woke up and began breaking camp too. A loud belch echoed over the pattering rain, and Clara let out a sigh. "Thank goodness they're going home today and won't be with us on the trail."

Tilly paused mid-zip as she finished readying her pack. "We really aren't leaving today?" She asked.

"Well, maybe—" she started, but then the thought disappeared, like a leaf carried down a river. Clara shrugged. "No, I think we should go on. It'll be good for us."

"Okay, well I'm not fucking sleeping in wet gear for three more nights." Tilly chewed her bottom lip, and Clara resisted the urge to tell her to stop, especially after feeling her own teeth dig into the inside of her cheek. "I have an idea. You're not going to like it, Mom, but it's a good idea. Trust me."

Before Clara could respond, Tilly was out of the tent, a curious Maddy trailing behind her. By the time she made it out of the tent herself, the two girls were chatting with Rocky, gesturing wildly. Rocky let out that space-stealing laugh and the girls laughed too. Then he disappeared into his tarp-smothered tent and emerged a moment later with a small black sack. Maddy hugged it to her chest. He shouted in the direction of Sonia and Brian's tent, walking over to rattle it for good measure.

The droplets sprayed off in all directions. Moments later, two hands reached out of the zippered door, delivering two more sleeping bags, dry and neatly rolled. They walked back to Clara triumphantly.

"They're heading home, so don't need their sleeping bags." Tilly shrugged. "We just have to give them our wet ones in return—and your phone number, so we can trade back when we make it out."

Clara shook her head, the corners of her mouth turning down in a frown. Even though she knew this was a great idea, a clever solve to the problem, she didn't want to use a stranger's things, least of all Rocky's. Sliding into the close space where he had slept just the night before felt a tad too intimate. But they really *did* need dry gear or this trip would be over before it even began. And they'd have to walk out with Rocky, which she definitely did not want to do. Tilly seemed to be finally opening up, less contrary. She wanted to reward that, not criticize it. She sighed. "Sure, all right yes. Good idea. Get our sleeping bags together. I'll take them over."

The rain had already slowed to a light drizzle and Naomi was only just emerging from her tent when Clara's boots crunched over the gravel and crisp undergrowth to where Rocky stood waiting. She couldn't escape the feeling that he was leering at her, and at Tilly over her shoulder. Something about him rubbed her the wrong way. She didn't want to be beholden to this man. But he was being generous, so what could she do? As he punched her phone number into his phone, he glanced up. "This your number, or your girl's over there?"

Clara snapped, "That *girl* is in high school, damnit!"

"Easy, lady. Chill," Rocky said, still smiling. Clara hugged the sleeping bags to her chest and spun on her heel, ushering Tilly along with her.

They passed Sonia on their way back. "Thanks," Clara said. "We definitely wouldn't have made it with wet gear."

"You might not make it the rest of the way anyway," a lilting voice spoke up. Brian ducked out of his tent's entryway, hoisting a black backpack behind him. He glanced at Clara's startled face. "The witches, remember?"

"Don't mind him, it's just some dumb thing he's seen on Reddit or some other bullshit," Sonia piped up from where she was pulling tent pegs from the wet ground.

"Just pulling your leg, lady," Brian said cracking a grin. "Have a great coupl'a days."

He turned to help Sonia take down the tent, and when Clara looked back at their tent pad, she saw that her girls had gotten things mostly packed up there too. And, predictably, Naomi was also packed, handing out homemade breakfast bars to the kids and tightening the straps on her pack. Even the clouds were parting, the rain only a faint patter now. Things were looking up.

CHAPTER THIRTEEN

THE TRAIL WAS a soggy wash. The mud clutched at their boots, dirt spattered up their pant legs past their knees. The rhythmic squelching of their steps was the only sound for the first few minutes. Naomi took the lead, as usual, then Thea and Maddy behind her. Aiden fell into step next to Tilly, who stiffened and studiously scanned the greenery to the side of the trail. Clara brought up the rear.

Brambles lined the path here, some kind of berry bush. Swollen fruit long past picking hung soggy and fermenting, those that had already fallen mixed into the dirt, staining it the color of blood.

Clara shook her head. Emilio had accused her on more than one occasion of focusing too much on the negative, and she refused to give him even the absent satisfaction of being right. She lifted her eyes. The sky had cleared just as Naomi promised, and robins flitted from branch to branch, flashing their red breasts proudly. She unzipped her cargo pocket and pulled out her phone to take a photo of them.

But before she could slide to the photo app, she saw the notification on her screen.

Saw this and thought of you!

From Juliana. She shook her head to clear it of the image of a terrifying Juliana from her dream last night. This Juliana was real: the one who sent her funny memes and talked her out of her emotional slumps.

It was a video of a cat falling into a pool and panicking, which then made it fall into the pool over and over again. The caption read, "When your anxiety makes things worse."

Clara's brow pinched. She was sure she'd turned her phone on airplane mode but then again, she always was kind of bad with technology. She looked at the video again and wondered if she should be offended it reminded Juliana of her. What was she trying to say? But as Clara watched it a third time, she couldn't help but laugh.

Suddenly a furious, loud sound pierced Clara's head, so shrill her vision went red, then black momentarily. The sound wound over on itself, a braid of auditory terror corkscrewing its way into her skull. She dropped her phone and clutched her ears, doubling over, panting.

Then all at once, like a thunderclap, the sound stopped.

Come. The whisper lingered in the negative space left behind.

She stayed hunched over, hands on her knees, pack knocking into the back of her head, until she caught her breath. After what felt like an eternity, she straightened up. She felt drunk. Or, worse than drunk, hungover.

Breathe in, breathe out.

She tried to find five things to focus on, a butchering of a strategy she'd picked up in some psych class in her undergrad. The slick brown of the mud, the green of the ferns and brambles that lined the trail, the sound of her family ahead, not yet aware that she'd fallen behind. That was three, two more. The distant call of a bird. The crunch of footsteps approaching.

Then Aiden was there, in front of her. "Ms. Gomez, are you all right?"

She tried to chuckle at his formality—after all, she'd changed his diapers—but her vision was fading to black, and her limbs felt wobbly, like her skeleton had melted away.

He caught her with a hand under her shoulder, Tilly swooping in to catch the other side. Supported now, Clara felt more blood rush to her brain. She cracked a smile, tried desperately to think of an excuse, a reason she'd faint like this, while also trying to press down the panic that something was horribly, horribly wrong with her.

She swallowed back bile. "Must not have slept so well last night." Naomi never faltered, never even took a day off sick. And this hike was Clara's idea. She wouldn't let a little headache ruin it for her.

Aiden fished in his pocket with one hand and brought out a Clif Bar. "You didn't eat breakfast and we've been going steadily upward for almost an hour. Your blood sugar is low."

Tilly rolled her eyes. "You aren't even accepted to pre-med yet, stop showing off." She returned her gaze to her mother though, a crease forming between her brows.

Aiden ignored her and handed Clara the bar. "You'll need water too. You okay to stand on your own?"

"I've got her," Tilly said, a bit too forcefully.

Aiden gave her a nod. "Okay." He let go of Clara and handed her the water bottle from the side of her pack.

She drank gratefully, the feeling returning to her limbs. She squeezed Tilly's shoulder. "Thanks, Sweetpea."

The teen scoffed and shrugged away, but Clara saw her face soften.

"We should probably catch up to the others. I told Mom to give the girls a snack too. They'll be just around the next bend. You all right to keep going, Ms. Gomez?"

"It's Clara, Aiden. And yes, I'm fine to hike. Thanks."

THEY DID INDEED catch up with the others around the next bend. The girls were nibbling on something yellow and chewy. Naomi held some out to Clara. "Mango jerky? Thea and I dried it ourselves."

"Um, no thanks," she responded, holding up her unfinished Clif Bar.

Naomi eyed her. "You doing all right? I knew we should have done a more strenuous training program leading up to this trip."

Clara felt the gut punch. Sure, she wasn't a hike-every-weekend fit freak like her friend, but she was strong and capable. She thought of the wrenching pain in her head, the dizziness.

"It wasn't—"

"She just had low blood sugar, Mom. In all the rush of the morning, she hadn't eaten anything."

"Can we keep going?" Maddy asked. "Naomi said there's a waterfall up ahead!"

"Course we can, love," Clara responded, this time taking the lead herself.

"Another hour or two," she heard Naomi say behind her, "then we'll break for lunch at the falls."

Clara forged ahead, her boots sliding across rocks and snagging on tree roots, but she wouldn't slow. She wanted to prove she was capable, that she didn't need to be led like a child. But it was something else too. That pull again, a drive to go farther, deeper. Something was niggling at her, a puzzle that needed to be solved. She had the feeling, like a word on the tip of her tongue, that the woods would reveal a secret if she could only go deep enough into them, if she would give herself up and let them swallow her. She felt the brambles scratch at her arms, foliage teeth she was passing as she made her way to the forest's dark, impenetrable throat.

"Doing great, Ms. Gomez." Aiden's voice shook her from her reverie.

"Yes, thank you," she said, leaving any thoughts of turning back long behind her. "Feeling much better."

AN HOUR INTO her surge forward, Clara became aware of her blisters. The back of her heel and across the tops of her toes rubbed raw, a burn with each step. But she gritted her teeth and pressed onwards. She couldn't stop. The forest wanted her, called to her. She knew if she could just peel back a layer, she would know something vital. Her breath came in bursts, the grade of the trail increasing incrementally with each passing minute. But she couldn't stop. Didn't even slow.

Come.

Come.

Come.

Footsteps on the trail, wingbeats in her ears, a chant, a rhythm. She was the forest and the forest was her.

Clara

"Clara!"

She spun, teeth bared, ready to rage at the interruption. But startled at herself and deflated. "What?" she said, a hint of the simmering anger still laced through her voice.

"The girls need a water break." Naomi shot her an odd look as she handed Maddy her water bottle and helped Thea with the spout on her Camelbak.

Aiden reached for Tilly's bottle in the outside pocket of her backpack, but she swatted him away. Clara raised a brow at Naomi, but she didn't seem to have noticed. Before high school, back when Naomi lived in the house down the road, Aiden and Tilly had been the best of friends.

They were "thick as thieves," Emilio used to say as they rocked Maddy out on the front porch, watching the two older kids rip up and down the street on their seven-speeds. Obviously, something changed, as things often do.

Maddy marched up to where Clara perched on a boulder, wiggling her blistered toes in her boots. "Mom, we were calling you for ages." It wasn't just a comment, it was an accusation. "But you didn't stop."

"You need to be stronger out here in the wilderness," she heard herself snap, as though the words came from someone else's mouth.

Maddy's face turned stony. There was a smear of dirt across one cheek, and sweat glimmered along her hairline. Clara swallowed back another biting remark with considerable effort. What was wrong with her? She took Maddy in her arms. "Sorry, hon. This is actually harder than I thought it would be."

"Yeah," Maddy said into the fabric of Clara's raincoat. "I just want to go home. My socks are wet. Thea and I both just want to go home."

"It's tiring, but I think you'll feel differently once we reach the falls," Naomi said brightly.

Clara cut in. "What's important is that we're together. We've already overcome the biggest obstacle of all, the huge rain storm and all our soaked gear. We've got three nights left and it's all downhill from here."

Maddy looked up the trail. "It's all *uphill* from here, Mom. And I've got blisters on all of my toes. And how do you know there won't be another storm? Or something worse?"

Indeed, as she spoke, Clara did feel a few small rain drops on her nose. As they'd climbed, the clouds had taken over the sky again, bathing everything in a shadowy, silver-gray light. But it would probably just be a quick shower.

"Let me have a look at those blisters, Maddy," Naomi said. She knelt by Maddy and started to apply moleskin to her toes. Yet another thing Clara should have thought of but didn't. She gritted her teeth.

"I don't know there won't be another storm, Sweetpea. But I do know that we can weather whatever comes our way. Right?"

Maddy shivered and looked away as she pulled her boots back on.

"You look cold. Probably means we should get moving again," Clara said.

"Clara's right," Naomi said, moving up the trail past where Tilly leaned against a tree, back to the rest of the group. "The sweat on you is making you colder. Can't stand still for long. Let's pick it up and work up a good lather." She marched forward, taking the lead spot once again. "We're nearly to the falls!"

Maddy and Thea fell in behind Naomi in an obedient stumble, their hands clutched together. The rest of them filed in behind.

Naomi kept a running commentary, perhaps to keep everyone attentive and motivated, scrambling forward to keep within earshot of what she was saying. Or perhaps just because she liked to hear herself talk. Clara could never be sure.

"'Broken Trail' was the name given to this path by some early explorers to the area. Anyway, apparently it used to function as a trade route between First Nations groups. When the first colonizers from the East Coast made their way through here, they used the trail as well. But after a huge rain, a landslide sliced right through it—just above the falls, where we're headed next—so the explorers called it broken. They couldn't figure out a safe way to pass for a while. Eventually, a trail was carved out and around the slide."

Naomi continued, "Obviously before opening the trail to hikers last spring it's been completely redone and made more permanent. Jay helped out with some of the restoration. He was really bummed when they had to close it after the murd—" Naomi glanced at the kids. "Sorry. I mean after what happened."

"You mean the *murder*," Tilly called loudly. "It's not a secret you guys are bringing us on the trail where Mom's crazy old patient killed that guy."

"Tilly!" Naomi cut a glance at Clara who held up her hands.

"I didn't tell her. And I think we should change the subject."

"Agreed," Naomi said.

A buzz began to grow in the back of Clara's head, that low drone that heralded either a panic attack or a headache. Her backpack yanked painfully on her shoulders and each step she took she felt she was trying to extract her feet from quicksand.

"What about the witches that guy said came to these woods? To escape being burned? When did that happen?" Thea asked while Clara tried to swallow past her sandpaper tongue.

Naomi tutted. "That's ridiculous, honey. There were no witches. *Are* no witches."

"Actually," Tilly said. "There are some pretty horrific true stories of colonizers chasing native peoples from their communities and into the woods under the excuse of witchcraft. So there may be truth in some of those rumors."

"But no one was *burned*," Naomi responded, earning her a glare from Tilly. "British Columbia wasn't even part of Canada when all those witch trials were going on back east."

Clara reached up to massage her aching temples.

"Unfortunately, all of this is much more recent. Even this century," Tilly shot back.

"Okay," Thea went on. "So what if witches *did* come up here? What if there *are* still witches in the woods?"

"Yeah. What if that's who killed that guy in the woods?" Maddy added.

Tilly laughed. "Nah, Mom's crazy patient did that. Didn't she? Good thing she's gone now."

Clara's exasperated scream sliced the conversation in two.

"Enough!" she shouted. "I'm not talking about this anymore." Her voice rose, shrill. "Witches did not kill that man. Juliana did not kill that man. Everyone needs to just shut the fuck up!"

Clara's phone buzzed in her pocket.

CHAPTER FOURTEEN

"CLARA," NAOMI SNAPPED.

"No," Clara said, ignoring her buzzing phone. "I'm done. Let's keep hiking. Get to the waterfall or whatever."

"I think maybe you need a break."

Clara plastered on a smile. "We just had a break. I'm peachy. As long as the talk of witches and fucking murder is all done."

"*Language*, Clare. You're scaring the kids."

Clara stopped and glanced at everyone. They'd formed a kind of semicircle around her. Aiden had his arms crossed and had somehow angled himself between her and Thea. Beside Thea, Maddy stared at her with wide eyes. Tilly looked her up and down with a sly smirk that Clara liked least of all.

Naomi stepped forward. "You're acting kind of—"

"Do *not* say crazy."

She shrugged, as though to say *you said it, not me,* and Clara wound her fingers in the hem of her jacket to keep from hitting her friend in front of their kids. Her teeth found purchase in the inside of her cheek and she bit down, hard. Clara had never been a violent person. It must have been the stress of the past few days—who was she kidding, past few months. She took a deep breath, as large as she could with the hulking backpack weighing on her like an anchor, and exhaled.

"I'm sorry. I'm fine. Let's just keep going. I'll have a stretch or whatever at the falls."

"Fine," Naomi said, but continued eyeing her. Aiden took the lead up the path. As the kids filed forward, Naomi hung back beside Clara. "If you aren't up to this—Honestly, Clare, you don't have anything to prove."

"I'm not *proving* anything."

"Well, you seem a little . . . stressed," Naomi said.

"Of course I'm fucking stressed. My husband left me and said he hasn't loved me for years. My kids fucking hate me. Maybe with good reason. I don't even *know* if Tilly has applied to any colleges, after all. I'm on leave from my job because I can't take the stre—"

"Yeah. That. Do you think talking about it might help?"

Clara's phone buzzed again. She shoved her hand in her pocket and toggled it to "do not disturb" mode. Her tongue probed the divots her teeth made in her cheek, tasting iron.

"No," she said. "I came out here to relax. To escape it all. To get through to Tilly and spend more time with Maddy before—"

"They won't go live with Emilio full time, Clara. Judges rarely rule in favor of the male parent, for better or for worse."

Clara stopped walking. "What's that supposed to mean, for better or for worse?"

"No, no. I didn't mean it that way! I meant obviously in your situation it's for better. But there are times when it may actually be better for the kids to be with the—You know what? Never mind."

"Yeah. Never mind. I said I didn't want to talk about it." Clara sped up, taking the empty space behind Maddy and Thea. Naomi didn't rush to catch her.

The trail climbed up and grew rockier. Tall, sturdy Douglas firs gave way to smaller trees. Red cedars, Sitka spruces. The path narrowed, twisting around boulders the size of a small house. Around one of these bends, the river roared at Clara, a raw and rushing moan that was barely filtered through the intervening greenery. They couldn't see it yet, but its presence was evident everywhere. Water beaded on the trees and damp moss hung from the branches. The moisture in the air soothed Clara like a balm on a burn. Her earlier anger at Naomi felt irrational now. Clara's jaw loosened, the joints relaxing.

Naomi finally fell in beside her.

"Been a rainy season, I guess," Clara said by way of an olive branch.

Naomi looked around and shook her head, bewildered. "Still, the river is *ferocious* right now. Let's give it a wide berth." She instinctively kept to the outside of the trail, ensuring she was between the kids and the steep drop off that began to grow on their left.

Vapor hung in the air, the towering rocks dripping with lichen and a slickness that would never fade. The ground beneath Clara's boots squished with each step, like a living thing, breath rising and falling.

"Time for snacks yet?" Thea asked.

"Almost," said Naomi. "Based on the map at the trailhead, we should be reaching the falls momentarily, then we'll have one quick climb and we can break for lunch up at the top."

The group nodded and picked up the pace, their hunger and desire to rest their feet driving them onward.

Just as Naomi predicted, they reached the river's edge in no time. It was a white wash, churning and rushing steadily downward, annihilating the dead trees that piled against the rocks like oversized pick-up sticks. Its roar was thunderous, and Clara had to suppress the urge to cover her ears.

Thea and Maddy ran up ahead with renewed energy, climbing with ease along the steepest section of trail they'd encountered so far, so steep an old chain hung down it. Clara stared in wonder, and not a small amount of fear, as the girls scrambled up. Naomi, Aiden, and Tilly followed, picking their footing a bit more cautiously. Clara clutched the rusty chain that ran alongside the steep climb, cold and rough in her hands. She pulled herself up bit by bit, boots sliding against the slippery rock. At one point, about three-quarters of the way up, a rock wobbled and she lost her footing, nearly plunging to the ground below. The chain chafed her palms, wearing a raw strip. She let out a small cry that was immediately swallowed by the river's thunder. Gritting her teeth, she managed to get her boots onto secure ground again and, after what felt like an hour of terror, she hurled her body over the last two feet and clambered up onto the flat rock that overlooked the falls.

"Lunch, please!" she called, gasping. "Oh, wait, I've got the lunch in my bag." She dropped her pack to the ground and leaned over to put her stinging hands on her knees.

Clara fished around for one of the pre-packed "easy backpacking lunches" she had prepared with advice from the internet and passed the trail mix, granola, jerky, fruit roll-ups, and crackers to Tilly and Maddy before grabbing some for herself.

"Tilly, maybe not so far," Clara said, as her daughter took her portion and wandered to the edge of the rock that hung over the churning falls. She gave Clara little more than a scowl over her shoulder and plopped as close to the edge as she could while still avoiding the heaviest of the river's misty spray.

Everything had a strange, muted, white noise quality about it, devoid of any color or sound besides the water's churn. The sky was a weathered white that matched the river below. The mists even made the trees blend into the slate gray of the rocks. Clara fingered the phone in her pocket and wandered to the tree line, where the rock gave way to a carpet of pine needles at the edge of the forest. She settled under a damp cedar. The old, weathered bark of its trunk poked against her back as she nibbled a bit of jerky and watched the others. Thea and Maddy were tossing raisins at each other and trying to catch them in their mouths. Raisins littered the ground around them, and Clara was surprised Naomi hadn't scolded them for it. She was busy tying something to the outside of her pack, and Aiden had wandered over to sit beside Tilly. Though they were only a few yards away, Clara couldn't hear them. Their words, like everything else, were swallowed by the river.

Juliana must have paused here, perhaps leaned against this very tree, or chatted with Gavin overlooking the edge of the water. Was there an ominous air at this point in their journey? This was the last point anyone had seen them, if Clara remembered correctly. Another group of hikers saw Juliana and Gavin fighting at the water fall, testimony that helped seal the case against Juliana. As though a woman couldn't fight with her partner and *not* murder them.

The fine hairs on her neck raised. A feeling of being watched sent a chill down her spine. A thought: *What if Juliana is watching me now?* She glanced around the clearing and into the forest, but saw no one. It was an absurd thought. Juliana had been texting her from Solara for weeks now. She was back, safe and sound, hating her new therapist. Clara pulled her phone out of her pocket to find she'd received six text messages. She had no idea how she was still getting service. And hadn't she turned it off again after taking that photo? Or maybe she'd forgotten to.

All the texts were from Juliana. The first one was a photo, a quick snap of Juliana at the trail head. Gavin must have taken that one.

The next was a simple text: *Miss you!! :)*

Then a longer text telling Clara she's been having a hard time, thinking a lot about her family and how much she'd like to see them again. How her new psychologist just wasn't listening to her, not as well as Clara used to. Clara tried to parse the words, but something wasn't making sense. Juliana had no living family, as far as Clara knew.

She had never spoken about her family before. Not in their sessions together and not in their texts. There was nothing in her file about a family either, other than a deceased grandmother.

Clara was about to scroll onto the next message, another photo, when Tilly appeared next to her. Clara dropped her phone to her lap and looked up. "Hey, Sweetpea," she said.

"And you give me a hard time about being addicted to my phone," Tilly said.

"I'm just . . . looking at pictures. I have so many good ones from the hike!" she said with false brightness. "Have you gotten any?"

Tilly shook her head. "I'm just letting you take them all I guess." She started off into the woods and Clara jumped up.

"Where are you going?"

"I need to take a piss. I'll be right back."

Clara glanced behind her at the group. "All right. I guess. Don't be long, okay?"

Tilly rolled her eyes. "Jesus. You telling me how long I'm allowed to piss now too? Just need to control everything, don't you Clara."

"No—That's not—I mean, whatever, Tilly."

Tilly scoffed and stomped away into the shadows.

CLARA SAT BACK down and returned to her phone. The next three messages were all photos. Juliana at night, in the woods. Clara swallowed. She could see the edge of a Solara-issued T-shirt peaking at the bottom of the picture. That must have been the night—that night.

Their night.

Her pulse raced. If anyone saw this picture on her phone, would they somehow guess she'd been there? Out here, with Juliana the night she disappeared? She glanced up across camp. Aiden gazed out at the river. Naomi and the two younger girls clustered together around a pile of miniature Uno cards.

All was as it should be. Naomi had never mentioned Clara's first jaunt into the woods. And neither had Dr. Benton. If they'd known . . . if *anyone* had known, Clara would be in much bigger trouble.

She took a deep breath in and let it out. No, no one knew what happened, and Juliana was back at Solara. She was just sending some old photos. Maybe it was her way of saying she wished she were here on the hike now. That made sense.

Clara typed out a quick response to that photo *Wish you were here!* and sent it off before scrolling to the next photos.

A low buzz built at the base of Clara's skull again. The next photo was an owl.

A one-eyed owl, perched on a branch.

It was fine. It was a coincidence. They'd been in the same place. Of course they'd seen the same wildlife.

But the next photo.

The next photo was of Clara. On the trail. Her yellow pack obscured her face and most of her body from view, but Clara recognized her hiking pants, her new boots, that oversized bright yellow backpack.

Her stomach turned.

How in the fuck?

Suddenly, a shadow passed over her. Clara jumped, banging her head against the tree.

"Jesus! You scared me," she said, putting a hand on her heart as Naomi took a surprised step backward.

"Sorry! Sorry. Just came over to see if you knew where Tilly was?"

"She's just gone to the bathroom. Should be right back," Clara said.

Naomi peered between the trees. "She went off the path?"

"I imagine she didn't want anyone seeing her pee," Clara responded with a laugh, but ice was creeping up her back. "Pretty sure you'd do that, too."

"Okay. But I know how to note landmarks and way find. It's easier than you think to get lost, Clara. I usually always recommend going with someone else."

"I'm sure she's fine." Clara couldn't get the photo of herself out of her mind. The shot, from lower on the trail, captured her backpack, her legs, one hand outstretched touching a Douglas fir branch. She shivered. "Maybe I'll just go check on her."

"Probably not a good idea. We don't need both of you lost."

"I can find my way." Clara bristled at Naomi's insistence on babying her. She stood to get on even ground. "Hey, do you have cell service out here?"

"Nope. Nobody does. This mountain is still a black spot for all carriers, thank goodness. You can't call her. We should just wait. I'm sure you're right, she's probably close."

Clara nodded, her fingers tapping the phone in her pocket, powered down this time. A thought was itching at the back of her brain, but she wasn't going to examine it right now.

Wasn't going to think about what the implications of her improbable text messages might be. She'd learned enough in abnormal psych to pass her tests—no need to dredge all that up again now for a self-diagnosis session.

"I'm going in. I'll just call her name a few times. She can't be out of ear shot."

Naomi pursed her lips a moment and then shrugged. "Okay. Yeah. But don't forget to pay attention to your way out. Like I said. Two people lost is a lot worse than one."

"Got it." She turned and traipsed off into the woods, not wanting to be around other people right now. Other people who might notice her spiraling off the rails. She ran a hand through her hair. *Get it together, Clara.* Her stress leave, this hike, they were all meant to make things better. Not worse.

CHAPTER FIFTEEN

CLARA LET THE shadows of the forest swallow her. The sunlight slanted through evergreen needles and orangey leaves, most of it gone by the time it reached the forest floor. The pine needles acted like sound insulation—even the roar of the river softened. She went further in, down a slope.

"Tilly?" she called, her voice sounding far away, even as it left her mouth.

The trees clustered close around her. Their limbs reached for her, grasping at her hair, her jacket, scraping along her cheeks like angry nails.

"Tilly?" she called again.

Landmarks. Clara remembered to look for landmarks. That way, when she found Tilly they wouldn't both end up lost. She took note of a leaning Douglas fir, a small rock covered in moss that resembled a troll, a rotting log.

"Tilly?"

Clara stood still a moment, listening for sounds of life.

There were sounds: the whisper of the wind, rustling of the leaves, but no footsteps. No response from Tilly. Maybe she should go back. She turned back toward the river, eyes peeled for the troll rock or the leaning Douglas fir. But all the trees looked the same. The boulders too. She spun a circle to reorient herself back to their picnic on the rock, but there was nothing but trees, trees, trees on all sides. It had only been a few steps, mere meters into the woods; she should be able to see the brightness of the clearing, but branches reached over her on all sides, stealing the light. She took a few steps in the direction she'd come.

But—was that really the right direction? It looked denser and darker, not like it would open up into a rocky clearing in a few feet. And the river's roar was muffled, barely there, seeming to come from the ground itself rather than any particular direction. Other than that, the forest was oddly silent, not even a bird singing or a twig snapping.

Clara chewed her lip, tasting blood. There was no need to panic, she told herself. Sound traveled differently here. That was all. She would calm down, find her way out, and everything would be fine.

But then she remembered her phone. Those calls and texts from Juliana had buoyed her, had kept her going even on her leave, even when Tilly slammed doors or ran away. The friendship she had leaned on in her darkest moments. Her heart began to pound in her ears. Was any of that real? Clara put a hand against a tree, felt the roughness of the bark, smelled it. That was real. She couldn't have imagined weeks of text messages, could she?

No, that was insane. *Maybe not the best choice of word*, she chided herself. She was just being silly, lost in the woods. Her bad sleep the night before was making her hysterical and panicky. This was a solvable problem. She could find Tilly and find her way out of here. Clara tried to remember all the tips Naomi had shared with her. How to way find, what to do in an emergency, how to use what you had in the moment. But what did she have? A phone she was too scared to turn on and a pack of soggy tissues?

She took a few more steps toward where the river should have been. She would go back, restart, find her way again. A rushing sound filled her ears. Her heart leapt—it must be the river.

But then it grew louder, the voice of the leaves, the trees, screaming into her ears. *Mommy!*

A word. One word.

"Tilly?" she called out again, her voice shaking.

Silence and then, "Mama!"

She followed the sound, rushing between the trees, her feet snagging against roots, branches scraping against her face.

Her breath came in bursts, but she surged forward. *Mama! Mommy!* She was coming. Oh, baby, she was coming! Tilly hadn't called for her like that in years. Tears pressed at the edges of her eyes as she gulped back sobs.

Somewhere out there, in the wilderness, her baby needed her. Clara's mind raced with all sorts of scenarios—a bear, a fallen tree, tripping in a hole.

Her boots skidded to a stop, the sudden change in motion nearly making her topple over in the opposite direction. There, not ten yards in front of her, stood a girl. Not Tilly, much younger. Maybe eight. Dark, tangled hair matted with leaves. Face pale, mouth hanging open in that way of overtired children. But her eyes were alert, trained on Clara. Scratches lined her arms. Whatever clothing she wore was torn and dirty beyond recognition.

Clara held up her hands, moving slowly, not wanting to scare the girl away with any sudden movements. "I heard you calling," she said quietly. "That was you, you I heard calling, wasn't it?" The girl nodded, mouth still sagging open.

"I'm—I'm going to help you," Clara said. Her heart pounded in her ears, and she tried to ignore the pressure building in her chest.

Clara was never good in emergencies. She always blanked and couldn't decide what to do. But she was the only person here now. There was no one else to follow. She had to act.

"Help me," the girl echoed back in a voice like rustling leaves. A quiet rasping.

"Yes." Clara's head bobbed in reassuring panic. "Yes, I'm going to help you. Where are your parents?"

"Help me," the girl said again.

Clara looked around, searching the woods for any sign of where the girl might have wandered from. "Yes, I will help you. If you'll just tell me who you're here with? Your parents or . . . or a teacher or something?"

"Help me."

Clara exhaled slowly. "Come with me. I'll—I'll take you back."

The girl's mouth snapped shut then, her lower lip beginning to wobble. She shook her head fiercely, like spiders were crawling through her hair. "Not back," she rasped. "Not back. *They* are there."

Her head whipped back and forth, now at a frenzied pace, until her whole body was shaking, vibrating. Clara stood transfixed a moment, then stepped forward, pressing through the barrier of her own inaction. Her hands found the girl's shoulders and fought against the tremors.

"Shh," she said, trying to soothe, but the girl shook so violently Clara could hear her teeth clacking against each other in a loud rattle. Was this a seizure? Tilly had a friend in elementary school who suffered from seizures and Clara had seen him have an attack once, but she had no idea what to do to help. She called out to the woods, "Help me!" But she knew Naomi and the others wouldn't hear her over the river's roar.

She must have been gone so long now, maybe they'd come into the woods to find her. Maybe they would hear her and come help. "Somebody help us," she cried out again.

The girl's knees began to give way, so Clara gently lowered her to the ground. "Help us!" she cried again. The girl thrashed on the ground, leaves and pine needles sliding away beneath her, revealing the dark brown mud below. Only the whites of her eyes were visible now, red veins webbing across them like fine lace.

Clara gasped. Was she watching this lost little girl die? Her own heartbeat pounded against her skull, loud and insistent, the paralyzing freeze of panic taking her over. But she wouldn't, she wouldn't let it. She spoke soothingly to the girl, held her shoulders. Clara flinched as blisters began to form along the girl's cheeks and arms, popping up in waves spreading out from her center. Smoke rose from her, as though she were burning, but there was no fire. Clara blinked and covered her nose, the smell of seared meat permeating the air.

White foam gurgled from the girl's mouth now, lining her lips. No, not foam, something else. *Maggots*. Clara's heart stopped. They crawled from between the girl's swollen lips, first just a few, then gobs of them. She let go of the girl's shoulders, crab-scrambling back on her hands and heels. A river of maggots and grubs flowed over he girl's pale, sweaty cheek and pooled into a writhing mass on the wet ground below. Her mouth opened further, splitting open, wider than a human mouth should go. More creatures now, scuttling cockroaches and slithering worms poured out, covering the girl's body and the surrounding ground.

God, no. This couldn't be real. She knew it wasn't real. But Clara's stomach roiled. The stench was awful. Char, rot, vomit, death. She retched and backed away further, covering her mouth with the back of her arm. It looked real. It smelled real.

Something grabbed her from behind, making her jump. It was just a tree. The girl was nearly covered by the swarm. Her body had stilled, but the insects and worms covering her gave a sense of unnatural, undulating movement.

Clara used the tree and climbed to her feet. She found her voice again. "Help!"

"Mom?" The voice wasn't far. And it wasn't coming from the girl on the ground. Clara's pulse began to slow. She knew that voice. Sassy and sardonic.

"Tilly! We're over here," she cried, but when she looked back to where the girl had been, there was nothing but a pile of leaves. No sign anyone had been there, writhing on the ground only moments before. One lone black cockroach made its way across the leaf litter, its tapping footsteps echoing loudly in Clara's ears. Where had the body gone? Clara put her hand to the ground. It was cold and damp, like every other patch of ground. She squeezed her eyes shut. What the hell was going on? She'd had anxious moments before, sometimes took Ativan, but she'd never *hallucinated.*

"We?" Tilly limped up—from where Clara didn't know—and leaned on a tree a few feet away.

"There was—" Clara shook her head. Her hands trembled. A dryness filled her throat, contrasting with her wet cheeks. She realized she'd been crying.

"You all right, Mom?" No hint of sarcasm. Honest concern. Clara looked at her daughter. Mud smeared across Tilly's left cheek and up into her hair. A tear trail wound its way through the dirt on her face.

"You were limping. Are *you* all right?"

"I—" Tilly looked away, her face pale. "I got lost."

Clara held her breath. "Me too. Can I have a look at your ankle?"

Tilly winced but nodded.

Rolling up her daughter's pant leg, Clara saw the swollen, purpling skin immediately. Pressing against the structured confines of the hiking sock and boot that contained it. Potentially the only reason Tilly was even still able to walk. She drew in her breath.

"Let's get you back and see what we can do."

"I think we should go home," Tilly whispered as the wind picked up, hissing across the tree tops.

"We'll see, honey. I'll take care of you."

Tilly nodded, her lips a thin line.

Clara offered her shoulder for Tilly to lean on and took one more look back at where the girl had been. No sign of her, no kicked up leaves, no writhing maggots. Just the pressure of Tilly's weight on her shoulder. It was her daughter who needed help. She needed to keep it together.

They took a few shambling steps, and suddenly the way back to the river became clear. Almost a trail, if slightly overgrown. A three-foot-wide path between the trees, and at the end of it, Clara glimpsed the gray of rocks shining in the sun. How had neither of them found it before?

CHAPTER SIXTEEN

Vancouver, BC
August 13, 1979

My Marie is a delight. She has her aunt's eyes, which catches me sometimes, and I have to pause. My sister would have loved this tiny bundle of light and joy, her namesake. Like the fat squirrels we used to feed nuts to and chase between the trees. I don't know if my Marie has her spirit, but sometimes I wonder.

This morning, Donald woke up early for the mill again. He works so diligently. But he does dote on Marie and me. I'm still sometimes surprised when he walks through the door—still unused to men around after all these years. And after what happened.

But Donald, he's something different. Last night he traced his fingers across the ridges of my scars and told me, "I'm following a treasure map to your heart, dearest Eleanor." And I nearly laughed because never before has someone ever said something like that to me. His love is a surprise, everyday a surprise.

He doesn't mind it either when I burn sage in the corners of the room or tuck flowers into his pockets as he heads off to work. Anemones and Yarrow and White Heather to make sure that he returns every day with all his fingers and limbs still with him. Protection against the machines of the mill.

I teach Marie as I collect the herbs and flowers during our days, grown in the window boxes and the tiny garden plot out back. I've become accustomed to the loud sounds of the traffic and the people on the street. Children yelling and playing, the odd plane overhead. But sometimes, on quiet nights, I still dream of those early days with my mother. A vase of flowers on the table, fire in the hearth. The melodies she used to sing as she stroked my hair at bedtime.

And I sing them now to Marie.

CHAPTER SEVENTEEN

THE CLEARING BY the river was visible, but still far. Clara knew Tilly's ankle was bothering her more than she let on, judging by the amount of weight on her shoulder. Their boots slipped and skidded on the slick stew of pine needles and mud underfoot. Tilly let out a hissing breath every other step and kept darting glances behind her.

Clara was also scanning the brush around them, on high alert after her . . . encounter. She swallowed. It had felt *so real*. She'd never hallucinated in her life, never even taken hallucinogenic drugs. Professionally, she knew that high levels of stress could cause episodes akin to a hallucination, but even despite everything, she didn't think she'd been under enough stress to cause *that*. Imagined text messages were one thing, but this dying girl was something else entirely. Clara tried to calm her shaking before Tilly noticed.

"So, what's going on with Aiden?" Clara asked after a few silent moments, eager to put her mind on something else. "You guys used to be so close."

"Mom," Tilly whined.

"Sorry. Sorry, I know now isn't the time." But Clara needed to talk, needed to fill the silent forest with one of their voices. "I was just surprised at how you've been treating him."

"How *I've* been treating *him*? Mom!"

"That came out wrong. I'm always saying things wrong. Sorry. I mean I was surprised to see that you two are clearly not friends anymore."

They stumbled forward a few more feet before Tilly spoke up. "I already told you we weren't friends. We used to be. But that was years ago. You obviously haven't been paying much attention." She laughed bitterly. "He's popular now. Apparently too popular to be seen with me. So, no. We are definitely not friends."

"What do you mean?" Clara's skin prickled, a strange, familiar fear. Ever since Naomi took her under her wing in eighth grade, she'd been worried Naomi would ditch her for someone cooler, more confident, less high strung. She never did, but even after all these years, Clara's jealousy reared up if Naomi mentioned another friend.

"It doesn't matter. It was a long time ago."

Clara chewed her lip, trying not to press more. She could see Thea's red jacket ahead against the backdrop of gray rock.

"I was drunk." Tilly said it almost like a challenge.

"Okay," Clara said, tensing. But she didn't take the bait, hoping Tilly would say more. They hadn't talked about Tilly's near-arrest that night Juliana went missing. As soon as Emilio brought Tilly home, Clara implemented a stricter curfew and social media restrictions.

But they never actually mentioned the police or what happened. Never mentioned that Tilly had been coming home smelling like alcohol a couple nights a week. She just thought . . . if she could just get Tilly under control it would all be okay.

"At a party." Tilly shot Clara another sideways glance. Another dare. Clara stayed silent as her stomach tied itself into knots. "I asked him for a ride home. But he went off with some guy and left me stranded." She shrugged.

Clara wanted to smack him. Aiden was a responsible kid, a good kid. He got good grades and played varsity basketball. "Maybe he forgot?" Clara offered, immediately regretting it.

Tilly shot her mother a withering glare. "Are you kidding me right now? He *left* me, drunk and alone, at a party in West Van where I hardly knew anyone. Anything could have happened."

Clara's stomach dropped. The silence stretched between them, familiar now after so many years of not talking about anything important. She could almost see it, the gulf between them.

A faint memory—one that she'd buried deep, deep down—threatened to bubble to the surface. A phone call to her father from a stranger's house phone. The blinking lights of an ambulance. Her mother's disapproving glare, the expression she directed at Clara nearly every day afterward.

Don't, Clara's inner voice warned. She shook her head, shoving the memory away again.

What was Tilly doing in West Van? "Did anything—"

"No," Tilly interrupted. "Nothing did. But it *could* have. I called an Uber and made it home on my own because I'm not fucking helpless."

Clara nodded. "That is true. You seem anything but helpless." So unlike Clara. Even now, with her injured ankle. "I'm proud of you Tills, for handling that. And everything Tilly. I'm just . . . proud of you. I think I haven't said that enough lately."

Tilly gave her a strange look. "Okay. Well . . . Thanks?" She released herself from Clara's shoulder and stood on her ankle with gritted teeth as they entered the clearing. "And now, here we are!" She gestured with mock cheerfulness to the group.

→→→←←←

"*THERE* YOU ARE!" Naomi said, her brow knitted. "We need to get going if we're going to reach the next camp before nightfall. It's safer if we get there with plenty of time to set up."

She had tidied the camp and all four of the others stood waiting, packs already perched on their shoulders. Tilly scoffed and hobbled toward her bag. Clara could tell she was trying to hide the pain in her leg—trying, but not succeeding.

"Just a little snag," Clara admitted. A little snag—a little girl dying, rotting, consumed by maggots, before disappearing. And, the very real problem of Tilly's possibly-broken ankle. She tossed the food she'd left by the tree into her backpack and went to help Tilly.

"Everything all right?" Naomi asked, softening.

"Fine," Tilly replied through gritted teeth. Aiden approached, reaching to lift her pack in assistance. "I don't need your help," she hissed, grabbing it from him and stumbling, nearly falling. Clara caught her with an arm around her waist.

"I think we need to look at that ankle," Clara said. She eased her daughter down onto a rock.

"What?" Maddy ran over, her pack dropped and forgotten on the rocks behind her. "You okay, Tills?"

Everyone gathered, concern wrinkling their foreheads and drawing their eyebrows together in unison. Naomi approached, first aid kit in hand. She knelt by Tilly's leg with a sigh. Or maybe she hadn't sighed, maybe that was Clara's overactive imagination too.

The roar of the river added to the buzz of anxiety that grew behind Clara's ears.

There you go again, letting everyone down, a voice in her head said, bordering on a growl. *Can't finish anything you start, can you? What will Naomi think?*

She shook her head to clear it of those thoughts. Her daughter was injured, potentially seriously. That should be her biggest fear. Not what her friend thought of her. Or that they won't finish this hike.

Although she couldn't deny her own surprising hint of disappointment at not being able to go further up the trail, deeper into the woods. She wasn't usually one to forge ahead and push into the wilderness, and yet she felt a yearning to not leave these woods. The thought of turning back made her feel ill.

"All right, Matilda, let's get this boot off you." Naomi gently held Tilly's calf aloft with one hand and used her other to loosen the laces as far as they could go. Slowly and carefully, she eased the boot off Tilly's foot.

Tilly let out another hiss, but so did the rest of the group as they laid eyes on the greenish purple stretch of skin Naomi had exposed. The ankle was already at least doubled in size, bulging unnaturally. Naomi's lips pressed together. "There isn't much in this pack that's going to help you, unfortunately. I'm going to give you a pain killer, but we're not going farther up the trail than this. We should figure out how to get you out as soon as possible."

The wind picked up, blowing a thicker layer of clouds in front of the sun and making the woods whisper. Clara shivered. "It's already too late in the afternoon to hike out. It took us, what, almost two days even to get here? And that was without someone injured."

Naomi raised her eyebrows. "Clara, I really think—"

"No. We need to keep our heads clear and not panic." But she was panicking. She was panicking at the thought of leaving the woods tonight. She was panicking about not finishing what she'd started—no, that made no sense. It wasn't that. She pictured that dark stretch of trail she'd run down before, pursued by the ravens. Hiking down in the dark would be suicide. "You have an emergency beacon, right?"

Naomi nodded.

"Activate the beacon. We can wait for rescue here. It will be safer."

Aiden stood. "Maybe I can run out tonight? Get help? I even have my trail runners packed. It'll be good practice."

"Don't be ridiculous," Naomi said. "Either we all hike out together or we all hunker down here."

Clara nodded. "Right. We all stay together. Here."

Naomi eyed Clara. "I'm still not certain this is our best course of action. You're not wrong that a hike out would be difficult, especially if the weather picks up again. But Tilly needs medical attention soon."

Clara nodded. "And the safest way to get it is if we wait here." Another breeze shook the trees until it sounded like they were saying *stay, stay, stay*.

"What would Daddy do?" Thea asked, sidling up beside her mother.

Clara wondered, too. Naomi's husband volunteered for Search and Rescue. Too bad he wasn't here with them now. Clara squeezed her lips tight before responding. "He's probably the one who'll respond to the beacon. He'll be here in no time, I'm sure."

"I want to go home today," Tilly said. "We *need* to go home. *Now*."

Her eyes darkened, and a look crossed her face, more afraid than Clara had ever seen her. Clara's heart beat a rhythmic chant in her head. It occurred to her then: Tilly had seen something in those woods too. Something that terrified her.

Clara swallowed down the spiny ball of fear that threatened to choke her. Maybe it wasn't safe to stay another night. If Tilly had seen something too, then it wasn't all in Clara's mind. But she couldn't come right out in front of everyone and ask. If she really was losing it, she didn't want it confirmed in front of the whole group, especially Naomi. She needed to get Tilly alone.

"She's right," Aiden said. "We should go today. We can all go. Carry Tills, camp where we did last night, and get out of here early tomorrow morning."

Naomi looked up from where she squatted over Tilly's ankle. She looked at Clara.

She spoke slowly. "I think maybe Clara is right. Jay will probably be on the receiving end of this beacon, and they're more than equipped to get a helicopter up here. I know we all want to do something, but maybe waiting is the safest thing."

"Hopefully it's just a sprain," Clara said, pushing a lock of hair out of Tilly's face. Tilly snorted at her and looked away.

Naomi squatted next to Tilly again, her brow creased. "I know it hurts, sweetheart. But we'll take care of you." She patted Tilly's knee, pulled a spare jacket from some pocket in her backpack and wrapped it around Tilly's shoulders. Clara bristled at Naomi's maternal, nurturing gesture. Clara should have been the one to say those things, to promise to take care of Tilly. Naomi stood. "Aiden, why don't you take the girls and find a good spot to camp. We should be back into the woods a bit, less exposed to the river and the elements."

The trio headed into the woods.

"But I like it by the river," Tilly said, her eyes darting to the shadows growing between trees. Her pupils dilated, consuming most of her irises. Again, that uncharacteristic fear. Clara took her hand.

"I know it feels that way, Tills," Naomi said, "but trust me, when the evening winds start, we'll want to have some cover." She peeled the wrapper off a fruit leather and handed it to Tilly. "Here, you didn't have much lunch."

Naomi caught Clara's eye and nodded toward the far side of the rock. They strode to the edge, watching the water rush and dive over the side. "I'm not sure about this plan, Clara. There's still time for us to start down the—"

"I really don't think it's safe to move her," Clara said, the words out of her mouth before she'd even thought them, even considered her angle.

"I think she might be in shock," Naomi said, her voice low despite the fact that Tilly wouldn't be able to hear her from there.

"All the more reason to stay," Clara said.

Naomi sighed and shrugged. "You might be right, but it just . . . feels wrong. But it is what it is. Let's focus on keeping her warm and fed until we can get help. I'm sorry this happened, Clare."

Clara's fists clenched and unclenched at her sides. She was never good with changes in plans, but she had no idea where this irrational anger was coming from. "Yeah," she muttered. "Me too."

"I'm sure we'll all laugh about this someday. It's going to be fine. Tilly will be fine. I've activated the beacon, so we can hunker down and wait. Keep warm, keep the spirits up. If the chopper doesn't arrive tonight, it will by tomorrow morning for sure."

Clara looked off to the horizon beyond the trees where dark clouds gathered, glowing purple in the slanting evening light. She couldn't help thinking how beautiful it was out here.

A FEW HOURS later, Tilly swung on a hammock Aiden had unfolded from an impossibly small sack and stretched between two trees. He had offered to lift her in, but she ignored him and hopped in awkwardly on her own, nearly overturning it in the process. Clara had willed herself to not intervene. He honestly seemed to be trying to make amends with Tilly.

Clara sat on a stump nearby, her shaking hands curled around the tea Naomi had brewed for her. As darkness fell and she watched Tilly sway in the hammock, a cold settled over Clara, and she wondered if she'd made the wrong decision. It was too late now to turn back. Whatever decisions had been made were final now. At the time, staying hadn't even felt like a decision. It was just the right thing to do. The only thing to do. But now that Clara stared down the prospect of spending another day here, perhaps more, her earlier drive to push farther into the woods seemed to have dissolved. She couldn't understand why she had it in the first place. She took a swig of her tea and stared into the darkness between the trees.

The air was thick with moisture, and it chilled her even through her layers of fleece and merino wool. At least Maddy and Thea would be warm. Naomi had them buzzing around the woods searching for large rocks—apparently things were damp and dire enough that she had okayed a fire outside of the official park fire rings. "A fire is another good way to attract attention and potential rescue," she'd said.

Clara was glad for the brightness of Maddy's coat as she tracked her younger daughter in and out of the tree cover. Too many strange things were happening. It could be all in her head, although she was beginning to think maybe it wasn't. And if it wasn't her imagination—the girl, her phone having service, Tilly's unexplained fear—she wondered what on earth it might be. Something . . . supernatural? Clara almost laughed at the thought. She was a scientist, had never even entertained the idea of anything vaguely supernatural. Either way, she didn't want to take any chances.

The idea that she was even considering something like . . . ghosts—there, she let herself think the word—was laughable. Clara didn't even believe in god. Though in the years she was with Emilio, she had consented to going to church every Sunday, obediently moving from standing to seated to kneeling with the rest of the congregation. But it had all been an act, another acquiescence to avoid conflict. And the discipline was good for the kids, she'd reasoned.

A yellowed leaf, mostly brown at this point, fluttered down and landed on the lid of Clara's travel mug. She flicked it off and took another sip, pondering. *Could* the visions she'd been seeing actually be ghosts? Could she admit to herself that ghosts could be a real thing that actually existed?

Clara rubbed her temples. She was getting too far ahead of herself, already thinking about ghosts and hauntings. The girl in the woods . . . Maybe she was just a lost girl who'd run off. Maybe she was a hallucination and Clara really was going insane. She wasn't sure which she hoped for more. And, if her suspicions about Tilly's fear proved to be right, how could it all be in her own head?

You're really losing it now, that growl in her head said, low and scraping, like metal against bone. Clara had always had a critical inner voice, as long as she could remember. It sounded sometimes like herself and sometimes like her mother, but this harsh, scraping edge to it was new.

A hand on her shoulder made her jump, a splash of tea leaping out through the small hole in the lid and onto her pants.

"Sorry, Ms. Gomez." Aiden darted a worried glance over to where Tilly swayed in the hammock, her eyes alert to the forest around her. "I'm going to go hunt for some firewood with my mom, so it'll just be you and Tills at camp until we're back. I just wanted to let you know."

"Aiden, I'm not an invalid," she snapped. That came out more forceful than she'd intended. She looked over at Tilly too. Maybe Clara wasn't an invalid, but Tilly wasn't going anywhere fast. Clara exhaled, blowing a lock of unruly hair out of her face. "Tell your mom we can hold down the fort."

"I know, Ms. Gomez. Sorry."

"It's Clara. And," she said, trying to soften her face, trying to shed the undercurrent of unexplainable rage that seemed to be crawling up under her skin, "thanks for your help. With Tilly. Heard you guys had something of a falling out."

He shrugged, looked away. Something in the look made Clara's blood boil, just for a moment before she clamped a lid on it.

Tilly was right, her thoughts seethed. *He did want to shed her.*

She forced the thought down and reminded herself Aiden was just a kid, like Tilly. It was all in her head—his look, his shrug, his implication that she couldn't get by without his help. She couldn't trust her thoughts anymore.

"Go ahead, Aiden," she said again. "Really, we've got this."

He nodded and strode away, tossing one last glance over his shoulder at Tilly, who pointedly looked away. Once Aiden and his mother were out of earshot, past where the two younger girls still wandered, collecting rocks and playing what looked like forest parkour, Clara wandered over to Tilly. She absentmindedly pushed the hammock, rocking her in a way she hadn't since Tills was swaddled in her bassinet.

"How's your ankle?"

"Fine, really. I wish we could leave now." Her voice was tight.

Clara looked up at the sky, already darkening toward evening. Even more so now that the black clouds had rolled closer. A few random sprinkles hit her cheeks. The dry leaves and pine needles whispered overhead. "I know sweetie," she said, patting her daughter's knee gently. "But it really is safer to stay." The words sounded hollower than they had an hour earlier. Clara swallowed.

"I don't give a fuck what you and Naomi think is safer," Tilly spat, looking into the trees. Then, in a smaller voice, "I just . . . I'm scared. There was something—"

She trailed off. It made Clara's skin crawl.

"What did you—" She breathed in. This was her chance. "Did you see something in the woods, Tilly? Earlier?"

Clara's insides slithered themselves into knots. She wasn't sure if she hoped Tilly had seen something too, so she could confirm she wasn't completely losing it. Or if she would rather it all be in her head, nothing more threatening in the woods than her own insane imagination.

Tilly met her mother's eyes only briefly before staring into the purpling shadows beyond the trees. Clara held her breath.

"No."

"Matilda, I can see something is bothering you."

"Maybe the fact that my ankle is twice the size it should be?"

"You know what I mean. Beyond that."

Tilly sighed, fidgeted with the zipper on her jacket. "You wouldn't believe me if I told you," she whispered. Her green eyes grew dark.

"You'd be surprised. Tilly," Clara was speaking more quickly now, insistent, "what did you see?"

"I—It was—"

A scream echoed through the trees, cutting her off.

CHAPTER EIGHTEEN

CLARA'S HEART THUDDED in her chest. Tilly's fingers clutched around her wrist in a terror grip. They both stared into the growing darkness around them. No one was visible through the trees for a moment. Not the younger girls' purple and red jackets orbiting each other, not Aiden's sandy hair bobbing his way through the trees, not Naomi's sleek, pink raincoat.

The scream echoed a second time, louder than the first, then footsteps tromped through the undergrowth. Branches cracking, a mad scramble. Finally Maddy and Thea exploded from behind a thick copse of brambles, out of breath, clutching each other.

"Something black," Maddy panted.

"It was a bear!" Thea's voice was shrill.

"Two," Maddy said. "A baby."

Clara swallowed back that spiny lump of fear again. Her skin itched. A claustrophobia gnawed at her, pressing against her skin like too-tight clothing. Even though they were out of doors, not a wall for miles, they were trapped.

"Mom said the bears are hibernating now," Tilly announced from the hammock, earning a glare from her little sister. But Clara could see that it was worry that creased Tilly's face, rather than derision at her sister.

Maddy, oblivious, dove into the argument. "We *know*. But there was *something* out there. Black and moving through the trees. And, Mom, it was *big*. A big one and then a little one following."

"Probably the boogeyman," Tilly said to Maddy, who stuck her tongue out. "Remember that time you were so scared of the neighbor's Halloween decorations you couldn't pee with the door closed for weeks? Oh, wait, that was just last month."

"Screw you, Tilly!"

"Okay, okay. Hang on, guys." Clara put a hand on Maddy's shoulder.

Clara pressed down her growing fear by digging a nail into the palm of her hand. She smiled. "It does sound like you saw something scary. There's lots of shadows at this time of night. So how about we get these rocks set up in a ring. A fire will definitely help ease our worries. And keep any animals away."

She didn't believe half of what she was saying. A fire wasn't going to fix anything except maybe the chill that had embedded itself into her bones. Where was that "wilderness woman" drive she'd had earlier?

She scanned the surrounding woods for any sign of a bear and made a note of where their hatchet stuck out of a nearby log. If a wild animal did approach, could she wield the hatchet against it? Would it be enough?

With a growing terror in the base of her stomach, she hoped a bear might be the worst thing they had to deal with.

Clara watched the girls pile rocks into a ring and she pieced through some sticks on the ground, looking for kindling. She had only ever made fires in the safety of the fire ring, and usually someone else lit them. Emilio or Naomi. But dammit, she could do things too.

"You girls keep working on putting those rocks into a circle. I'm going to go grab the stove and a couple headlamps, and we'll get dinner going too." As she walked over to the tents, she darted glances between the trees. Thea and Maddy had been known to let their imaginations run away with them, but she'd also seen the real fear in their eyes and couldn't discount that maybe they *had* seen a bear. Or something even worse.

Maybe she'd made the wrong choice, suggesting they stay here. When she thought back, she couldn't remember why she'd been so sure it was the right thing to do.

It didn't matter now anyway. Doing something. Being busy. That was what was important. Idle hands did the devil's work, as Emilio's mother used to say disapprovingly when the girls got up to mischief in their younger days. Imagine if she could see Tilly now, stealing liquor and sneaking off. Clara ran a hand through her hair. Of course it would all be blamed on her. And perhaps it was her fault. Emilio always had said she was lacking something, a certain gene that would make her *want* to give up her body, her independence, her profession for a year each time they wanted to have a child. A gene that would make her love doing laundry, love tidying the kitchen. All those things should have come naturally to her, according to him.

Clara pushed those thoughts out of her head and bent into the tent to find the Primus stove. The hollow clanking of wood hitting the ground announced Aiden and Naomi's return. She zipped the tent closed and found an old stump to set up the stove. "Pad Thai or"—she held the second bag closer to her head lamp—"Forever Young Mac and Cheese?"

"Don't care. I'm sure they're both gross," Tilly sighed from the hammock. She had her phone in her hand and appeared to be scrolling through photos. Clara thought of her own phone and the strange photos that had come in. She was dying to ask her if she had a signal. She wondered what Tilly was looking at if not her social media. It's all she seemed to do these days when she was home.

"Any response on the beacon?" Clara asked instead, as Naomi arranged the wood in the fire ring the girls had finished. A gust picked up a lock of Clara's hair. She zipped her raincoat tighter. Earlier she'd felt a peculiar sadness at the thought of being rescued two days early from these woods, but now all she could think about was leaving. Why was she always making the wrong decisions and not realizing until it was too late?

Naomi shook her head. "It's a one-way signal. And with the rain coming in, they may have to wait until morning."

Clara nibbled her lip. "What if I was wrong, Nay? We maybe should have tried to make a go for it on our own."

"If there's a storm coming, it's probably even better that we didn't try to get out ourselves," Naomi said.

Far from soothed, Clara poured boiling water into the Forever Young Mac and Cheese, trying not to let Naomi's words affect her. The rain was picking up now. She wasn't prepared to hunker down and weather another storm here with rescue uncertain.

Aiden rushed to tie a tilted tarp over the makeshift fire pit to provide some shelter from the downpour. Maddy and Thea took refuge—both from the rain and whatever they thought they'd seen in the trees—in the tent already, huddled together around a lantern and a book. By the light of the smartphone in her hand Clara could see Tilly nibbling her lip to almost bleeding. Once again, she questioned her decision to stay.

"Do you think Jay will make it here tomorrow?" Clara asked.

"What's the rush all of a sudden? You were the one insisting we should stay." Naomi straightened, cracking her back, and pulled a box of matches from her pocket. Clara noted a hint of snark in

Naomi's voice. If she hadn't wanted to stay, she could have told Clara off. She should have disagreed with her.

"What's the rush?" Clara echoed, her attempt at relaxation draining out faster than the nearby falls. "I mean, apart from my daughter's broken ankle to this shit weather to—now dark things lurking in the woods and terrifying our kids? Like, I'm kinda done, Naomi. It was a good idea—an okay idea. But it didn't turn out—"

"Woah," Naomi held up her hands. "This hike was *your* idea, remember? You asked me to come along for support. And it was *your* choice to stay after Tilly got hurt."

Was it her choice? Clara grimaced. It hadn't felt like a choice, more like a need. Staying had felt like the obvious answer. "I did *not*. I didn't want you here," Clara said instead, her voice bordering on a growl, close to the scraping quality her inner voice had taken on lately.

Naomi's face turned stony. "You're lucky I *am* here."

Clara scoffed, turning off the Primus.

"Sorry," Naomi said, releasing a long breath. "That was harsh. I think we're both stressed. I've known you a long time, Clare. We've been through a lot together. We'll get through this too."

Clara blinked away her surprise at her outburst. She hadn't meant to raise her voice at Naomi. "I just wish none of this had ever happened." Clara sat on a log and put her head in her hands. "I wish we'd never come here. I mean, what a ridiculous idea! I don't even like camping."

"Listen, okay, I'll admit it, maybe this didn't turn into the spectacular trip you'd hoped it would be. But Tilly seems stable. We can still make the most of it while we wait. We're still spending time together. You and the girls. Like you said you needed. And also you and me. It's like old times, before Jay and Emilio. Back when it was just the two of us. We used to have so much fun." She squeezed Clara's shoulder.

"We did. Sure. But not in the middle of the woods with no way out."

Naomi squatted by the fire and her match turned into an angry blaze as she touched it to the fine shavings she'd tucked in the middle of the wood stack. "There *is* a way out. Just not tonight. I know things are hard right now."

Clara scoffed.

"I don't mean just Tilly's ankle and the rain. I mean everything, Emilio, Juliana—"

"No." The word raced out of her so fast, like a door slammed. Naomi looked up, blinking.

"Clara, you should talk about it. You've been keeping so much in for so long."

Clara sighed and stared up to where the tips of the trees scraped the purple sky. She *should* talk about it. She knew that. At least some of it. She didn't want to talk about Juliana. Or whatever Naomi thought she knew about her. But Emilio . . .

Clara glanced around—all of the kids were engrossed in their various activities. Either out of earshot or paying too much attention to other things to hear. "You know, he moved in with Becca a week after he left us?"

"Wait, Becca?"

"His financial adviser. *Our* financial adviser. That bitch."

"Oh shit. That's our advisor, too," Naomi mumbled.

"I know. You recommended her to us. Thanks." It was meant to be a joke, but the word came out barbed. Naomi didn't seem to notice.

"That's what I've been saying this whole time. Fucking Emilio. I always knew he was a total asshole."

Clara darted a glance over to where Tilly was still engrossed in her phone. Hopefully she couldn't hear them. "It was a dick move. He was a good dad, though. Still is." It pained her to admit it, but it was true. He was good to the girls. She checked her watch and opened the bag of mac and cheese. She let the steam escape and then started scooping glop into camp bowls. She looked up at Naomi. "You certainly tried pretty hard to get us together, considering you apparently thought he was an asshole the whole time," she whispered. A lump rose in her throat, but she swallowed it down. She wouldn't cry over Emilio. Not now.

Naomi shrugged, sitting back on her haunches. "We were like *twenty* when I set you up. Back then it didn't matter if he was an asshole if he was hot. I just knew he'd be good in bed. I didn't know you were going to up and marry him."

Clara's body tensed. Something ugly tickled at the edge of her consciousness. "You just knew . . ." She met Naomi's eye. "Exactly how well did you *know* that?"

The other woman shrugged again and jabbed a stick into the fire. "Sometimes you can just tell."

A wave of nausea roiled through Clara. It wasn't very far below the surface, that itching her beneath the skin, but she wouldn't peel back any more layers. Wouldn't expose any more ugliness. Now wasn't the time.

Is it ever the time, Clara? How much shit are you willing to just shovel under the rug?

Her hand shook as she lifted the mugs of sticky mac and cheese.

You're weak, Clara. You barely stood up to Rocky when he was pawing your teenage daughter. Won't stand up to Naomi now. You just can't handle all the dirty truths around you.

Her skin tingled suddenly with the memory of Emilio's hands on her, his hot breath in her ear, her nails in his back. And she wondered—didn't want to wonder, didn't want to know—if Naomi had those same memories.

Instead, she stomped off to the hammock to hand Tilly her dinner. She swallowed back the acrid bile in her throat and called out to Maddy. "Dinner, Mads. Come on out. Fire's warm."

But Clara wasn't. A coldness had enveloped her. She chewed absently on the pasty noodles from her bowl, the shell-shaped macaroni like bland cardboard in the pastry sauce. Was her whole life a lie?

Naomi stared too intently at the fire, barely looking up when Aiden handed her a plate of whatever gourmet backpacking food he'd whipped up. He shot Clara a sympathetic glance that let her know he'd overheard the whole thing. That just made it worse. Her stomach roiled again, and she knew it wasn't just from the over-salted mac and cheese. She felt the ground tipping beneath her. Her fingertips dug into the meaty bark of the log she sat on, nails catching on the rough edges and bending backward. Salty glue stuck in her throat, she couldn't swallow. Wingbeats in her ears. A buzzing.

She ran past the edge of the firelight, made it behind a tree and hopefully out of earshot, before she emptied her guts onto the wet ground. She heaved again, her knees in the mud. Raindrops pelted her back and tears stung her eyes.

A hand on her back, Clara glanced over her shoulder. Naomi. The distant fire painted shadows across her face.

"I'm fine," Clara rasped.

"You don't look fine. It's been a tough go. I'm here for you, you know."

She shrugged Naomi's hand away. "I know. Like you've always been."

"Exactly. I'm always here for you."

"That's the problem," Clara mumbled, wiping her mouth on the back of her sleeve as she stumbled away.

"What?"

"I said, that's the problem." Rain ran over her coat like tears, soaking every part of her not covered in overpriced, waterproof gear.

"You're *always* there. *Always* somehow knowing what's right for me. Apparently better than I know myself."

"Why won't you let me help you?"

Clara's wet hair stuck to her forehead as she spun to face her friend. "I *do* let you help me, Naomi. *Too much.* I mean . . . I can't tell what's right anymore, which version of me is actually *me*. Did I cheer in high school because you got me on the squad? Did I go to UBC because you were there too? Did I marry Emilio because—" She left unsaid, *because* you *were in love with him?* She cut herself off before she could bare herself that way. Instead, she said, "I think you've helped enough." Her voice was cold. "I just—I have a lot to figure out, and now my daughter is injured and we're stuck in the godforsaken woods. I think—I think we should have gone home. I don't know what I was thinking."

Naomi blinked. "Is this because of what I said about Emilio?"

"No—Yes. Yes of course it's that. You can't just casually tell me that you fucked my husba—ex-husband and expect that to be fine."

"But I didn't—"

"I don't want to hear it."

Naomi stomped a foot on the ground, mud flying from her boot. "Will you *listen*, Clara? How can you say that? I did *not* fuck Emilio. He—" She pushed a wet hair out of her face. "He came onto me once—only once, after Jay and I were already together. *Before* I introduced him to you, by the way. But it went nowhere."

"So I was the consolation prize you handed him instead."

Naomi paused, her body still. "No. Clara, don't be like that!"

"You hesitated. I was, wasn't I? The consolation. No wonder he left me eventually. I could never live up to what he'd really wanted. I could never compare to you. I'm surprised we lasted so long. My life is your seconds, the pieces of things that weren't quite good enough for you to keep, you passed on to me. My whole *life* is your fucking *hand-me-down.* Jesus." Clara pressed her hands to her face and started to turn away.

"Damnit, Clara. You need to take some responsibility. You're a grown ass adult. You can't blame everything on me."

"But *you* did this! *You* said this hike was a good idea. *You* agreed with me that we should stay. *You* introduced me to Emilio."

"Which is it, Clar? Which are you blaming me for? All of it? This hike was *your* idea, a way to recover after . . . after what happened with Juliana. And, if I remember correctly, *you* said 'I do' at your wedding. Not me."

Clara was soaked now, rain mixing with her tears, pattering like thunder on her hood. She felt battered, empty. Alone.

"I don't know what to think anymore." She sniffled. It was a little deranged, what she was saying to her friend. Could she really claim that Naomi had orchestrated her whole life? That sounded like textbook paranoia. She should know better. But she couldn't deny how she felt. True, Naomi hadn't pitched the hike idea, but she'd encouraged it. And Clara couldn't imagine what possessed her to come up with such a plan in the first place, other than to impress Naomi. It's what she thought Naomi would want her to do. Maybe her whole life was made of decisions to do what she thought Naomi wanted her to do. Had she ever even once made a decision for herself?

Naomi stood still, letting the rain pound against her bare head. It ran in rivulets down her forehead as she watched Clara with searching eyes. Clara was about to walk away when her friend came and wrapped her arms around her, their raincoats crinkling and squeaking together.

"I'm sorry," Naomi said, "I really am sorry about all of it."

Clara's muscles relaxed. "Tomorrow—if Jay doesn't come in the morning—let's just leave on our own. We can do it. Together."

Naomi nodded. "Sure. Yes. I think that's a good idea."

"Tomorrow, we'll leave this place," Clara said, more firm this time.

Naomi smelled like campfire and damp, but beneath that, the scents Clara always associated with her: spice, exotic flowers, clean sheets. Her heart did a flip in spite of itself, the anger slowly melting away, washed by the rain and Naomi's embrace. She tried to cling to it, but it was slippery, slithering away and leaving her empty.

Naomi rested her head on Clara's shoulder for a moment before pulling a few inches away. Her breath steamed against the cold, wet air. "Let's get back. We'll get out of this. Together. You'll be okay, Clare." She took Clara's hand and they strode back into the light of the fire.

Clara suddenly had that itchy feeling of being watched. She glanced over her shoulder, thought she saw someone standing by the next tree: dirty face, long dark hair, a hint of a feathered tattoo peeking above the neckline of her shirt. But Clara blinked, and the image was washed away in the rain.

CHAPTER NINETEEN

"MOM!" MADDY'S VOICE sliced through Clara's sleep. She swallowed back the lingering, acidic reminder of the previous night's events. Once again, she woke to the tent walls shaking with the incessant pressure of the rain, an assault of tiny, liquid bullets against the thin barrier.

Clara glanced around her. Maddy wasn't there. Tilly was sprawled half off her sleeping pad, her bad foot elevated on her pack. The swelling had worsened overnight and her ankle was now a sickly shade of blue-green, or maybe that was just the reflection of the nylon walls that surrounded them. Sweat caked her brow and Clara hoped it was from the humidity in the tent and not an infection.

"Mom!" Maddy called again. From outside. Her voice shrill.

Clara's pulse pounded in her ears. Her vision tunneled. What was happening now? She zipped up her raincoat and crawled outside into the deluge. It was impossible to tell what time it was. The clouds hung low and dark, caressing the tips of the trees and soaking everything beneath. Rivulets of water snaked their way along the muddy ground, weaving in and around the piles of leaf litter and pine needles.

"Clara, there you are." Naomi jogged over, each step sending up splashes of muddy water. Maddy and Thea came up behind her, Maddy's face white. Their raincoats suctioned to them like second skins.

"What's going on?"

"We have a slight problem," Naomi said, her voice emphatically even.

"Oh?" Clara tried to catch her breath, but a tide of panic washed over her.

"The food, Mom! Didn't you hang up the food last night?"

"Of course I hung up the food," she replied, more sharply than she'd intended. After they'd fought last night, Naomi offered to hang Clara's food since there was no bear box here. But Clara insisted she could do it.

And she *could* do it. In fact, she *did* do it. Exactly the way she had learned to, and exactly the way Naomi had done hers. Clara had even double checked it by the light of her headlamp later that night to make sure their knots were identical, their placement the same. The food bag had been dangled over a high branch and anchored by rope to a lower branch, nice and strong, so no bears or other wildlife could get at it.

"Come on," Maddy said. She led the way into the woods, further from the river, to the tree where they had secured their food. The bag lay on the ground, its dark blue, waterproof fabric shredded into ribbons. Foodstuffs lay torn open and scattered across the ground.

Clara swallowed. It was four days' worth of food, rendered a soggy mess by rain and mud. She closed her eyes and massaged her fingers into her forehead a moment before looking back at the tree. The anchoring branch she had used was snapped off, a clean cut, almost as though it had been sawed free. "How is this even possible?"

Her eyes followed the trunk up to the branch where their food had hung. There, dangling as it had been last night, was the orange bag containing all of Naomi's food and supplies. "Fuck," she whispered under her breath.

The rain pressed down, threatening to smother her. She felt its weight on her shoulders, her lungs, her head. Tears pushed against the back of her eyes. *This isn't my fault*, she wanted to scream.

Isn't it? That voice. That voice! Clara wanted to rip it from her skull. She pulled at a fingernail with her teeth. Clara's vision swam, the trees around her seeming to move and shift. She blinked it away, focusing instead on the tattered bag on the ground. At the base of the tree, she noticed a footprint. It was in a patch of mud shielded enough from the pattering rain to remain mostly intact.

"We can stretch our supplies for an extra day, maybe two," Naomi said as Clara squatted to inspect the print, "which should be more than enough, but—"

"I thought we were leaving today, one way or another," Clara replied, not wanting to rely on Naomi's good planning and smug generosity for too long. "If that's the case, we have more than enough food."

Naomi glanced at her feet, where the rainwater beaded along the waterproofed leather. "That's the other thing—"

She cut off; nothing but the incessant drone of rain filled their ears for a few moments. Then the rumble of thunder echoed through the trees. Resounding, rolling cracks that made them all jump. The ground shook, it was so loud.

"It's this storm," Naomi started again, gesturing to the sky as the thunder crescendoed and then faded.

"I thought the helicopter would come today."

Now you can stay. Now you can stay and stay and stay. Clara resisted the urge to plug her ears, knowing that wouldn't keep the voice out anyway.

Naomi shook her head. "Choppers can't fly through this. They may send people on foot. We have to just sit tight. Jay knows our route."

The pounding in Clara's head was louder than the storm. She stood and shifted her weight, lifting one boot and then the other out of the squelching mud that threatened to swallow her feet.

The buzzing returned in the back of her skull, and her breath came in short bursts. *Not now*.

She took a breath.

"Sit tight? With half as much food as we should have? And by the way, it looks like someone did this on purpose." Clara eyed everyone assembled, one at a time. "One of us or . . . or maybe someone else we don't know is out here. Look. There's a boot print."

Naomi and Thea squinted at the tree. "I don't see anything but mud," Naomi said.

"Right *there*. That's a print."

"It could be," Thea said with a shrug.

"It could be anything," Maddy said, and Clara tried her best not to glare at her daughter.

"It could be one of ours from when we hung the food," Naomi said. "It could be anything, like Maddy said. The point is, we're short food so we need to be careful."

"My *point* is that someone did this on purpose. Look at the branch."

"Clara. You're acting—"

"Don't. Whatever. It doesn't matter. Tilly needs a fucking doctor. You said we could leave today. We *are* going to leave today."

"*You* where the one who said you wanted to wait—that it was safer to wait! So we waited!"

Clara spun. "Can't you send messages with that beacon? I mean, isn't this the twenty-first century? We're never truly alone or out of technology's range and all that?"

Naomi shook her head. "Emergency beacons use a different frequency, like a morse code SOS. Unfortunately, only satellite phones have two-way communication capabilities."

Clara lifted her arms and dropped them again. "That's ridiculous. We don't have a two-way beacon. Great. So do we even know if anyone can see our distress signal?"

"It appears to be working properly." Naomi lifted the device out of her pocket and showed the blinking red light. "And even if it's not, we're only meant to be out here for four days. As soon as Jay realizes we aren't back at the right time, he'll come for us. Beacon or no beacon."

Clara massaged her fingers into her forehead. Only a satellite phone would have two-way capabilities, Naomi said. But Clara had sent texts. Or maybe that was all some kind of hallucination . . . or something weirder. But she had to try, right? They had to get out of here.

"We'll be out as fast, and as safely, as we can," Naomi was saying, her voice rising over the thunder. "When we talked last night, I didn't anticipate the storm would worsen."

Thea leaned close against Naomi's side. "I'm scared."

"Won't Jay see this storm and know we're in trouble?" Clara pushed.

"Maybe, but I think he'll assume—I mean, he'll *know* we can handle it. It's fine," Naomi replied, her lips set in a thin line. "We have shelter. We have food—*enough* food. The rain will let up soon."

WHEN SHE ARRIVED back at camp, Aiden had already lit a fire under the slanted tarp. Tilly's swollen foot and the edge of her sleeping bag stuck out of the hammock. Clara was happy Tilly was up and about, but she couldn't deny the welling panic she felt about not being able to leave. And even more than that, she was still playing over and over her decision to stay. The weather had been fine at that point. What made her so certain they should stay in the woods last night?

But maybe it was like Naomi said. Things looked different last night. Back then it seemed they'd only have to weather the night and then be rescued. Easy peasy.

But as a drop of cold rain snaked itself into her neckline and down her back, she knew this would be far from easy.

She leaned behind a tree on the edge of camp and fished out her phone, staring at the glowing apple symbol as she waited for it to boot up, then search for service. She watched the three dots bouncing for an eternity before they disappeared and were replaced with the 5G symbol. She had it.

Immediately, a notification came in, then another. Texts from Juliana.

No other calls. No emails. No texts from anyone else. Just Juliana. Clara rubbed her eyes, shook her phone, and looked again. Still clear as day.

I miss you! You must be almost halfway by now.
SEE YOU SOON

Clara swiped them away like they burned her. She navigated to her contacts and tried to call Jay, but the call didn't go through. She tried another friend. Emilio. Even Dr. Benton. None of the calls could connect. The 5G symbol had disappeared. She tried 911, but not even emergency calls would go through.

Repulsed, dizzy, she tossed her phone into the mud and stomped on it, again and again and again until she heard a crack.

She smoothed her hair back into her ponytail and sat beside the fire, staring at the orange flames.

"Morning," she said to Aiden, her voice thin.

"Morning."

She darted a glance to Tilly, who appeared to be napping. "You heard the news?" she asked Aiden.

He gave her a blank look. "When I woke up, everyone was gone. Figured I'd start a fire. Tried to help Tills into the hammock, but . . ."

"But she hasn't forgiven you for ditching her to hang with the cool crowd," Clara finished.

Aiden shrugged, whacking at the fire with a long stick.

Like mother, like son, Clara's thoughts burbled, on their way to boiling over. She took a breath. No, that's not what happened. She'd always feared Naomi would ditch her, but she *didn't*. When Clara's dad died, Naomi was there for her, every step of the way.

"Never mind," she amended, trying to recover but failing miserably. "Did you hear? The food's ruined."

Aiden looked up, confused. "What?"

Another rumble of thunder echoed after his question. "The food's ruined. Well, most of it anyway. And your mom says it's unlikely rescue will come during this storm." She swallowed back an apology. "We won't be out of here today. Maybe not even tomorrow."

Maybe not ever. Clara wanted to find the camp knife and carve that voice from her skull.

Aiden's Adam's apple rose and fell with a quick swallow, and she was reminded that Aiden was only a child, too. With his own fears. She massaged her forehead and looked at him, trying to soften her face.

"That's bullshit. Tilly needs to get out of here." He looked at Clara. "You're right. Everything Tilly said is true. I screwed up, but I've been trying to make it right."

"I know," Clara said. "I can tell. Everybody makes mistakes."

"I just wish she knew how sorry I am. I'll run down and get help."

"That's quite the gesture. But this storm seems like it will be pretty bad."

"Screw that. I've hiked through rain before. I know the north shore really well. I can get to Dad and get a chopper here by tonight, tomorrow morning at the latest."

"Your mom said it isn't safe. And help will come anyway once your dad realizes we aren't back. Losing you on top of everything else will not help a thing, Aiden."

"You think my mom knows everything, don't you?" Aiden said, giving her a sidelong glance. "I don't think we should stay in these woods."

You can say that again. For once, Clara and her inner voice were in lockstep. And it sounded strong, clear, and like herself.

The trees closed in around her, her pulse pounding in her ears. She stood and wandered over to where Tilly reclined in the hammock, swinging herself by pulling on a poor sapling growing nearby.

"We're not getting out of here today, are we?" she said.

Clara shook her head. "I'm so sorry, Tills."

"When can I say 'I told you so?'"

"We'll figure something out. How's your leg?"

"Fine," she said, hiding a wince as she lifted it to show Clara. More sweat beaded on Tilly's brow, and Clara knew now it wasn't just the humidity. "I'm just enjoying my downtime. Phone's dead now, though."

Clara's breath caught. "Did you have service? Any . . . messages?"

Tilly gave her an odd look. "No." She said the word slowly, dragging it out. Tilly swallowed. "The woods—I think there's something strange happening here."

That cold feeling in Clara's stomach again. She'd been so focused on solving the immediate problems—no food, Tilly's injury—that she could almost ignore the other stuff. She glanced over Tilly in her hammock out to the woods beyond. The shadows seemed to move and whisper, figures darting between the trees.

"It's just our eyes playing tricks," she said, hollow.

"What is? What's our eyes playing tricks?"

Clara hesitated.

"What is it, Mom? Did you see something?"

"I . . ."

"Well, I have. Somebody texted me. Mean things. Crazy things. And I shouldn't be getting texts, right? No service?"

"What did they say," Clara asked, her voice a whisper as she was trying to catch her breath.

"And our first day, some crazy old zombie witch lady shows up right in front of me. Holding a frying pan. A fucking *frying pan*. One of those old heavy ones. Totally my eyes playing tricks, right?"

"Wait. What?"

Tilly hesitated. "That's how I fell," she said, her eyes on the woods. "Her dress was all muddy and she only had one eye. Only one eye! But why is it the frying pan that freaks me out more?"

Clara's body tensed. She glanced over her shoulder to where Aiden stoked the fire. *One eye.* "Tell me exactly what you saw."

"I just fucking did!" Tilly's eyes raked the tree tops before turning away from Clara, gazing out into the woods beyond. "Told you you wouldn't believe me. Now go away. I'm tired."

"Listen," Clara hissed out a whisper, "I *do* believe you. Something *is* going on. But I'm gonna get us out of here, Sweetpea. We're gonna be all right."

Tilly glanced back, her face rearranged until she looked like the little girl she once was. She grabbed Clara's hand, nails digging in. "I hope so. I hope you're right. Because—" Tilly bit her lip. "Because the text messages all said one thing: *it wants us.*"

She couldn't help herself. She leaned closer. "*Who* wants us?" Clara thought about the number on her own phone, Juliana's number. Her stomach turned. But Juliana was back at Solara. They'd been talking. Juliana was safe back at Solara and wouldn't be texting Tilly threatening things about the woods. Clara pressed her fingers to her forehead. That just wouldn't make sense. They had no service anyway. But if Tilly was receiving messages too, then it wasn't all in Clara's head. And that didn't make sense either. "Who were the messages from, Tills?"

Tilly's red hair scraped against the hammock as she shook her head. "I don't know," she whispered, "but it plans to keep us."

CHAPTER TWENTY

LUNCH WAS A meager affair. After Tilly's admission, Clara couldn't imagine eating anything. Her stomach was a tangle of knots. And the uncertainty around how long the food would have to last laid another anxious cloud over camp. The kids ate some of the hard crackers Clara had managed to salvage with some sort of packaged spread. Naomi passed around bags of trail mix. Fortunately, there was no shortage of water. It ran in tiny streams all along the ground and around their tents. Came from the sky like a faucet. Everything was drenched.

Clara shivered within her thin rain jacket. And not entirely from the cold. She glanced to the hammock where Tilly nibbled a cracker and stared at the forest beyond.

Naomi, jaw tight, shuffled a deck of damp Uno cards by the fire and handed them to Maddy and Thea. When she had returned from rescuing the food they'd salvaged, Aiden wasn't around. Clara told Naomi about their conversation—about how he volunteered to go for help, and she was sure Naomi blamed her for his departure, no matter how many ways she assured her she had actually told him not to go.

Clara watched the girls. It was probably just her anxious imagination, but Maddy looked paler and thinner than when they'd left home two days before. Bony shoulders poked sharp angles in her rain jacket. Purple circles rimmed her eyes. No one had slept well the night before, Maddy especially. She'd tossed and turned and cried out in her sleep numerous times.

Clara wandered over to Tilly, still in her hammock. "Wanna come eat by the fire? It's chilly out here."

"I'm fine," Tilly snapped. "I like the hammock."

Clara eyed the rings under her eyes, the greenish pallor to her skin that she hoped was just a reflection of the tarp overhead.

"I can support you on my arm. Might be good to get up and around."

"I said I'm fine, Mom," she said, handing Clara the cup and plate from lunch.

"Are you sure your phone is dead, Tills? I want to see the messages."

The girl shook her head. "It's dead, Mom." Her voice was so small.

"We need to talk," Clara said.

"I'm sorry about the cops. And Dad," Tilly blurted, catching Clara by surprise.

"That's not what I—"

"I'm sorry about sneaking out. And saying I loved Dad more than you. I just want to make sure you know, in case . . . in case something happens."

"Tilly, nothing's going to happen. I promise."

"Something already *has* happened."

Clara's breath whooshed out like a popped balloon. "I know," she whispered. "I know."

"Now, I'm going to nap," Tilly said, her eyes drooping.

Clara marched away, swallowing back the lump that rose in her throat. She rinsed the dishes robotically and sat by the fire, teeth digging into the inside of her lip. She should be able to fix this. But she was never very good at fixing anything.

"I wish you hadn't told Aiden to go get help," Naomi said again, looking up at Clara.

"I didn't," she replied with a sigh. "He was concerned about Tilly. And I guess they had a falling out and he saw this as his way to make things right."

"As if he knows the best way." Her words had bite, and Clara wasn't sure if it was directed at Aiden or to her.

"I did tell him not to go."

"Now we'll just have two parties to rescue," Naomi spat. "If we're lucky."

Clara bit her tongue before she could come out with a rebuke. Warring with each other would fix nothing. Her chest felt strained, wanting to burst around her unsaid words. She took a breath. "All I know is everything sucks right now, and we're all just doing our best to help. I know you're worried about him, but he said he's done this kind of thing before."

"And you just take everyone's word for it." Naomi rolled her eyes.

It was eerily close to what Aiden had said earlier.

You never know anything at all, do you Clara? Always taking the word of whoever is closest, even if they're a child, the voice in her head jabbed, returning to its old, grinding self.

"He's an adult, Naomi. He's going to do what he wants regardless of what I say."

"You said you were going to take more responsibility for your decisions now, didn't you?"

Clara let out a huff. "It wasn't *my* decision that he left. Not sure how many more different ways I can say that. And maybe—yeah, sure—maybe I did want him to go. Maybe I *do* hope it's the right decision. But did I tell him to go? No."

Without allowing time for Naomi to respond, Clara stood and walked away from the fire to the edge of the tarp. The rain came thick, a wall of water hemming them in. She felt the pressure again, the tightening of her skin, that claustrophobic feeling. Water and trees as far as her eye could see. They were trapped.

Wind whipped up the incline from the river and sent the tarp shuddering above her. She reached an arm out beyond the protective roof and felt the rain rush over her hand. The shushing of the drops against the shelter seemed to fade, to come from farther away, like her ears were adjusting to a higher altitude. Then the threads of a voice bounded among the trees like an echo and coalesced for Clara to hear. *H-h-h-help.*

A feeling of being watched snapped her eyes up. Not five feet in front of her stood a stooped, shivering figure. A matted mass of black hair shaded her face. Blood ran in rivulets down her arms and legs, exposed by her cargo shorts and T-shirt, also stained with red.

Clara's breath caught in her throat. For a moment she couldn't move—she was transfixed, as though impaled. She glanced behind her, but no one else seemed to have noticed. Naomi stared at the fire while the girls played Uno, Tilly was still in her hammock. She thought of the girl who had blistered and died in front of her.

H-h-h-help. The voice bounced around her brain again.

Clara raised her hands and took a hesitant step forward. "I don't—I don't know how to help you." She spoke quietly. If all these visions wanted was help, maybe she could help them. Whether or not this figure was real, she wasn't sure. Was she offering to help a ghost? A hallucination?

The figure stood taller and raised an arm to push the mass of hair from in front of her face. Black eyes and exposed teeth. Sallow cheeks.

Not me.

The face—it was Juliana. Clara's hand went to her mouth, but she couldn't suppress her cry. "You!"

Not ME. Juliana's voice echoed again. She reached a long thin arm to the side, finger extended, pointing. Clara's gaze followed.

There. From the trees watched a stern looking woman in a faded dress. A heavy pan in one hand, dripping onto the ground below. One of her eyes was swollen shut, a deep scratch arcing over it from eyebrow to cheek. Behind her, a child. She peeked out and Clara recognized her too. No maggots this time.

The woman turned her good eye on Clara. It burned, flaming almost orange. She moved swiftly, narrowing the distance between them in fits and starts, like a tape skipping. Clara stumbled backward, but when she looked up again, Juliana was gone along with the other two, disappeared into the rain and fog.

"Watch it!" Thea called just in time to stop Clara's backward steps from knocking over their Uno game and landing her in the campfire. Clara regained her balance and slumped onto a log beside Maddy. She hazarded a glance to the edge of the tarp, but saw no sign of the stern woman or the little girl. Or Juliana. Clara's mind spun, trying to piece together how she was seeing Juliana in front of her. Here. Was this all part of her hallucinations? She briefly entertained the thought that Juliana never actually went back to Solara, that she had it wrong all this time. Could she have survived out here? All those weeks since Clara left her? No, that didn't make any sense. She'd been left here with nothing.

Maddy looked up from her game, and for a moment Clara could have sworn she saw the same fire the ghostly woman had in her eyes. But it was probably just a trick of the light, a flicker from their campfire.

Clara shook inside her rain jacket. Fear and hunger and cold combined to rattle her bones.

AFTERNOON SLID SLOWLY through the trees, time passing almost imperceptibly. The sky barely brightened, the sun hidden behind dark gray steel wool. Clara paced the perimeter of the tarp, peering into the darkness for any sign of Juliana. The rain did slow, though, shortly after lunch, and the younger girls made a game of racing through the trees.

"Stay closer," Clara called out, but Naomi shushed her.

"They've been cooped up in tents and under tarps for almost a day now. They need to move their bodies."

It was true, but all the same, as Maddy's tiny frame flitted in and out of view, Clara felt like the girl was slipping out of her fingers the same way she slipped through the trees, despite the puddles splashing and peals of giggles to always let her know the girls were still nearby. But it wasn't enough to ease her tension.

"Sure they do, and then we end up with another injury," Clara couldn't help saying. *Or what if Juliana takes them?* She kept the last thought to herself. She couldn't very well tell Naomi she thought she'd seen Juliana in the woods.

"They'll be fine, Clare. We've had so many setbacks; let the girls run off some steam." She smiled, but her voice belied a similar exhaustion to the one Clara felt in her own bones.

Clara tried to exhale, but a hint of panic lingered below the surface. Only a shadow, but there nonetheless, waiting to emerge from its cover.

Naomi patted her shoulder and Clara jumped. "Jeez. You okay?"

"I . . . no. Not really."

"Clare, you can talk to me."

She looked at Naomi, thought about their conversation the other night. She'd opened up about Emilio finally, only to find out that Naomi had suspicions this whole time. A gulf had opened where there used to be trust. Naomi was her very best friend, had been since they were thirteen and hiding under the bleachers giggling about boys. But the power dynamic was always the same. After the giggles, Naomi would go out and date the boys and Clara would sit in her room alone. She'd been living her life as Naomi's shadow for a long, long time.

"It's Juliana, isn't it?" Naomi asked, startling Clara's gaze from the fire.

"What do you mean?" She tried, and failed, not to sound like a cornered animal.

"I know it's taken a lot to process her death," Naomi said.

Electricity crackled along Clara's limbs. She went rigid. "I don't—"

"I know, I know. You don't want to talk about it. You've been saying the same thing since Dr. Benton called you almost a month ago with the news. I know you're the psychologist, but I think it's been long enough. You can't keep it inside forever. It's tearing you apart, Clare."

"What are you talking about?"

"You refused the mental health support Solara offered you as part of your leave package. You won't talk to me. You've been getting more and more erratic. I think this needs to come out. I'm so worried about you."

An unexpected sob welled itself up Clara's throat, like a spider dragging itself from a filling sink, but Clara managed to swallow it down again. Prickly, spiny. She gagged. "You're wrong."

"About what?" Naomi put her hand on Clara's leg. Something solid, real. Did that mean what Naomi was saying was real, too?

"She's . . . Juliana's not dead. I just saw her, and . . . and we've been texting. And she's waiting for me to come back. She really hates Dr. Phillips and complains about him all the time. And when my leave is over, I'm going to go back there. I'm going to help her.

That's what this trip is all about. I'm just . . . like, trying to understand her so I can better support her when I'm back."

Naomi's forehead creased. She took Clara's hand. "Clara. She died. Juliana is dead."

"That's not true," Clara said, her voice rising. "I just saw her. Over there! I just saw her because I brought her to the woods and left her here and this is all my fault."

"What on earth are you talking about? Saw her *here*? No, Clare. She died that night a few weeks ago. The night Tilly got arrested. Remember? You called me right before Dr. Benton phoned with the news." The look on Naomi's face turned Clara's stomach. All twisted up with pity.

"No. No. That's not—No." Clara put her hands on her ears. "Stop."

"Clare, I'm worried about you," Naomi said.

Clara dropped her hands from her ears and took a deep breath. "I'm fine," she lied, giving Naomi a firm nod. "Fine." But beneath the act, her insides were churning.

She thought of her phone; vibrating in her pocket, smashed in the mud. Thought of the messages Tilly mentioned. Thought of how strange it was that no cops ever showed up after she helped Juliana escape; that Dr. Benton never questioned her about Juliana's disappearance.

It was because she didn't disappear that night. She died, alone, in Solara.

Clara remembered the message from Dr. Benton that she'd put off listening to for so long, the request for her to call him back. He sounded so sorry—*I know you two were close*. She remembered it all now. He offered her paid leave. That's why she was home. *That* was the stress.

Juliana wasn't out here in the woods with her.

Juliana was dead.

CHAPTER TWENTY-ONE

CLARA WANDERED OVER to Tilly's hammock, numb and spiraling after her conversation with Naomi. She wanted to see something real, normal, to have Tilly spew insults or tell her she was a terrible mother. She wanted to wake up, for all of this to be a bad dream.

But when she arrived at the strip of green cloth, she found Tilly asleep. Her eyes moved quickly back and forth under their thin blankets of skin, chapped lips parted emitting a rasping breath. Clara put a hand to her daughter's forehead to find it radiating warmth.

"No. N-no, you can't," she whispered in her sleep.

Clara tried to soothe her. "Shh-shh." But her blood ran cold in her veins. She couldn't soothe her properly, knowing how precarious their situation actually was. Waking from her nightmare wouldn't save Tilly—they were *in* the nightmare. Her vision telescoped, the edges going black.

She couldn't reconcile the fact that Juliana was dead. Of course Clara was familiar with dissociative amnesia, but this was something different. She hadn't suffered a long-term trauma that would lead to such a thing. And the text messages. The *phone conversations.* Clara had heard Juliana's voice, listened to her advice. All while she was . . . dead. And, despite her usually staunch disbelief in the paranormal, she had already all but admitted that there must be something more going on here. Something like a *haunting.*

And maybe Juliana was the haunting.

Tilly darted a clawed hand out from the safety of the hammock and dug her fingers into Clara's arm, nails biting into the damp nylon of her jacket. Clara jumped.

"She's coming," Tilly hissed, eyes still closed. "They're coming."

Then she slumped back into the hammock, limp as the wet leaves at their feet.

Clara held her breath. So many fears, too many fears. They poked through her like rods, keeping her in place.

It was just a dream, she told herself. *Tilly was just dreaming.* But she looked to the woods nonetheless. Something was out there among the trees, she knew, watching them. Despite the rain clearing, the shadows had darkened. Could evening be approaching already?

A beat of wings in her chest again, a whoosh through the branches above. Looking up, she caught glimpses of ghostly white, circling, circling. Her pulse pounded in her ears. *Run run run*, it said, but she stood paralyzed.

Tilly cried out, "Mom!" just as her eyes snapped open. Clara spun and saw Maddy standing behind her, near enough to kiss. A toothy grin cracked the girl's face, but her brows pinched low, twisting her expression into a snarl.

"Maddy? I—"

A glint in her hand. The girl swung and Clara's side bloomed in pain as she wrenched out of the way. Clara put a hand to her torso, it came away dark, crimson. *This can't be happening.* Maddy lunged forward in a jerky stumble toward Clara, the camp knife flashing in the glow of the campfire.

Clara raised her arms protectively. "Maddy, stop," she cried.

"*Look out!*" Tilly yelled, just as Clara felt her heels collide with the logs near the fire. The earth shifted away from her and she tilted backward, nothing to grab onto to right herself. She fell into the embers, smashing her tailbone against the rocks Thea and Maddy had arranged so neatly the day before. Pinpricks of stings bloomed larger as the embers ate their way through her raincoat and into her flesh. Maddy hovered over her before squatting down and grabbing her arm. She brought the edge of her knife against Clara's wrist.

"Maddy!" Clara gasped.

The girl faltered, pain etched across her face. "Mom," she whispered. "Help." Clara's vision went blank as flames licked up her back.

Stop drop and roll. Stop drop and roll. The voice of Tilly's old kindergarten teacher sang through her head. She lurched her body to the side, rolling out of the fire pit and scattering embers as she did so. The air filled with the scent of burned plastic and hair. Where the fuck was Naomi? Clara rolled and rolled through the wet leaves and then got to her knees, her body wavering. She put one foot to the ground, as though proposing, and looked around wildly for her attacker.

Attacker? It was *Maddy* for Christ's sake. What the hell was going on? Wingbeats overhead, that damn owl circling faster and faster, lower and lower. Louder than an owl should be. Clara's head spun, her balance threatening to send her tumbling again. The owl let out a heinous screech, a woman in trouble.

As Clara's vision cleared, she saw Maddy approaching again, her limbs jerking as though she were a windup toy. She advanced, teeth bared and knife drawn. "Feed the forest," she said in a voice that wasn't her own.

"Mom!" Tilly hobbled across the camp site faster than Clara could have imagined possible.

"Feed the forest,." Maddy said again and it seemed to come from the air all around them, the trees, the earth, the wind.

Clara swallowed, trying to make sense of the scene. Footsteps approaching. Naomi and Thea running up from the edge of camp. Their coats blinking in and out of trees. Where the fuck had they been?

The swoosh of feathers through the branches above. Tilly closing in on Maddy. Clara got another foot on the ground and stumbled forward like she was drunk. Too slow. Too late. Never enough.

There was a crack and Maddy crumpled to the ground, the knife flying.

"What did you do?" Clara cried, looking at her daughter's body slumped in the damp leaves.

"What did *I* do?" Tilly asked. "I fucking punched her so she didn't kill you!" She ran her hands over her face. "Is she okay?"

Clara gathered her thoughts, now strewn across the silent forest. No wingbeats, no owl shrieks, no footsteps. Naomi and Thea stood at the edges of the site, staring, probably thinking they'd just walked into the dysfunction of Clara's family they had always suspected simmered below the surface. Nothing out of line here, this fucked up family always just punches each other to the ground and burns each other up in campfire embers.

She wanted to address them. Her first inclination was to smooth this over like she did everything else. But there was no fixing this. And her kids needed her more than she needed to keep up appearances with Naomi. She pushed down the inner voice telling her she couldn't handle this.

"I'm sorry, Tills. I don't . . . I don't know what—"

"She was possessed is what." Tilly slumped onto one of the logs near the fire. "Get me some twine and I'll help you tie her up."

"*Tie* her *up!?* Matilda, that is your sister."

"You can't keep acting like everything is normal here! That was not Maddy. I know my sister, and that thing with the knife was *not* her!"

"What do you mean it wasn't Maddy?" Thea asked, cautious, lingering around the edges of the conversation. Clara helped Tilly to her feet, relishing the feel of Tilly's weight on her, despite the ache in her side. They all squatted around Maddy. Naomi pressed an emergency ice pack onto a bruise that bloomed around her eye near her temple and put a finger to her wrist to take her pulse. Clara pressed a hand against her jacket to quell the pain where Maddy's knife had slashed her.

Naomi looked up at Clara. "What did we just see?"

Clara swallowed, unsure. She didn't want to say what she really thought happened: *some spirit from the woods—maybe my old patient even—possessed one of my children and tried to kill me. Then the other one knocked her out.* Naomi would think she was insane . . . more than she already did. But she didn't have any other explanation. Was she insane?

Maybe you are insane. Look at your child. Look, Clara. Look *at her!*

Clara eyed her daughter's body, splayed on the ground below her. The scene in front of her wavered as though it were underwater. They were all drowning here.

"She will probably have a concussion," Naomi said after a moment of hesitation. "But otherwise, she's just knocked out. What happened, Clara?" She asked again. For the first time, Clara realized Naomi was out of her depth too.

Tilly bent down and reached for the ice pack. "How about I take that, Naomi, and you help my mom patch up the hole in her side before you start interrogating her."

Naomi nodded, lips tight, and pulled a roll of gauze from the first aid kit. She had Clara shrug off her raincoat, which elicited a gasp from Thea. Her shirt was red and slick with blood beneath, pocked with burned holes. Naomi gently lifted it and applied the gauze. She turned to Thea. "It looks like more blood than it is, because it mixed with the rain. Clara's going to be just fine." She turned back to Clara, her expression contradicting her words to Thea. "I'm going to look at these burns too," she said.

Clara's torso felt broken, stung by a thousand bees, and the buzzing in her head grew. Naomi's words echoed: *Clara's going to be just fine*. But would she? Would any of them? They were coming apart at the seams, perforated and broken.

Thea nibbled on a nail, looking on. "I want to go home," she said, and Clara felt that statement in her bones. She stared at her daughter, splayed out in the muck, and wished they'd never come.

CHAPTER TWENTY-TWO

THERE WAS TOO much discussion, in Clara's opinion, of whether they should tie up Maddy's unconscious form.

"She could try to kill one of us again," Thea said.

"Listen, we have no idea what's going on here. It might be some kind of reaction to the business with Juliana. Or Emilio," Naomi said, tying off the gauze. Something sour rose in Clara's throat, but she swallowed it down.

"Are you fucking serious right now? This has nothing to do with Dad." Tilly scowled. "It's these woods you brought us into. Something possessed Maddy."

Thea whispered, "Possessed?" just as Naomi let out a huge guffaw.

"No, honey," she said. "No one is possessed. Listen, we're all just a little shaken up. We're stuck"—she held up her hands at Thea's worried look—"but *only temporarily*. People are rescued from these woods all the time, and—"

"People also *die* in these woods all the time too, don't they?" Tilly responded. "I mean, what are we even doing here? We're here because Mom's old patient murdered someone. Right here. Possibly right at this very waterfall." She shot Clara a glare.

Clara shook her head. "Listen, no one is going to die here."

Clara's words sounded degrees firmer than she felt. She was still shaking, her hands balled into fists at her sides. Naomi rubbed some kind of ointment onto the burns across her back, making her flinch with every touch. She replayed the scene over and over: the blank look in Maddy's eyes, her vicious grin, the knife in her hand, the flames of her torch. She had *almost* wrapped her head around Juliana's . . . death.

Now, to be confronted with the fact that Juliana might be haunting them and maybe even *possessing* Maddy? She couldn't imagine why. Or how. She didn't know how any of this paranormal stuff was even supposed to work. And Juliana always seemed to like Maddy and Tilly, always asked after them and wanted to hear what they were up to. She wouldn't—

"Clara's right." Naomi patted Thea's hand. "Aiden's gone for help. I have the beacon on. We're going to be rescued one way or another. All we need to do is hunker down and stay safe."

Silence descended as their eyes wandered over the scattered camp. Maddy's form slumped between them, now leaned against one of the logs.

"If we need to stay safe, we should tie her up," Thea said, drawing an eyebrow raise from her mother.

"Listen. No one is possessed," Naomi said again. "And *no one* will be tied up. Maddy probably just needs some emotional support."

Clara bristled. "Yes, we're not tying anyone up, but Maddy is *fine*, Naomi." *Maddy's the good one*, she almost blurted, forgetting herself. Instead, she said, "We have been dealing with things, thank you. This is . . . something different."

"Sure we have," Tilly scoffed.

Damnit. Clara flashed her daughter a look.

She had thought she was breaking through, thought they were getting somewhere, but Tilly pulled back just as distant as before.

Naomi finished dressing Clara's wounds and handed her back her jacket. "I refuse to tie anyone up, and that's final. Let's gather around the fire. Maybe we can tell stories. Pass the time until we're rescued."

"But no ghost stories!" Thea responded, with a glance toward Maddy.

"Sure, no ghost stories," Naomi replied.

"I'm not sure it's a good time," Clara said, hunching over Maddy's still-unconscious form. Panic welled in her chest as she took Maddy's limp wrist. "Are we just . . . waiting for her to wake up? Is there nothing we can do?"

"Not with what we have here," Naomi said. Then, more quietly, "Let's make things as comfortable as we can. I think the kids are all shaken."

I *am shaken*, Clara thought, her stomach turning over at the sight of her child lying there. Panic clawed at the back of her throat.

"All right, story time!" Naomi said with false brightness. Tilly hobbled over to sit on a log by the fire with Thea. At least the campfire story idea provided a welcome distraction from the current fucked up situation. Maybe Naomi was right.

Before Naomi could start, though, Maddy's eyes began to flutter and then open, to Clara's relief. She did not like seeing her baby's form lying so limp and lifeless. It reminded her too much of the dream she'd had two nights before, when she'd imagined the tent full of blood.

But back then, the horror was only in her dreams. Now, their reality had turned horrific.

She brushed Maddy's hair off her forehead. "Mads? Maddy? Are you . . ." She wanted to ask if she was back to herself but had no idea how to phrase that.

"Mom?" Maddy asked, her voice full of groggy fear. "What happened? I didn't mean—" She let out something between a sob and a cough.

Tears burned behind Clara's eyes. She pulled her daughter into her lap. "You're all right sweetie. We're here and you're safe. We're all safe." Tilly gave a snort but said nothing.

Maddy sat up straighter, wiped a trickle of blood from beneath her nose. Wide-eyed, gazing at the trees beyond, she said, "We're not safe. None of us are. She wants us. She told me. In here." Maddy pointed to her temple. "She wants us all to burn."

Clara's blood ran cold. The unmistakable echo of what Tilly had told her the day before sent tingles of terror weaving down her arms. "Who, sweetie? Who are you talking about?" Clara asked, while Thea huddled under Tilly's arm.

Maddy blinked at her. "The girl. The mother. All of them."

Clara swallowed and glanced at Naomi, who wore a look of uncertainty for possibly the first time in her life. At Naomi's loss of composure the ground seemed shift beneath Clara. She tightened her arms around Maddy, wincing as her daughter's frame pressed against the wound she herself had inflicted only moments before. Tears threatened again. Fireside story forgotten, she held Maddy against her shoulder and rocked her.

Naomi stuck another log on the fire, which was losing its battle against the encroaching darkness. Nearly a whole day had passed and they weren't any closer to leaving this place. The woods were vast, but they were hemmed in, stuck. She felt danger circling all around, hungry, pushing at their shrinking bubble of safety.

She was reminded of a movie she'd seen ages ago, some idiotic horror film Emilio had rented when they were first dating, about a couple lost at sea when their dive boat left without them. They clung to each other in the cold darkness and rolling waves as sharks circled ever closer.

Of course, ultimately, the sharks devoured them.

What sharks waited outside the false safety of this fire? Clara wondered.

Approaching footsteps shook Clara from her reverie, and her grip on Maddy tightened further. She noticed Naomi tense almost imperceptibly next to her as well.

"Mom, you're crushing me," Maddy complained, wriggling from her arms. A twelve-year-old once more.

Clara reluctantly let her go and got to her feet. Whatever was coming, she would face it head on. She knew Juliana. If that's who was lurking out in the shadows—even the ghost of her—Clara wouldn't let her get close. Naomi slid something to her side, facing away from the children. The camp knife. Clara realized then that Naomi's confident control of the situation was sliding. The woman was rattled. Naomi was supposed to be her anchor. The change made Clara dizzy, the pressure of panic digging its hungry talons into her chest.

"Who's there," Naomi called out as the noises grew nearer. A light appeared in the darkness.

"Mom . . ."

"Aiden?" She fumbled with the knife in her hand, securing it into her belt once again.

Clara's head spun—had he returned already with help? Were they saved? But he had only been gone since the morning, and she knew deep down that he wouldn't have made it back so quickly, even unencumbered by a heavy pack and younger kids. Her hands searched the air around her reaching for something to hold onto in this tossing storm. She found Tilly's shoulder and leaned on it. The girl scowled at her but held her weight anyway.

"I tried. But you must have heard it, felt it. We should have realized. It must have been what we thought was thunder," Aiden said, breathless.

Naomi shook her head, glancing back to where Clara stood, wavering, before looking back to Aiden. "What are you talking about? Felt what?"

"The landslide. The whole mountain . . ." Aiden's eyes widened in disbelief. "Mom, half the mountain slid away. I made it past the first wash, but that was barely anything compared to the next. And the river's overrun its bounds almost everywhere. I've never seen anything like it." Clara's stomach flipped. *Stuck.* She waited to hear Naomi's new plan, what they could do next. She must have a plan. They couldn't stay here. Not with the *haunting*.

But Naomi just wrapped her arms around her son. "I'm so glad you're safe. Don't you *ever* go off like that again on your own. You should know better."

"But, Mom, we had to try. We still have to try! Tilly needs—"

"I don't care. If something happened to you—How do you think you could help Tilly if you're lost? Or *dead*? You couldn't help *any* of us. We're going to stay here. We're going to stay here as long as it takes to get rescued."

Thea stood. "But how long will it take, Mom? We can't stay here forever. The food . . . Tilly."

Naomi turned on her daughter. "We will *stay*," she hissed, her teeth bared, a cloud passing over her eyes. Then, recovering herself a bit, "We'll stay as long as it takes. We're safe here. We'll be rescued."

"It might be worth trying again," Clara said. "Tilly's gotten worse. And—" How could she phrase what she wanted to say? How could she explain that Juliana seemed to be haunting them? "I just think it's not safe here. For any of us."

"*Clara*," she snapped, but then clamped her mouth shut.

Naomi's hands squeezed into fists and released over and over again. She turned back to Thea and brushed a hair from her face. She exhaled slowly, deliberately.

"I will keep you safe, guys, if I have to die doing it. Which," she quickly amended, "I doubt I will have to do. So let's stop worrying about things we can't control and worry about something we can control. What should we have for dinner?"

Maddy slid her hand into Clara's. "I'm not hungry," she whispered. Clara nodded, watching Naomi turn from her children to find the camp stove—her face dropping from confident, protective mother to completely lost in half a breath. Clara knew she had to do something.

You can't. You can't do anything. You never could. Give up.

No. This was her moment. She shifted her boots in the mud below.

Give up, Clara. Stop it with your ideas. You'll only make more messes.

She reached up and smoothed her frizzed hair back into her ponytail. No. She clamped down on that inner voice with as much finality as she could muster.

She bent forward. "You should still eat, Sweetpea," she whispered to Maddy. Keep yourself strong." Then, to the larger group. "Let's inventory our food and portion it out so we know it will last at least . . . four more days. Just in case. Not that we'll be here that long. We're going to try to find our way off this mountain." *Before it's too late*, she thought, then continued. "We should also inventory our first aid kits. And reserve most of the anti-inflammatories for Tills. And, I guess, wound dressings for me. And if we're stuck here for days, let's fortify our camp. Gather as much firewood as we can, set up all the tarps we brought to make a little encampment. And let's pull more logs around the fire." She looked at Maddy against her side and Thea across the fire pit. "Let's make it as comfortable and homey as we can. We'll get through this. Together."

Just then, the skin on the back of her neck prickled. She turned to see a face watching her from the edge of the woods. Black eye, blank face. Then wingbeats, so soft she thought maybe she'd imagined it. Maybe just the blood rushing in her ears.

Still, she scanned the blackness for a few extra moments before jumping to help Naomi.

⟶⟵

A FEW SCOOPS of freeze-dried noodles and half a handful of nuts was all she and Naomi doled out to the kids for dinner that night. Thea and Maddy were quiet, scooping noodles into their mouths and chewing absently, eyes on the fire. Aiden leaned against a tree beside Tilly's hammock, rocking it gently and chatting. Earlier, he had taken the younger girls off to gather the firewood without being asked. The wood sat piled next to their fire ring, which Clara had repaired after the incident.

Incident. The word echoed inside her skull. It was the word Dr. Benton had used in his voicemail. *There's been an incident. Please call us back at your earliest convenience.*

Juliana had been here, strode these same trails. And now she was dead. Dead. The thought still felt foreign in Clara's mind as she gnawed the flesh of her cheek instead of noodles. What had Juliana seen here? What had she *done* here?

And why was she—or this apparition of her—back?

To find you. To bring you. To consume you.

It was the wind, the whispers of leaves and the creaking of branches against each other. She shook her head, frizzed strands of hair tickling her cheeks. Naomi slid down on the bench next to her, sipping from her Nalgene. They'd both forgone dinner to save the food for the kids.

"You all right?"

Clara let out a bitter chuckle.

"That was a dumb question, I know."

"It's okay. Thanks for checking in. Are *you* all right? I haven't seen you so rattled."

Now it was Naomi's turn to give a bitter laugh. "Honestly? I don't know what the hell is going on here." Their eyes drifted over to Maddy where she sat finishing off her dinner.

We'll probably all die here, Clara's mind rasped. But she pushed it away again. *Shut up*, she told the voice. *Shut up shut up shut up.*

"Me neither." The words tickled the back of her throat—*haunting, Juliana*—but she couldn't bring herself to tell Naomi. She still didn't fully believe it herself. She didn't have any proof. "But we'll make it. We have to. For the kids."

Her friend nodded, a muscle in her cheek working. She turned to Clara again. "I know I already told you last night, but I really am sorry," she said.

"It's okay," Clara said, meeting her gaze.

"It's not. You were right. I always took it for granted that you went along with my plans without question. That you did what I wanted you to do almost all the time. I—Clara, I love you. I worry that I've hurt you."

"You know, I've known you a long time. It's inevitable that we've done things to hurt each other. But you were also right last night about me taking responsibility. My life is my own. Not yours."

"I know. That's what I'm trying to apolo—"

"No, you misunderstood me. My life is my own, so if I went along with your plans, that was *my* choice. It's so much easier to blame someone else when things turn bad, but you never forced me into anything. And even if something *had* happened with you and Emilio, that is ancient history. I can't blame the demise of a whole multi-decade relationship on something you may have said thirty years ago."

Naomi nodded. Swallowed. She turned her eyes back to the fire. "You know you're the best friend I've ever had."

Clara wrapped an arm around her. "Me too," she whispered. "Me too."

CHAPTER TWENTY-THREE

THE RAIN BEAT down, ceaseless, and the temperature plummeted along with everything else. Clara shivered in her coat as she rounded up the dishes for washing. Tilly dried them for her and then returned to the hammock, letting Aiden help her back into it this time. She winced every time she tried to put weight on her leg, and when Naomi did her usual checkup, she shot Clara a look and shook her head. Even the younger girls had taken to wandering around solemnly, laughing less. Thea stuck close by Naomi's side, and Maddy had a glazed look about her, dark circles growing under her eyes like storm clouds.

The rain would clear tomorrow, Clara decided as she ran the rag across the dishes. And when it did, they were going to make their way back down the mountain. All of them. Together. They would climb up and over the landslide if they had to. It would take a long time, but they could do it. They couldn't sit around here while their food supply disappeared and Tilly's leg became infected. A great fog had lifted from Clara, and now that it had, she couldn't imagine what had driven her to want to stay after Tilly's ankle injury. What had she been thinking? Yes, Naomi had a beacon and, sure, a helicopter rescue *felt* preferable to hiking down a mountain, but obviously no chopper was coming. Anything was better than sitting around here, fraying at their edges, while Juliana and whatever else threatened them from the shadows. It had been long enough. Despite everyone else's morose mood, Clara felt instantly lighter as soon as she made the decision. Her hope took flight for the first time in days. She had a plan.

She told the girls a bedtime story that night, once they were all tucked cozy and safe into the tent. One about a fish who longed to explore on land, so when he awoke one morning to find his fins had turned to feet and his gills to lungs, he jumped at the chance. But he soon found himself lost and alone, in an unfamiliar world where danger seemed to lurk at every turn. But then he befriended a mouse and made a life for himself on land.

It was nice to hear Maddy giggle again. And even if Tilly rolled her eyes a few times, she eventually settled in against her pillow and drifted off to sleep, her face looking much less strained than it had earlier.

Clara lay awake listening to them breathe for a long time after they fell asleep. As though she had willed it, the rain slowed to a patter and then stopped altogether. She tossed and turned a few times, trying to find a comfortable position that didn't irritate any of her wounds, until settling on her side opposite her bandage. Tomorrow, they would leave. With that comforting thought, she let herself drift off to sleep.

A STRANGE, CRISP smell permeated the tent, and Clara woke to find a body curled into hers. She opened her eyes to find Juliana's face inches from her own, their sleeping bags whispering together, unzipping. Her eyes were dark, the scent of exotic flowers, Clara was drowning. Their lips met, a swelling wave of a kiss.

Clara pulled back. A bolt of fear ran through her. *Where are the kids?*

Juliana pulled her closer again, hands swirling, rushing river rapids over her back. Clara moaned despite herself, but then she pushed Juliana away.

"What are you—Juliana?" Sleep blanketed her mind in thick down, her reactions slowed, her thoughts jumbled.

"Shh," Juliana whispered, her lips brushing Clara's ear. "Relax. Just let me in." She ran her hands over Clara's skin and Clara began to sink again, beneath the surface, buried under the thick loam of sleep.

But when Juliana's hands scraped over the scabs on her back, she jolted alert. "No. Get out. Get out of here. You aren't meant to be here." She was climbing out of quicksand, gasping for air.

Juliana's face flickered in the darkness, morphing into Naomi's and back again, before cracking open into a wolfish grin. Her laughter peeled into the night.

CLARA WOKE TO screams.

She reached to either side of her and felt her girls. They were there, safe. They too roused in response to the bloodcurdling sounds rending the night. Maddy had her sleeping bag pulled up under her chin, eyes like saucers in the dim glow of the tent. Tilly lurched for the tent's zipper but fell short.

Heart pounding, Clara wrenched the zipper open and emerged into the night. "Stay here."

The crisp, cold air bit at her, stinging her eyes. The moon, full, sliced silver through the trees. The screams didn't stop.

They wove in and out of each other before unbraiding into distinct voices.

"Mom!" It was Aiden's voice, strained. "Stop!"

Thea quietly crying.

A growl lit the night. Human, but also . . . not.

The blood drained from Clara's limbs. Numb-handed and stumbling, she forced herself toward their tent, fear like a talon around her lungs. Wingbeats in her ears. Wingbeats and . . . laughter? Echoes of her nightmare, but made real.

The tent shook with movement. Aiden's large form pressed against the maroon wall, silhouetted as someone flared up the lantern. "Mom!" His voice was laced with panic, high and breathless. Nothing but that animalistic growl again in response.

Clara saw everything in freeze frame, gray scale. Her hand on the zipper. The tent open. Thea white with panic, her arm dark with blood. Aiden standing in front of her, arms spread wide. Naomi sprawled. Knife glinting in her hand and teeth bared, she growled again.

"Kids," Clara said quietly, "out of the tent." Thea dove from behind Aiden out into the cold night with a whimper. Aiden made to follow, but as he reached the threshold, Naomi lunged again, knife catching the lantern's light. Clara leapt at her friend, her only thought to keep the kids safe.

The edge of the knife caught her in the arm like a bee sting, nothing compared to the ache in her other side, but still she cried out. She grabbed Naomi's wrist and lunged, pushing her body out of the way as the woman slashed again, spit dripping from her lips. Naomi's eyes glinted, her mouth pulled back into a cruel smile.

"I have to make you bleed for the forest," she hissed in a voice not her own. "Slice you open, watch you drip, drip, drip. Just like I did all alone in my room. Drip. Drip. Drip. And once I'm back, everyone else will *burn.*"

What the hell? Vaguely, Clara was aware of Thea's terrified cry behind her as Aiden pulled her further away. And of her own girls piling out of the tent and watching from a few paces away as she struggled with Naomi at the tent entrance. They fell to the ground, scrabbling at each other in the mud.

The knife slid from Naomi's grasp, clanging against the gravel tent pad. Clara kicked at Naomi with her heel, her need to protect herself and the kids stronger than her desire to not hurt her friend. She connected with Naomi's midsection, earning a grunt of pain from the other woman.

Naomi's teeth dug into Clara's forearm, making her scream, her body going tense and then slack. Naomi took the opportunity to scoot away and get back to her feet, grabbing the knife once more.

"This body is stronger than yours. And faster. So much better than your pathetic little daughter's. You chose your friend well." Her face spread into a wolfish grin again, made all the more macabre by Clara's blood dripping from her teeth.

Clara slid back a few paces, looking up in horror. "Naomi! Stop!"

"*Wrong!* Not Naomi." The Naomi hissed. "Wrong wrong wrong!" She waved the knife back and forth in front of her like a joke. "Naomi is gone. Tucked . . . somewhere back here, maybe." She shrugged and pointed to the back of her skull with the blade. "It's good to see you, Clara. *Think* about it. You know me. You wanted to help me. You wanted to *save* me." She laughed, a dry and rasping sound. "And now . . . well, now you'll do that and more." Leaning forward, she grabbed Clara by the hair and ran the edge of the knife gently along her jawline. "You were so eager to tell me of your beautiful, innocent daughters, your asshole of a husband. It was everything I needed. So perfect it was almost as though Auntie planned it herself."

"J-Juliana," Clara whispered, trembling. "H-how?"

Naomi—who Clara was now certain was actually Juliana—leapt to her feet, jabbing the knife in the air. "*Right*! Turns out you do have a few brain cells kicking around in there. And for that, your prize is . . ." She grabbed Clara's arm and raised the knife. She pressed it against Clara's wrist and hummed, "*Two and one, a family spurned, let them burn, and we'll return!*"

A crack sounded and Naomi stumbled to the side, eyes going wide as she dropped the knife once more. Aiden stood behind her, holding a huge branch. "Go," he shouted, and Clara pulled herself to her feet and sprinted away. Glancing back, she saw Naomi try to right herself, only to be hit by Aiden again. And then he ran with Clara into the darkness.

Everything was a confusion of tree limbs and incoherent whispers as she and Aiden searched through the surrounding darkness for the other kids. Moonlight lit enough that she could still see Naomi's slumped form in the center of camp, but the girls had disappeared. Panic welled in her and flowed over, hot and blinding. Her breath came out in short gasps.

The lump on the ground began to move, twitchy at first, and then smoother, rising to a low crouch. "Oh, Cla-raaaa! Clara, where are you? I can *smell* you. You're *mine.*"

Clara held her breath, not even letting the slightest exhale give her away, and yet through the darkness it seemed Naomi was facing right toward her.

"I'm coming for you, you little sack of flesh." She took a step toward them in the darkness.

"Shit," Aiden muttered from beside her as they caught sight Maddy and Thea, only a few feet from Naomi, huddled behind a tent. Louder, he called, "She's over here!" and took Clara's hand, pulling her through the woods. Clara darted a glance over her shoulder. The bait worked.

Naomi was only a few paces behind, diving through the underbrush like a natural predator. Beyond, she glanced Tilly gesturing to the girls from beneath a rotted log.

Good. Naomi was mad enough to follow her instead of searching for the kids. They would lure her away. Aiden pulled further ahead, a trail runner and sprinter just like his mother. Clara's heart pounded, her lungs burned like a house on fire. Her muscles protested with all their might. At the best of times, she wasn't a runner, but after days of sleeping on the ground with barely any food, it was a wonder she wasn't collapsing to the ground. Slivers of moonlight sneaked through the tree branches and flickered off Aiden's back, giving her a beacon to follow through the dark. Still, she slipped and staggered over slick tree roots and jutting rocks. A vine snagged her, and she stumbled forward onto one knee, battering her already broken body. But still, Naomi came. Clara pushed herself to standing again and willed herself onward.

She let out a frustrated grunt and forced her legs to move even faster, to ignore the stiffness and fatigue plaguing her body, the metallic throb in her side. She saw the edge of the forest far ahead of her, heard the roar of the river.

Another roar echoed up from behind her. Naomi's exasperated snarl. "CLARA!" She ran faster. The voice was too close, licking at the back of her neck, clawing at her limbs.

"No," she yelled, willing herself faster, faster.

She broke the tree line and saw Aiden in her periphery, launching out with another branch. Naomi's shins hit it, and her body tumbled forward, arms flailing, face first into the rocky outcrop. She hit with a resounding smack.

"Mom?" Aiden cried, fear and remorse and hope mingling there. He glanced at Clara. His shoulders rose and fell beneath his merino under layer, hair mussed and sleep still clinging to his eyes. "What's going on? What's wrong with my mom?"

Naomi writhed on the ground, rolling over and spitting blood and teeth shards. She let out an exasperated grunt and snapped her broken nose back into place with a crack.

"I don't—" Clara started, but Naomi rolled and planted the knife into Aiden's calf. He let out a bloodcurdling yell as Naomi rose to her feet, stumbling a bit and laughing as though drunk.

"You stupid, stupid boy." Blood sprayed from her mouth with each word. "You're making this harder than it has to be. Your mommy's gone. Fucking give up." Her voice gurgled, wet with blood and saliva. "You're all making this harder. You can't fight the inevitable. None of you are getting out of here alive."

Aiden limped away, grimacing as he dragged his wounded leg behind him and yanked the knife out. He let out a whimper as he tore off his shirt and tied it expertly tight around the wound. He straightened. "My mom is not gone. I don't believe you," he said. Clara could see his shoulders shaking, whether from the cold or the terror or the pain, she didn't know.

The creature inside Naomi laughed again. "You think you can get me out?" She spread her feet, bouncing on her toes, a fighting stance. "Try."

He shook his head, shoulders sagging even more, defeated. "I'm not going to fight you."

Clara's heart broke. "Naomi, come back to us. You have to come back to us. Aiden is your *son*, goddammit."

She turned those dark eyes onto Clara again. "I don't have to do *anything*. I'm free now. I figured it out." Naomi tilted her head to the side.

"Well, mostly. I still can't figure out how to get in *you*. Frustrating. But, oh well, this is working better than I'd planned. I thought I might be able to do it with Maddy, but she was too weak. I shouldn't be surprised your offspring were all spineless, Clara." She leaned in closer. "First, I'll slaughter you two and feed you to the forest, then I'll go for the others and light them up. Auntie said that should be enough." She glanced away, as though lost in thought. "That should be enough."

"Naomi, Aiden is hurt. Thea is scared. We need you. Remember when we used to sit on the porch and rock Aiden and Tilly together? Remember Jay? Come back to us."

Something wrestled on Naomi's face. The sneer slid a bit, her eyes softened and then tensed into a look of horror. She glanced at Aiden's bandaged leg in the moonlight. "I . . . I—Oh god."

"Mom," Aiden pleaded. "Mom, I need you." Tears ran over his cheeks.

"I'm here, baby." She started toward Aiden with jerky steps, as though overcoming some invisible force. "I'm he—No, no. She's ba—"

The jerky steps turned fluid once more as Naomi bared her teeth and lunged at Aiden. He raised the knife in front of him, shaky. "I don't want to hurt you, Mom."

"I'm not your *mother*. I will bathe this forest in your blood and watch your sister burn. I will release those trapped here and replace them with your sorry souls for eternity."

She dove at him once more and expertly wrestled the knife from his hand. Aiden stood, arms raised defensively. The rapids roiled white like angry spirits behind him. "Stop doing this!" he cried.

I have to do something, Clara thought from the edge of the clearing, her chest tight, body paralyzed.

Naomi dove forward again, advancing on Aiden. His face was a mask of confusion and terror as his mother lunged with the knife, narrowly missing his side. Naomi bared her teeth as Aiden dodged another slice.

He stepped dangerously close to the edge. Clara had to act. The spray from the waterfall soaked his pajamas to his skin, blood coated his left leg from the knee down. It mixed with the mist and ran in rivulets over the stone, dark, curling tentacles.

"Mom!" he cried again, his voice cracking. At once shifting from almost-adult to child.

Naomi lunged again, and a stripe of red blood bubbled up through the skin of Aiden's forearm. He teetered on the edge of the cliff.

Do something, dammit!

Clara hovered, transfixed, her heart gripped by some unseen force. It was never fight or flight for her, always freeze. A buzzing filled the back of her throat, back of her skull. Her vision narrowed.

No. She pressed forward through the invisible barrier and hurled her body at Naomi. She'd meant to knock her away from Aiden, to knock her to the ground or knock her out somehow until she recovered, as they had when Maddy had her episode—had been possessed.

But instead Naomi's body hovered weightless for a moment on the edge of the cliff before sailing over the falls. Clara's momentum brought her to the edge too. She fell, knees cracking against the rock, to keep herself from tumbling over as well. She reached a futile hand out, as though she could catch her friend who was already swallowed by the gaping mouth of whitewash below. A rush of blood filled her ears, and then Thea's cries from the tree line where she stood in Maddy's arms. Tilly watched from behind with wide, haunted eyes.

Clara looked to Aiden. "I'm—I . . ."

"My mom," he said, hollow.

"I—" Clara stammered. She couldn't recover herself. How do you face the children of the person you just killed? *Killed.*

At that word—at that thought—Clara's whole body was overtaken with shaking. Had she ended a life? She gagged, as if to dislodge what she had just done from her throat, from the timeline at all. She wanted to rewind, gain back the last few seconds. Her head spun, spiraled, and contorted, folding in on itself. Thea's screeches lingered in the cold night and Clara pressed her hands to her ears. She couldn't breathe.

"I'm sorry," she croaked, and began stumbling back toward the forest before Aiden could respond. Because, what else could she say? She had no response for him. She gagged again, all of her mistakes lodging in her throat, thick and viscous. She tasted metal on her tongue.

"You saved me." His voice came from behind her, hollow. "It was a split-second decision. She was—"

"She was *your mother*." The words pushed past the clog in her throat, coming out strained, flattened.

Aiden's face registered them like a slap, tears springing to his eyes. He put his hands to his eyes. Still half asleep, Clara realized. Still wondering if this was real. Was it?

"Is she gone?" he whispered, trembling.

Clara didn't respond. Couldn't.

She had saved them, true. But had there been another way? Her skin felt too tight, like she had walked into someone else's body. She replayed the image of Naomi being sucked below the waves over and over in her mind.

"She's a good swimmer," Aiden said weakly. "Strong."

"She is," Clara responded, watching the way the water roiled and rolled over the rocks. "She's a strong person."

She *was* a strong person. A hole in the pit of her stomach. The gut punch certainty of a sudden loss. Clara was reeling, but four pairs of eyes now locked on her in the moonlight, all tired and hungry and scared. And she was now, supposedly, in charge.

CHAPTER TWENTY-FOUR

Vancouver, BC
October 29, 2001

It has been one year now since my granddaughter came into this world. I think about that day often, the way it broke me. The way it gave me new life. I've never been a stranger to silver linings, brightness hidden behind a tragedy, to sudden changes caused by misfortune.

"A woman's body is made for child bearing," my mother had told me years before. "Do not feel that means you must bear a child, sweet Eleanor. For the choice will always be yours. But if the time ever comes that you will, trust in your body. For it knows the way."

I whispered it to Marie that day—"Trust your body"—when her pressure waves grew closer and closer together and I knew the time would be soon. But she cried out in a pain more vicious than I had expected.

The girl within her was upside-down and backward, the doctor had explained to me. "Stubborn," he had said. And now, having known her for a year, I can attest that she is indeed all three of these things. Always too quick, too stubborn, a bit too much. As tough to raise as a wild bear. But maybe that's just my old age. I can't keep up anymore.

It's difficult to remember this day—not because I can't, but because it hurts. Even with all the assistance of modern medicine, these white walls and astringent smells that still felt so foreign to me, my Marie didn't make it through. I remember holding her hand as she pushed and cried and breathed. I watched as her life, and her blood, drained out of her onto the operating table. So much blood. I will never forget it, surging rhythmically over the edge of the table. Splatters on the white floor below. The smack and patter of rain.

Marie had taken my words to heart, insisted on a natural birth, had signed all the papers indicating she understood the risks. "Take good care of her," she whispered to me. Her last words.

They covered her with a white sheet and handed me the small, wrinkled bundle. Pink face and black eyes, deeper than the depths of the deepest lake. She smelled of pine needles and earth. I pulled her close to my chest. She smelled like my mother.

"I will name you after her," I said, "my fierce little Juliana."

CHAPTER TWENTY-FIVE

THE MOON BATHED everything in silver, as though they were trapped inside a tear. Clara's hands and voice shook as she gathered up the children, and they limped back toward camp. She felt hollowed out, a husk, outside of herself. The pines towered around her, glowing in the ethereal light.

None of this could be real.

"In the morning," Aiden said through his chattering teeth, "in the morning, you'll go downriver and look for her, right?"

The thought hadn't occurred to her. She was so certain Naomi wouldn't have made it that she hadn't even considered it. The crush of water, cataracts created by the churning current, the rocks and debris. It would be a miracle if Naomi made it out alive. But Aiden was right. Naomi was a good swimmer, and strong. A tiny fire of hope ignited inside her. And even if what she found wasn't good news, Naomi had their only rescue beacon. "Yes, I'll go and search."

"Tonight." Tilly's voice was firm over the rushing of the waves and Thea's whimpers. "Go tonight, Mom."

"I—" It was the middle of the night. The moon hung high, lighting their way back to the tents. "I should check all your wounds and get you to bed safely."

"Mom," Tilly hissed in her ear. "If there's any hope for her, you have to go tonight. Go *now.*"

The words stabbed into her. Her knees turned to jelly. It was true. If they waited until morning, it would certainly be too late. But how could she take care of four injured and terrified children *and* make her way down the side of this mountain to see if their mother's body washed up somewhere below? Not to mention, Juliana could seemingly take control of any one of them at any time. It seemed an impossible task.

"I'll check their wounds. *Our* wounds, I mean," Aiden amended. "I guess I am the most qualified here."

"You're just a—"

"I've interned with EMTs all through high school. I can do this better than you can."

Clara gave a quick nod, conceding. "Thanks. And you're right." She put a hand on his shoulder, small and vulnerable in the night, and gave a little squeeze. "Your mom would be proud."

"She *will* be proud. When you find her." He looked at her with hopeful eyes, terrified and serious, but hopeful. She felt the weight on her shoulders and was surprised to find it felt more grounding than crushing, like an anchor rather than a wave. She gave another nod and patted Aiden's shoulder before releasing him.

"We should all stay together," Aiden said. "In one tent. Ours is ruined anyway."

Clara nodded. Four kids huddled in a three-man tent wasn't too cramped, and she felt safer leaving them if they were all together. Thea shook like a leaf in the corner of the green tent, eyes glassy and glazed over. "Keep her warm," Clara whispered to Aiden as she settled them all inside as comfortably as possible. "I think she's in shock." The look on his own face told her that Thea wasn't the only one.

Maddy leaned forward, tears and mud streaking her face. "I don't want you to go. What if—what if *it* comes back. What if it's . . . *me* again? And I do something bad?"

Clara had no answer. She swallowed. Leaving them alone felt wrong deep in her soul, but she was pretty sure Juliana was after her more than the others. *I have to make you bleed for the forest.*

Tilly suppressed a shiver and leaned forward toward the tent opening. "We're good, Mom. I'll take care of her. Just go," she said, her jaw tight. Her eyes had a glassy sheen, but Clara could see she was fighting the pull of fever.

Clara's insides twisted. She hovered on the threshold of the tent, stuck in the mire of indecision. But she didn't have that luxury anymore. She was in charge now. Left alone to make all the choices when every choice was wrong. But Tilly was right, if she didn't look for Naomi tonight, it *would* be too late. And all five of them couldn't make it down the river.

"One sec," she said and went over to Naomi's disheveled tent to collect the other sleeping bags. Back in her own tent, she laid them out across the kids' legs. Aiden was bandaging Thea's arm. "No stitches," he said, all business, applying a few steri-strips. "Not for her. But . . ." His tired eyes wandered to his calf as he lifted it from the bedding. The shirt wrapped around it was soaked through with blood already.

"I'll help," Tilly said, unzipping the first aid kit further and pulling out some alcohol wipes.

Clara swallowed. "I should stay. Didn't Jay always say that as part of his safety talks? Stay put?"

"Jesus, Mom. This is a different situation! I'm sure Jay wasn't talking about when someone goes over a damned waterfall. We don't have time to wait."

Clara cringed, staring at the kids with her brow tight.

"*Please* go. We got this," Tilly said again. "I'm good at sewing, remember? I made that quilt?"

"Aiden's leg is not a quilt!" Clara said, a forgotten memory of a small, proud Tilly holding up her quilt tickling the edges of her thoughts. Tilly had worked so hard on it and did it without any help.

"We can handle it, Mrs. Gomez," Aiden said. His voice was firm, but the crease between his eyes exposed the thin veneer of his confidence. "Consider it doctor practice."

"Go," Tilly said, breathless. "You have to find her, before—" She cut off abruptly, but her eyes held the rest.

On the other side of the tent, Maddy snuggled next to Thea. "Try to get some sleep," Clara said, bending over to plant a kiss on each of their foreheads. She tucked the blanket up around them, her heart hammering in her chest at the thought of leaving these kids alone in uncertain woods after everything that had happened. She fished out her headlamp and a map and left all the food for the kids. They needed it more.

"Don't talk to *anyone*. Okay? And—" She had no advice for if one of them turned like Naomi did, like Maddy had. Her only consolation was that their only real weapon, the camp knife, went over the falls with Naomi. "Just . . . be safe. I'll be back by morning."

As she strode off into the darkness, she couldn't escape the feeling that she was leaving her heart behind her. She wondered if that's how Emilio felt walking away from them for the last time, from the home they'd made together. Had he felt torn in two, like a vital piece of him had been extracted and left behind? Clara doubted it. Regardless, she was marching off half a human now. Less.

But, maybe that was best for where she was going. She felt something waiting in the shadows, lurking at the edge of her consciousness, like a cat ready to pounce. *Pounce on* me, she thought. *Do it. Just leave the kids alone.*

Her headlamp bobbed across the wet, uneven ground like a scared animal, leaping from the base of a tree across the leaves to a rotted log, and then launching up to the treetops above before dropping once again. Clara's blood whooshed through her ears in time with her hurried breaths as she made her way back to the top of the falls.

Another light flickered through the trees, warm and inviting. It calmed her pulse and sent her tensed up shoulders sliding back into place. Dawn, finally climbing up over the edge of the rocks.

But, no, Clara realized. That couldn't be right. The sun would be rising above the mountains behind her, not up over the lip of the waterfall. She quickened her pace, almost leaping with joy. It had to be the rescuers. The rain had held off long enough. Maybe they had finally sent the search party. She was running now, her jacket snagging on branches, but she didn't care.

They were saved.

CHAPTER TWENTY-SIX

AS SHE NEARED the tree line, Clara realized her mistake. The crumbling of her hope was weighty enough that she fell to her knees at the edge of the forest, letting out a cry of frustration. No rescue.

She stared at the brilliant ball of fire that hovered at the cliff's edge. A girl, about Maddy's age stood in the center of the flames, her skirt crumbling to ash and face blossoming with blisters, mouth a black, gaping hole. Clara stared. A voice thundered in her head with the rushing force of water.

The river. Trust its flow.

It was different from Clara's other thoughts—not the rasping, growl of a voice she'd heard since entering these woods, nor the overly critical mix of her mother and herself. This was lower, more insistent. Almost a feeling instead of words themselves.

The girl turned, then, and dove over the falls, arms above her head and feet pointing skyward.

And just like that, she was gone.

Clara rushed forward and leaned over the edge in time to see the flame extinguished by the water below, no sign of a girl or a body. The sobs she'd managed to hold in all night bubbled out of her then, lopsided and ugly, water rushing over the rocks. She doubled over, put her hands on the stone beneath her and yelled out, angry and wild, into the dying night.

"Why are you doing this!?" she cried. "Leave us alone!"

No answer but the distant hoot of an owl, the constant rush of the water, the sharp ache in her side. She stood, wiping the dirty back of her sleeve against her nose and stumbling away from the edge. Exhaustion pressed down on her, but she had to carry on. It was all on her now. She had to find Naomi and get everyone out of here. They wouldn't be safe until they left these woods behind them. Far, far behind them.

Clara inhaled, watching the shadows slide down the snow-covered peak in the distance as the sun rose behind her. She would get them out of here if it killed her. With sure hands, she brushed back her matted hair into a ponytail. She zipped up her raincoat, tightened her hiking boots, and started making her way down the side of the falls.

The vision—ghost or whatever it was—had said to trust the river's flow. Was she trying to lead her to Naomi? Show her a way out? She had to admit, she did feel a strange certainty moving alongside the flowing body of water. The more time she spent near the river, the safer she felt. Perhaps if only because the roar of it kept out the voices in Clara's head. But she couldn't deny a tiny flicker of positivity. Maybe it was the fact that dawn had brought the sun instead of another rain storm. Or maybe the fact that she seemed to be doing something. Moving in a direction. Getting things done. She was getting her head on, as her father always said.

This vision had been different somehow too, Clara reflected as she grabbed the chain and slid her feet over the edge, searching for purchase on the rocky outcrops and roots that jutted out from the cliffside. The girl in the flames was older than the one Clara had seen in the woods earlier, and the light around her had calmed Clara, rather than igniting a panic. It was the first that gave any guidance. The first that hadn't tried to lure her further into the darkness between the trees.

Armed with this thought, Clara felt less alone. Perhaps not all the forest was out to get her. Perhaps she wasn't alone. Perhaps she could do this.

Eager, she increased the pace of her descent, but suddenly the ledge she'd propped her foot on pulled away from the wall. Her hands slipped from the chain, and she was airborne. For a moment she hovered, horizontal, before her body slammed into the hard dirt below with a lung-deflating crash.

The world spun around her, trees looming above like giants taunting her, leaning this way and that at dizzying speed. Her ears rang and sparks lit the edges of her vision. The burns on her back stung with the impact, blisters popping beneath her, sending flames up her spine.

She groaned, curling onto one side, trying to get her lungs to fill again. And once they did, her body spasmed with a coughing fit, which sent shivers of pain along her ribs and across the gaping wound in her side. She lay curled there for ages, days maybe, trying to find the strength to push through the pain and carry on. The cold seeped through her jacket, making her shiver. She was going to die here.

Move, her inner voice chanted, her own again. Calm and commanding. *Move or you'll freeze.*

She thought of the children back in the tent, terrified and awaiting her return. Teeth gritted, she pushed up to a lopsided sitting position. Her shirt and jacket were damp, soaked through with blood. When had she last changed the dressing? Before bed? Or had she forgotten? The bandage was completely saturated, the wound openly weeping.

It didn't matter now. Nothing she could do but carry on. She got up. Slowly, one knee at a time, then one foot at a time, hands on her knees. She tested her lungs, inhaling shallow breaths at first and then standing. No limbs seemed broken, which was lucky, but her ribs throbbed painfully. Her head buzzed, ears still ringing, but she swallowed and carried on down the river, more slowly than before. She kept her eyes along the banks, though didn't expect to see signs of Naomi's body—signs of *Naomi,* she amended—just yet. The rapids were still rough and churning at this point, but calmed further down and opened up into an area with eddies and pools along the banks that gathered fallen trees and other debris. If she was going to find anything, she guessed, it would be there.

And then what?

She scanned the roiling gray-white water as it washed over the rounded rocks, rising and falling and weaving in on itself like a pack of angry wolves. Everything in its path was bowled over, broken, rocks battered and softened into smooth curves.

No one could have survived this, Clara. Give up. The rasping growl sounded quieter, further from her, easier for her to push away.

No, she thought back, summoning the force of the rapids. The growl didn't return.

Still, there was no sign of Naomi, alive or otherwise. She spied branches and sometimes whole trees thundering along, snagging on the rocks before righting themselves and carrying on. But no sign of anything that hadn't originally come from the forest. She held onto the shred of hope, though. She couldn't lose Naomi now. She couldn't return to the kids empty handed.

As she hobbled down the path, Clara fantasized about finding Naomi alive and back to her normal self. Healthy, unhurt, dry and ready to tell Clara what to do next. Cheerful and energetic and filled with plans for getting out of these fucking wet, haunted woods. Clara had been too hard on Naomi, "painting the devil on the wall" as her father used to say. Seeing malicious intent where there was none. If Naomi came back to her, she would be a better friend. She would do anything.

Shit!

She skidded to a stop, her boots digging tracks into the muddy ground as she almost ran into the figure in front of her. Heart thudding, Clara took in the woman, hunched in profile, hair fallen long and unkempt over her face.

The woman's head swiveled revealing a face rust-colored by the blood she wore like a mask, covering everything but her jet black eyes. The woman crooked a red finger at Clara, sanguine lips curling back into a sneer.

Stay! The voice was rushing water in Clara's ears.

STAY. The thunder of the falls, pressing outwards inside her skull, threatening to make it explode.

"Juliana." Clara almost gasped with relief. If she was here, she wasn't back with the kids.

"Good to see you again," Juliana said and laughed, the wet, gurgling rasp of a mud puddle, but sharp as ice. "It was nice being in your friend. And now it's your turn."

"No," Clara said, but then realized she wanted to keep this specter of Juliana busy as long as she could. Keeping her here would keep her away from the kids. "My turn to what?"

Juliana smiled, wolfish. "Your turn to help me, just like you wanted. You'll help me and help me and help me. And then I'll help *them*." Clara's head ached, a migraine threatening, dark spots floated in her vision. It felt like fingers were digging into her skull, prying away layers of bone to get to the meaty center.

"Help . . . who?" Clara asked, hands shaking. Her mind raced, pulse running wild as the river. "Gavin? He's dead, Juliana. And so are you. I know it now. You're dead." Their conversation sounded like a mockery of the ones they'd had so often back at Solara.

Juliana straightened, the grin wiped from her face in the blink of an eye. Anger creased her brow. "*You don't know what I am*," she thundered. "You don't know why I'm here. I need to help my family."

Clara's brow rose. "Your family? But you have no—"

"I do." Juliana's voice was loud enough to vibrate the dirt at Clara's feet. She resisted the urge to cover her ears.

"Okay. I get it. Family is important. If you'll let *my* family go, I'll help your family, wherever they are." She let her features soften. "You're right, Juliana, I always did want to help you. And I still do."

Juliana mimicked her, mocking, "*Wherever they are.* They're my family, and I need you and yours to release them." Her voice raised to a fever pitch, outgrowing her vocal tract and seeming to come from the trees itself. "Gavin wasn't enough. I tried, but he wasn't enough. It's stronger if it's the same, Auntie told me. The same as it was for her. So I needed more, but where could I find more souls when I was locked away at Solara?"

Clara shook her head, thinking of all the times she showed Juliana pictures of her family, knowing it wasn't professional. Knowing she shouldn't.

"Then *you* came, dear Clara." Juliana stepped closer. "They're growing stronger, now. I know you've seen them, Great-Grandma and her daughter. Soon, they will be able to cross back over. They've been waiting *so* long."

Clara curled her fingers into fists and released them again. "You're not real," she whispered. An idea began to form in her head, seeded by the look on Juliana's face when Clara told her she was dead. Juliana may be everywhere. But she wasn't actually *here*, couldn't physically stop her or she would have already. She had no body, apart from the ones she borrowed, like Maddy's and Naomi's. But they weren't expecting her, and Clara was.

"I assure you I am real." The voice came through the trees overhead. Juliana's figure flickered and reappeared a few paces closer, making Clara jump. But also solidifying her idea. It wasn't actually Juliana's corporeal being. That was probably buried somewhere, or cremated. The migraine threatened again at the base of Clara's skull, those digging fingers, but Clara balled her hands into fists and pressed it away. She would not let Juliana in.

Clara twisted her feet in the mud, changing her footing, held her breath and then charged. "You aren't *real*. You can't hurt any of us. Get out of my way," she yelled to the image. And then she ran right through it. A wave of nausea and confusion flowed through her, along with a moment of crippling darkness and anger. But then she was through, stumbling on the other side, no Juliana in sight. Not ahead or behind. Clara inhaled and exhaled a few times, her shoulders rising and falling. Her whole body shook as she doubled over and dry-heaved, hands on her knees. But she'd done it. She'd proven Juliana couldn't keep her here.

Clara eyed the sun, finally fully cresting the mountain behind her, and guessed that at least an hour had passed since setting out. Though, in truth, she had absolutely no idea. A waterproof watch was one of the items on the supply list Naomi had given her that Clara had crossed off as being "optional" because it was too extravagant. "We can use my phone to tell time," she'd said to Tilly. Clara shook her head now at the memory. How naive she'd been. How ill-prepared. Always expecting someone else to double check things for her. Forgetting that, now, there was no one to do that. She was all alone.

But not even Naomi could have predicted this.

Clara stared at the path ahead, but startled at a thought—she had bested Juliana here, but had that sent her right back to the kids in the tent? Clara was able to keep her from taking control of her body because she knew to expect it, but maybe the kids didn't.

Oh no.

She spun, her boots pressing into the soft mud of the trail as she sprinted upwards, tracing the steps of their slow slog up only days before. Her heart thudded in her ears, thankfully drowning out all of her imagined scenarios of what Juliana might do to the kids if she didn't get back in time. Her eyes scanned the path for rocks or roots that might trip her up.

That's when she saw the footprints.

CHAPTER TWENTY-SEVEN

FOOTPRINTS.

At first she thought they might only be shadows, or divots the overflowing river's spray had made in the mud. But they fell at regular intervals, wet and shapeless near the river, gathering form as they led across the trail and up into the forest. Clara's heart leapt.

Up into the forest.

She stared at the mucky dips, trying to divine if they could be Naomi's. But who else would have walked right out of the river?

The footprints disappeared between the ferns on the far side of the trail. She hesitated. If they were Naomi's, she had to go after them . . . right?

Clara's teeth ground into the inside of her cheek. But the kids. Juliana. That should be her priority. If the prints were Naomi's, then she was walking, and hopefully she could find her own way back to camp. Clara started jogging back up the trail toward the kids.

"Clara!" The call made her stop dead in her tracks. It came from the higher elevations, where the footprints headed. "Clara!"

"Naomi?" she called out, rushing into the weeds. "Naomi?" But there was no answer other than a rustling of leaves up ahead.

Heart in her throat, she eyed the trail beside the river. This would be fast. If Naomi was here, close enough to call, then Clara could get to her in mere moments. And together they'd be a better match for Juliana.

She looked one last time at the sun glinting off the river's rapids and then dove into the dark forest beyond. The scent of pine needles and rot filled her nose, and the temperature dropped with every step she took away from the river's edge.

Clara stumbled upwards, her feet sliding in the muddy underbrush. She saw what appeared to be another print in a patch of soggy moss and it sent her further still. After a while, Clara slowed to a stop and took in the forest around her. She'd been climbing steadily for . . . how long? It felt like only a few minutes, but her muscles burned as if she'd been climbing for days. Time felt slippery. A footprint had appeared each time she thought about turning around, but she hadn't seen any evidence of Naomi for at least twenty paces.

Doubt pressed in as she looked back at how far she'd come. The river snaked its way through the woods well below her. She could only see tiny, flickering snippets of it through the thick tree cover. Had she really heard someone calling her name? Had she heard Naomi? Surely she would have caught up to her by now.

"Hello?" she called into the shade of the woods. "Naomi?"

A squirrel hiding in the ferns leapt away from her yells, but otherwise no one responded.

Clara's eyes flicked across the leaf litter, mud, and pine needles at her feet. There was no sign anyone had passed here. No more prints, no broken branches. Nothing but undisturbed nature: bugs eating rot, bigger bugs eating those bugs, slime molds digesting plant matter. But there was no sign of Naomi. She backtracked to where she'd seen the last print, right between those ferns, but the ground there was blank, untouched moss. It must have been a different two ferns. There were many.

But there wasn't a single boot print anywhere. She walked a wide spiral from where she'd been, thinking she'd see at least one. She was just following them, wasn't she?

Finally, her eyes did catch on a series of three prints in a row, only to realize that they were her own. She cursed and kicked a pine cone down the mountain.

"FUCK!" she yelled to the valley. And then, "Naomi! Where are you?"

Tears stung her eyes, close to freezing. She slumped against the base of a tall Douglas fir.

"Okay, Clara. Calm down," she said out loud to herself. "What's the next logical step?"

"The next logical step," Naomi's voice was smooth like honey in Clara's ear. She startled and spun to see Naomi, dressed in a cream skirt suit leaning against the tree over her shoulder. She seemed to not mind the mess the bark would leave on her pristine outfit. "The next logical step . . ." Naomi repeated, expectant.

Clara gaped. She swallowed, the cold sandpaper of her tongue scraping against her hard palate. A light rain began to patter the leaves above her.

"I," she rasped, "I could follow the slope back to the river and try to find the trail of your prints again, I guess. Any way I go down, I'll eventually hit the river. What do you think?"

Naomi laughed. Her hair cascaded around her face in dark waves, seemingly untouched by the rain. "What do you think?" she echoed.

"I can't search forever."

"Can't search forever," Naomi agreed with a little nod.

"Oh god," Clara said. "How long have I been gone? The kids! Juliana was headed for them I think. I should go back now."

"Go back," Naomi whispered, the smoothness of her voice fading into a dry, leafy rustle. "Go back now."

Clara scraped her tongue back in another dry swallow and tore her eyes away from Naomi long enough to tilt her open mouth up to the thickening rain. Why hadn't she brought a water bottle with her? She'd left it with the kids. Left everything with the kids, because she had held hope that this would be a quick journey. Half a day at most. But even through the clouds, she could see the sun was already slanting away from the mountain. It was well after noon. How had so much time passed?

"I can't go without you," Clara said, tears pricking the edges of her eyes. Naomi's white skirt suit took on a translucent quality, showing bits of forest through it. Clara reached out to grasp at her, to not let her go, but her hand met nothing but cold air.

"Go without me," Naomi whispered, now barely audible.

"Where should I go?" Clara whined. "Where are you?"

"Where would I go?" Naomi detached herself from the tree, nearly fully transparent now, and started off down the mountain, her cream heels hovering above the mud. "Where would I go?" she repeated over her shoulder. After a few steps, she disappeared completely, leaving no trace, not even a heel-print in the wet ground.

Clara sighed, pressing the heels of her hands to her eyes. Her stomach tightened, reminding her that she hadn't eaten anything since lunch the day before. Where would Naomi go? Clara felt her absence like a physical void carved out of her middle.

The kids were waiting for her. She had to move. Clara began her descent, following after the mirage of Naomi. She would go back to the river, retrace her steps.

"I wasted so much time," she said to the trees, watching their shadows grow long. Exhaustion settled on her like a second skin. She had to focus. *Think*. Clara didn't see Naomi along the river bank, so if she had made it out, where would she go?

To camp. Which is where Clara should have been waiting the whole time. Of course Naomi would survive and head back to the kids. It was stupid to think she'd be stuck in the river needing rescue. Stupid to think Clara needed to leave the kids and go after her. She was always making the absolute wrong decision. Tears stung the edges of her eyes.

What if when Naomi reaches camp, Juliana has already been there?

Or what if Juliana is still *in* Naomi and Clara has left the kids as sitting ducks for her? She was so certain Juliana was after *her*, but maybe she'd been wrong. The thought sent a splinter of ice down her spine.

She picked up her pace, first heading downhill to the river, but then realizing she'd never make it back in time that way. Rain pattered against her torn rain coat, the drops steadily increasing in size. She wouldn't make it back in time anyway. Why didn't she just give up? Just lie down on the mossy rocks beside the river and let it swallow her?

She bent, crumbling to her knees. *I can't go on.*

But then, a stronger voice, crackling like fire at the base of her skull. *You must. You can. You will.*

Clara stood again, straightened her jaw. She could do this. She glanced to the side, into the darkness between the trees. She dove along, ducking under brambles and leaping over fallen logs, branches whipping her face and snagging on hairs that had fallen loose from her ponytail.

Why had she left the kids alone? She should have thought this through. It felt like an impossible choice. Finding Naomi seemed like the most logical next step in that moment. Now she was left even worse off than she'd begun. *Dammit*!

She let out a cry as her coat snagged on a branch and spun her hard against a tree trunk. Her stab wound splintered with fresh pain as though another knife had been thrust there, so intense for a moment her vision went black. But she recovered, regained her footing and staggered on in a dizzy, lopsided lope. She ran as fast as her broken body allowed her. The wound in her side became a friend, a hiking companion. A reminder that she was alive, still going.

Her mind—hungry and pained as she was—wandered as she ran. Replaying random old memories as though swiping through pictures on a phone.

Her father—back when he was still playing the mountain man—baiting a hook by the edge of a stream, the blood from the giant nightcrawler trickling down over his fat fingers. Her mother, placing her in front of thc vanity mirror and painting her face for a family photo session, tut-tutting about her pimples as she dabbed blood-red lipstick across her mouth. Emilio, running a tender finger along her hairline to replace a fallen hair, whispering silly, lovely things in her ear.

She balled her hands into fists. Really, it was his fault they were in this situation. Not hers. Not Naomi's. If he hadn't—If he hadn't *left*, then she wouldn't be so panicked about Tilly, wouldn't have gotten caught up with Juliana. Wouldn't be in these godforsaken woods, hungry and terrified. Wouldn't be—

Clara's toe caught a root and sent her sprawling forward. Mud sloshed into her open mouth, a rock cut into her cheek. She lay there, breath wheezing into her lungs with an audible whistle, until she felt she could move her limbs.

She straightened up, wiped the mud off her face as best as she could, and scanned the woods, waiting for her dizziness to subside. Soaking ferns shaded by towering Douglas firs and cedars carpeted the ground, with clusters of mossy boulders jutting out at irregular intervals.

She shouldn't have left the path. Shouldn't have followed those footprints. Of course Naomi could take care of herself. And now,

Clara was lost. *Lost*. She finally had to admit it, she didn't know where camp was except for a vague direction based on the slanting of the ground beneath her feet. The rain was driving now, obliterating everything that wasn't right in front of her. She could have walked right past it an hour ago, maybe not twenty feet from her, and not noticed.

Her skin felt too tight, that feeling of needing to move but being stuck. She took a moment to catch her breath and zip the raincoat up to her chin. The temperature had dropped even more quickly than the sun, and now her breath made white bursts in the water-logged air. Twilight had fallen like a blindfold, when Clara was sure it should only be noon. Her muscles throbbed and a pounding built in her skull.

Clara moved slowly now, stopping every so often to listen and look for signs of camp, but nothing looked familiar. Or, rather, *everything* looked familiar. Each rock seemed identical to the last. She'd seen each tree hundreds of times before. She walked on for longer than she expected, calling out to the kids, and found herself still alone in the forest, soaking wet. Her teeth found the grooves she'd carved into her cheek over the years, filling her mouth with a metallic taste. Her stomach rumbled. *Shit,* she thought, shivering. *I'm so hungry I'm relishing the taste of my own blood.*

She kept moving even though all the emergency information Jay and Naomi gave her said to stay put if you're lost. She should have stayed put to begin with. Now, it was too late. The moment for staying put had passed. Although the idea of holing up beside one of these trees, just sliding down to its base and snuggling into the leaves was incredibly tempting.

Her senses became inconsistent, both dulled and ultra-sharp at the same time. The trees passed her like the warbling, tilting forms in a funhouse mirror. When she looked up at them, she could see each individual needle, one thousand shades of green twinkling above her. Birdsong seemed to echo both outside and inside her skull, at times approximating laughter, other times bells.

"Matilda! Aiden!" she called out, and the words refracted in her ears as though passed through a reverb machine, coming back to her broken and reformed.

She was shivering so hard she worried her bones might rattle out of her skin. Her side was crusted with blood, her underlayer shirt chaffing against the burns and stab wound.

Just when she felt she couldn't take another step, a roof came into view.

CHAPTER TWENTY-EIGHT

*T*HANK GOD, SHE thought, her knees going slack at the sight.

The tiny shack sat where the trees clustered together to create a protective canopy over the decrepit structure. Clara reached up to flick on her headlamp, but though the button sparked that satisfying click under her index finger, no light appeared. Taking it off her head, she tried the button a few more times, then banged it against the heel of her hand. Still no light. "Shit," she mumbled. Maybe it hadn't been charged enough? Or the bulb died in one of her falls? She turned her eyes back to the prospect of a shelter. She should carry on to the kids, but if she kept going like this, she wouldn't make it much farther. She looked more closely at the shack.

Most of the roof had collapsed in, along with the better part of two walls. Shingles hung askew, exposed studs reaching up like rotted, gray teeth, supporting nothing but sky. Moss and fungi had taken over, an orange slime mold making a home and a meal of what was left of the single windowpane beside the door. A door which, somehow, remained on its hinges, even if slightly off kilter. On the door, the word BITCH was carved in letters so jagged and slashed that Clara felt the aggression of it like a gut punch. The word echoed around in her head, every instance of it being used against her stacked on top of the last, a full deck of insults thrown at her, at all women, over a lifetime. Bile rose in her throat, the acrid taste mixing with the dried blood that caked her lips.

She shivered in the evening chill and limped over rotted boards that may once have been a small porch. Detritus littered the ground at her feet—odds and ends of a life long gone. An old tea kettle, bent spoon, broken jar, the head of a ball-peen hammer. All from bygone times. Clara scanned for signs of something more modern—a craft brew bottle or cigarette butt left by some wayward camper—but she found none. If she had hoped to find anything more than shelter in this house, she now knew she wouldn't. She took another dry, metallic swallow. This cabin may not help her get out of the forest, but it might be her salvation from the rain

The door was right in front of her, stabs of BITCH inches from her face, the scent of age and decay in her nose. A hole, where there used to be a doorknob. She didn't need to knock, but the urge was still there. It felt odd, the idea of stepping over the threshold of someone else's space, even if that someone was long dead.

She shuddered—what if they were long dead but still inside? What if a body waited on the other side of this rotted piece of plywood that served as a door?

Never mind. She had seen bodies before. She thought of the bloodied scenes that littered her dreams lately, the specters that haunted her in these woods. Behind her closed eyes were nothing but bodies—may as well find a real one.

The thought sent a rattling cackle from her mouth, one that she stopped short. *Fucking keep it together, Clara.*

She was unspooling like a thread.

She pressed against the door with a shaking hand, but it stood fast. She pulled against it, but the single hinge it still hung on was rusted. When she threw a shoulder against it, the door creaked inward a few inches but then stuck against something on the other side. She could probably just press in one of the fallen walls, but something about that didn't feel right.

Fuck it, she thought, and rammed a shoulder against the door, stumbling into the space beyond and cringing back a cry of pain as the wound in her side puckered. Clara blinked. Despite the missing roof, the single room inside was even darker than the surrounding forest.

The first thing that reached her senses was the smell—rot, mildew, death. Then, slowly, the sights of the tiny cabin. They came to her in flashes: fireplace with stones missing and scattered on the dirt floor, table leaning against the wall, rotted pile of rags that may have once been a bed, a chair with one broken leg, a bright pink rucksack—

Wait, what? Clara's heart pounded.

The rucksack leaned against a corner, flap open and straps splayed, perhaps tossed there in a hurry. It wasn't fresh, soaked through as it was with a blackish mold setting into the nylon closest to the ground, but newer by decades than anything else in or around the old cabin.

Her first thought was of food, her stomach registered it even before the signals reached her brain. It cramped and flipped inside her middle, leaving nothing but nausea behind. On her knees, she scrabbled with the sack's zipper beneath the open flap, the rusted metal scraping against her twitchy fingers. A wave of saliva washed over her parched tongue.

Old clothes, wrinkled and dotted with black. Lightweight pots and pans, Nalgene with water sloshing, plastic box containing various fire starters, first aid kit. She dug faster, numbly registering that if there had been any food in this bag to begin with, the animals would have retrieved it for themselves long ago. But she continued on, pulling out the jumble of items two at a time: a flip flop, extra gas canisters for a stove, a water filtration system. Then a crinkle of plastic against her fingers, like a wrapper. Maybe jerky, granola, dried fruit. Her mouth watered.

She grasped the plastic in her shaking grip and yanked it out. A freezer-sized Ziploc, filled with what appeared to be dried flowers and pulverized herbs. Her heart sank, but she held the bag to her face and squinted. *Edible?* The colors of the flowers still shone vibrant in the dim light. Most she didn't recognize, save for the common marigolds and lilies she remembered her mother planting in their yard.

Eat them.

She had no clue which flowers were edible, but her stomach rumbled and she knew she'd have to fill it eventually. So she grabbed out the dried blossoms—purple and orange and yellow—and crunched them between her teeth, bitter and fragrant and dry. She swallowed back the powder they created on her tongue with a swish from the old Nalgene bottle. Her stomach burbled in response, and she sat back on her haunches, winded from swallowing great gulps of water. A strange sensation took over her as she swallowed the last drop. She felt the forest around her, outside these flimsy walls. She could hear the trees whispering to each other, almost feel the roots slithering beneath her feet. And more than that, the vibrations of it all thrummed into her too, as though they were all connected.

Hunger temporarily—and barely—satiated, she decided to make use of the first aid kit as well. It was still fully stocked, bursting with alcohol wipes and gauze pads, band aids and Polysporin. It would be good to redress her wound and rest a bit before heading back to the kids. She wouldn't make it unless she regained her strength.

Clara removed her tattered jacket and top layer. Then, with trembling hands, she began to peel back her blood-soaked base layer and bandage. The old blood had dried into a caked, sticky mess, scabs and blisters breaking with each inch of fabric she pulled back. She arched her back uncomfortably to try to see the wound. Fresh blood—and some other greenish-clear fluid Clara preferred not to think about—oozed from its center. The skin around the gash was swollen and angry. She tore open an alcohol pad and sucked in a breath through her teeth as she swiped it over the area. The second swipe brought a stifled scream.

The pain was immense, her stomach tightening and sparks of light flicking along the edges of her vision each time she neared the wound. But she kept at it, wiping until most of the caked blood was removed and the wipe was stained red. Dizzy and panting, she tossed the alcohol-soaked wipe into the fireplace and dug out some gauze and Polysporin. Smearing on the antibiotic ointment proved almost as painful as cleaning the wound had been. And her gag reflex triggered each time her fingertip slid across the broken edge of her skin, the tactile sensation of the slash against her finger almost worse than the pain in the wound itself. Finally, as gently as she could, she layered on the gauze and taped it down. The burns on her back itched, but she knew that there wasn't much she could do with those on her own, so she left them open to the air. She put her hands on her knees and breathed in deeply a few times until the world stopped spinning. She wasn't good with injuries at the best of times, even on other people.

Clara pulled her bloody shirt back over her goose fleshed body and looked around the cabin, at the partially emptied rucksack, the fallen roof, the blackened fireplace. Her mind spun. She would make a fire. Rest awhile. Regain her strength. Hurry itched under her skin—she knew she needed to get to the kids. To save them from Juliana. But exhaustion stalled her out.

She returned to the rucksack to find a fire starter. As she lifted the bag, another plastic Ziplock slid out of a side zipper pocket with a great thunk against the dirt floor. A book lay protected inside. Two, Clara realized as she picked up the bag and brought it closer to her face.

One was an old, leather-bound journal, with corners that appeared to be damaged by teeth marks, the leather long overtaken with rot and age. The other was a much newer notebook, weathered, yes but the smiling, sky-blue cloud on the cover and the words "Dream Big" were still visible against the silver background.

Curiosity poked at Clara's brain as she fingered the bag in her hands. She peered up through the broken roof at the purpling sky. The rucksack may not have yielded real food, but it wasn't useless. Tiny sparks bloomed across the fire starter Clara had piled at the base of the fireplace. She added small bits of wood from the fallen roof and piled on larger bits once those boards were lit. Smoke billowed toward her in great, thick clouds, but the wood eventually caught. She breathed a sigh of relief as she held her stiff, cold fingers up against the flickering flame.

The turquoise sleeping bag she'd pulled from the backpack was almost dry, sequestered as it had been in its compression sack. Clara wrapped it around herself and leaned toward the dancing flames with the journals in her lap. She decided to open the more weathered journal first. She slid it out of the bag, careful of the worn parts. The leather felt aged, soft and pliable, but rough in the places it had been scuffed or stained. Untying the cord, she let it fall open to a random page, somewhere near the middle.

I'm passing on this history and tradition now, telling my child so she can tell her children and they can tell their children. So future generations can know the events that occurred in those woods. So they can hear my story and find the strength we all carry within ourselves to move forward from the past, no matter how filled with pain it may be.

The writing was not as old as she had expected from the wear on the cover. The date of the journal entry, scrawled a few pages previous, was from 1980. She flipped ahead, to a page nearer to the end.

I've been glad to see that Marie's daughter is interested in the olde ways as much as my Marie was. It is important to pass on this lineage to our bloodline, so that we may continue on. The knowledge must not be lost. This is why I escaped the men who came for us, why I left the woods. I did not know it at the time, and my questions about it haunted me.

Why did I survive when my family did not? Why did I live to carry on after they were gone? But now, watching my granddaughter name the herbs and assist me in mixing the ointments and reciting the incantations, now I know. I was the knowledge-keeper and this is the way of things. We all serve a purpose in this life. One step begets another.

Clara shut the book with a crack. The writer of this journal had also escaped the woods. *These* woods? She rubbed her eyes.

She flipped to the front of the book, and there in neat hand she read, "This journal belongs to: Eleanor Crawford."

Shadows flickered around her, leaping and spinning across the walls in distorted patterns like frolicking nymphs of the forest. The moisture in the wood hissed and popped like whispers. Like chanting. She let out a giggle that echoed back in her ears like an auditory recursion. A memory floated to her. Standing in a department store dressing room while her mother zipped too-tight dresses around her. Hours of passing the time sucking in her stomach against rayon-spandex blends while she watched her form echo back and forth in the many mirrors of the small room—a Clara watching a Clara watching a Clara watching a Clara—all the way down. A Clara recursion.

The giggles turned to guffaws now, the shadows to claws. Clara's heart skipped—did she really see that? But the laughter didn't stop. It came from somewhere too deep within her to stem the flow. A river burbling out of her mouth. A flood. She fell to her side, cheek against the dirt floor, body spasming. She tried to stop it. Tried to recover herself. Tears formed in the corners of her eyes, spilled over. Her vision blurred, the shadows loomed closer, claws turned to faces, mouths agape and filled with teeth.

Breath caught in her throat, her lungs seized. Panic descended. She reached up to her mouth to stem the flow of laughter—to stop this madness—and they met with something wet and filmy. She pulled them away and saw red, dark and rusty in the fire's light. A river of blood from her mouth, down the front of her jacket.

The cabin filled with her scream.

CLARA AWOKE TO the talcum powder scent of her mother. She tried to turn her head, but it was stuck fast.

"Looks like you've made a mess of things," her mother tutted as she sliced a metal comb through Clara's hair. Lydia was never one to mince words.

Remorse welled in Clara, her eyes filling with tears. She readjusted her position to make her mother's brushing hurt less. But it always hurt, no matter what.

"Your hair's filled with knots again, dear. What have you done this time?"

"Camping, Mother."

"How many times have I told you that camping is for ruffians? You should have let that idea die with your father."

A jolt went through Clara. Lydia yanked particularly hard with the comb.

"Did you condition last night?"

Clara shook her head, as much as she could with her hair pulled back in Lydia's vice grip. "You know I was camping."

Her mother scoffed. "You never listen. All your life, I knew you couldn't be trusted." Lydia scraped her hair into a tight up-do and came around to face Clara in her chair. "There. Now at least your hair looks presentable. What would people think? Seeing you walking around like that." She made a disapproving clicking sound with her tongue. "Now what are we going to do about all this blood? You're a mess, dear."

Lydia was just as Clara remembered her: powdered face, light eyes, perfectly pink lips. Her hair lay in waves around her face, which managed to carry the wisdom of the woman's age but without any of the wrinkles. Lydia took care of those with a series of injections every few weeks.

"Clara," she said, "you let your mama take care of things. Remember what can happen if you don't." Lydia's skin tightened around her face until it became waxy, and Clara could see the impression of her skull underneath. "Last time you made the decisions, your father died."

It was a knife through Clara's chest. She remembered the day, though she'd spent most of her life trying to forget it. It was meant to be a happy day, her graduation. She'd felt so mature—and so close to finally moving out from under her mother's tight grip. She'd planned to go home after the ceremony, but Naomi was throwing a huge party, so she hitched a ride there, telling her mother she would be home by curfew. But as the hours ticked by and drinks went around, no one seemed to be leaving any time soon. So Clara phoned her dad, afraid of what Lydia would say. He headed to pick her up, but never made it.

While she waited on the front steps of Naomi's house, a drunk driver plowed into her father's old Ford on the far side of town.

"That's right," Lydia said, pulling her sleeve over her hand and roughly wiping Clara's cheek. "You did that. *You.* And now you're about to get the rest of your family killed too, with all your bad choices." Her eyes had sunk back now, barely visible. Her lips peeled back in a smile that wasn't at all happy, teeth chattering at Clara. *You did this. You.*

The shadows closed in.

CHAPTER TWENTY-NINE

CLARA'S HEAD POUNDED—expanded, compressed—like her brain was too big for her skull. She pressed her hands to her temples for the umpteenth time that morning as she tried to unwind what had happened.

All she knew was that she had been here entirely too long.

She'd woken tangled in the sleeping bag, with her face pressed against the raw, dirt floor. She was so cold, it took her a few minutes before she could fully move herself upright, first by wiggling numb fingers and toes and then rubbing warmth into arms and legs. Her mouth tasted of bile, sour and acidic.

The cabin was a shit show. It had been in a state beyond disrepair when she'd found it, sure, but now . . . Crisp autumn morning light peeked through the broken roof, showing the scene in high definition. The area in and around the fireplace had turned to a blackened pit, ash and wood strewn everywhere. Camping gear and rotted clothing littered the dirt floor. Twin puddles of vomit and something dark and viscous—*blood,* Clara thought and then wished she hadn't—bookended the fireplace. The bag of dried herbs lay beside where she'd woken, petals and leaves and seeds spilled into the dirt. Her stomach roiled at the sight, and she pressed those temples again as the room spun around her.

She shoved most of the useful tools back into the backpack, along with the sleeping bag. The journals she tucked back into the Ziplock and slid into an outer pocket. She had to get moving.

Forgetting the children. Never could be trusted.

"*Enough*," she screamed to the empty cabin. "I'm *not* forgetting my kids! I'm doing *everything* for them." Clara waited a moment in the silence, but her inner voice didn't respond.

She hadn't forgotten the children, of course, but . . . what happened? She got lost and then nearly poisoned herself with strange flowers. She put a hand to the wall as another dizzy spell wracked through her. Her stomach pinched, even hungrier than before. She'd eaten those stupid flowers because she was starving, but now she was even worse off.

She slid down to the floor before she fell. It would be so easy to just stay in the cabin. It was safe here. Sheltered. She could rest. Her hunger was so pervasive it wasn't even a drive to action anymore, just a constant throbbing ache. She could stay here, she thought. Calm and safe. Until it ended her. But no, she had to go. She shouldered the candy-floss colored backpack. It felt weird, like she was sliding into someone else's skin, someone else's life. It occurred to her suddenly to wonder why the backpack was even there. Who had it belonged to? Surely not this Eleanor Crawford who wrote journal entries in 1980. Perhaps the owner was also the owner of the other journal. Clara wished she had peeked inside.

What if it was Juliana's? Wouldn't the cops have found it when they combed the area after Gavin's death? *Murder*, she now allowed herself to admit. Juliana absolutely could have done all the things the judge said she did. And she played Clara so well.

But Clara wasn't playing anymore.

Pulling the door open, she peered outside and blinked in the daylight. Had she only been in there one night? The whole world had changed. All of the deciduous trees were completely bare, no lingering leaves clinging on with their last breath. No, they now lay on the ground under a protective layer of sparkling frost. The conifers were dusted with ice, shining silver. Winter had descended, literally overnight.

Clara suppressed a shiver and took a step toward the threshold, but movement caught her eye. Near the edge of the darker copse of pines. Something large. Shadowy. The branches shook where it passed, a tinkling of needles ringing, swishing. The creature turned in profile and Clara stopped dead.

A bear. Lumbering through the trees. A smaller shadow behind it, trailing merrily.

Or, not so. They were thin, haggard. Fur matted. The mother bear stopped, raised her massive snout to sniff the air. Its cub followed suit, rising up onto his hind legs.

Bear! Clara's mind screamed, but her body did nothing but stand, staring. They were less than ten feet from her.

A snapping of a stick as the cub lowered back down pulled her from her shock, and she slipped back into the relative safety of the cabin like a sharply inhaled breath. A peek through one of the weaker parts of the wall showed her the bears hadn't noticed her. They continued on, sniffing the ground, sniffing the air.

She held her breath, vision still swimming from the effects of the flowers and her empty stomach, and squeezed her eyes shut, massaging her temples again.

She was stuck. Couldn't leave this cabin to go back to the kids or to even look for food. Stuck like she was in her life, always making the wrong damned decisions. Fine, she'd just have to wait the bears out, then.

What were they even doing there? Frost on the ground—they should have been on their way to hibernation. She watched them move, slow, twitchy, erratic. They did not look well. Red spider-webbed across their eyes and drool ran down their gums and onto the frosty ground below. Her teeth found the inside of her cheek and dug in.

She was separated by a rotting wall and no more than ten feet from two starving bears. Lowering herself as soundlessly as she could, she slid back to the floor. The backpack still clung to her shoulders, as any motion to remove it would probably alert the bears to such succulent prey nearby. Instead, Clara held her breath.

Ten minutes may have passed, or two hours. Time was irrelevant here. The sun slanted through the broken roof and the shadows made their daily march across the floor, but how much or how little, Clara couldn't tell. She had drifted off—long enough, she thought, for her neck to develop a painful cramp—and was awoken by a rustling sound nearby. A scraping, really, on the outside of the cabin's wall. *Rustle, rustle, scrape.* And behind that, heavy, heaving breaths. Clara froze. It must be the bears.

The bears rubbing against the cabin. Slowly, so slowly she felt her muscles would spasm and give her away, Clara raised herself an inch at a time until she could peer through the hole. And sure enough, just below her eye level was a mass of matted fur. Streaks of blood and mud and sweat marred the glossy brown coat. The smell of rotted flesh wafted through the slats on the wall, and Clara suppressed a gag. Had they been injured in the slide? Perhaps awoken from their slumber beneath the stream of rubble that slid down the mountain's side? A surprising pang of pity rocked her as she watched another mother struggling to survive and keep her child safe in this unforgiving forest.

The larger bear snuffled against the house, digging its great paws into the ground, rooting for something. Perhaps there used to be a garden here and the roots still lay under the ground. Whoever used this cabin so long ago must have had a food source. Could they have planted potatoes or carrots that continued to grow? Clara's stomach growled. She held her breath and counted.

Then, just like that, after a count of 239, the bears turned and sniffed the air and followed their noses into the forest. But Clara kept counting. To a thousand and then two thousand. And when the bears didn't return, her muscles finally relaxed from the tense knot they'd wound themselves into. But then her stomach cramped, a sudden reminder that she still had no food. If the bears found a garden, Clara would too. Carrots were roots. And beets. She could eat roots.

She licked her cracked lips, her dry tongue making them sting, and she shrugged off the rucksack. Cautiously, she slipped through the door and around to the side of the house where the bears had been.

The air had taken on that frozen, whitish-yellow tinge of the first freeze of winter. Too much sun and not enough warmth, like being burned with cold fire. Shadows were stark; frozen leaves crunched underfoot.

Sure enough, the ground by the side of the house had been scraped away in great gashes, leaving an uneven hole. Grayish-black forms were visible over the lip of the depression, leaning together haphazardly. They may have been turnips or beets, but as Clara approached, she knew her first impression had been wrong. So, so wrong. They weren't turnips, and she definitely couldn't eat them.

Bones. Piles of them.

Two skulls stared back at her with gaping empty sockets and slack jaws, that cruel, fleshless smile all skulls seemed to retain. The grinning skulls were charred black. The hair prickled along her arms and legs like lightning, but she stood motionless, as though actually struck.

A scream built in her lungs, but all that came out was a wheeze. She was in a nightmare and needed to wake up. This couldn't be real. None of it could. She reached a two fingered claw up under the sleeve of her rain jacket to give herself a good pinch, and yet here she still was.

She shook herself, exhaled. Panic helped no one. It made sense, actually. Maybe whoever had occupied this cabin was buried here.

With another shaky exhale, she approached the bones and crouched down. There were two skulls and a tangle of other long and small bones. Clara studied them as the light slanted further sideways in the waning afternoon.

One of the skulls was smaller, miniature, a child. A pang of horror went through her, the coldness of grief radiating from her center. Her heart contracted, repulsed, and yet she couldn't help her brain from spiraling into thoughts of childhood death. *What if it were my child? What if they suffer a similar fate?*

Her stomach turned. She hadn't seen her Maddy and Tilly in . . . how many days? Could it really only still be just one? Or was it more? And when she last saw them, they weren't doing so well. Weren't safe. She pictured Tilly, thick film of sweat on her brow and swollen leg propped up. Maddy, wandering blank-eyed around camp with Aiden's knife.

Clara put her hands to her face and screamed. The forest swam on for days in all directions. She was tiny, and somewhere out there in this sinister and shifting sea of trees, her girls needed her. And here she was, staring at old bones and rooting through a stranger's things.

Bile rose in her throat, a bitter call to action. She needed to fix this. She needed to find her girls and get the fuck out of these woods. Before it was too late.

Clara was about to stand, when she wondered, *Who had lain them to rest?* She reached a hand out to the smaller of the skulls and said a little prayer—in her own way—that this child's soul was at peace. It seemed like the right thing to do.

Just as she placed her hand on the blackened brow, a scream lit up the forest. She ran, rucksack bouncing painfully against her burned spine, unsure of what she would find, what horror awaited her. What if the bears had found the kids?

The screams continued like an air raid siren, a macabre breadcrumb trail that led deeper into the woods behind the cabin. She sprinted over ferns and slid on slick, ice-covered roots.

The stench reached her as she cleared the first layers of thick trees. Charred meat and smoke and rot. She gagged, pulling the neck of her jacket up over her nose and mouth. Smoke filled the air, braiding itself with the screams. Then she saw the flames, through stinging, watery eyes. They were sharp and harsh and sent a panic through her, a contrast to the warmth of the flames she'd seen around the girl by the river. She stumbled into a small clearing, rucksack swinging wildly on her back. The tape holding her bandages gave way, a sharp pain stung her side. Recovering herself, she rubbed smoke from her eyes and looked up to find three flaming pyres. One stood empty, but a woman and a girl occupied the other two, mouths agape as flames licked up and over their skirts, blistering their faces and hands, and turning their hair into incendiary halos. Their bodies thrashed and writhed against the bonds.

Clara stood a moment, transfixed by horror, before she realized that the girl was the same one she had seen in the woods that first day. She'd seen the woman too, with her apron and dripping frying pan. This was just a vision. An echo of what must have happened here once. It twisted something in Clara's chest. Something horrible happened in these woods, and ripples of it continued on, but that would not happen to her own children. She wouldn't let it. Clara's hands balled into fists at her sides. The echoes of this awful event stopped with her.

She took one last look at the burning women in front of her. They were beyond saving, but her own kids weren't. With difficulty, Clara turned away from the victims in front of her. She eyed the angle of the sun, the slope of the ground, and with surprising clarity, she marched toward camp.

She had no more time for wrong choices

CHAPTER THIRTY

ALL RIGHT, CLARA. Get your head on.

It was what her father used to say to her when they were about to undertake a new project, solve a new problem. When he asked for her help repairing the old plumbing under the sink, *get your head on and go get the wrench*. When they were lost on a road trip, *get your head on and come look at this map*. When he was coaching her through her college applications, *get your head on and get those essays written*. He trusted her to do the right thing when she "had her head on." He trusted her, period, in a way her mother never had. In a way even Clara hadn't.

Now, she just needed to get her head on and trust herself. She had been running unmoored, unraveling through the woods for days, hours, years, she didn't know. Her steps behind her were a tangled thread, netting her in. And what did she have to show for it? Nothing. But she could solve this. She solved problems for a living, albeit usually other people's. A friend—not Naomi, she realized—had told her in college: "Any decision you make is the right one, as long as you commit to it." That was Clara's real problem. It wasn't that she was unable to make good choices, it was that she was so afraid of making the wrong choice, she let everyone else choose for her.

She adjusted the straps on the rucksack. It wasn't so different from her life outside the forest. Finding herself hemmed in by the consequences of her bad choices. Or, rather, her non-choices. She so rarely made a decision on her own, without following what a parent or friend or lover told her to do. No wonder she had so little authority as a parent. She was a child herself.

Even now, shivering and alone in the woods, she desperately wanted Naomi to swoop in and take charge, to tell her everything would be all right. But she only had herself now. She had to take stock, to trust herself.

I used to tell you that all the time.

"I know, Dad," she said, glancing to where he strode beside her, stepping over the ferns in his khaki pants and loafers. "But what if you were wrong? Bet on the wrong horse?"

"I know I didn't. You can do this, Clara. You can do anything."

She scoffed. "Says the person who's literally *dead* because of my bad decisions."

He stopped in his tracks, mud squelching up the sides of his brown leather shoes. "*You* did not kill me, Clare. A drunk driver did."

She shrugged, tears pricking her eyes. "You would have been home if not for me."

"And you may have been in the very car that hit me. Or you may have been behind the wheel yourself. You did the right thing."

"I never do the right thing." She faced him.

"You sound like your mother."

Clara shot him a glare.

"Your mother always meant well, but I know she was hard on you."

"Understatement of the year."

"I'm sorry about that, Clare. And I'm sorry I wasn't there for you when you needed me." He put a hand on her shoulder.

The tears that pricked her eyes overflowed. "I'm sorry too. I'm sorry I even went to that stupid party," she said.

"We can't change the past," he said. "But you can let go of it."

Her throat contracted in a sob. "I can't. It's who I am."

He wrapped his arms around her. "I'm proud of you. You're a great mother, even in this hard time. And you're a strong person. Toughest I've ever met. Just look at you."

She wet his shirt with her tears, and when she finally pulled back, she saw he had the same translucent sheen as her vision of Naomi. "No, no. Don't go yet," she said.

"I'm not even here," he said. "I'm dead, remember?"

"I'm learning that's less permanent than I thought."

He tapped her forehead and then her heart. "I'm here, Clara. I'm you. I'm the voice inside your head. Just allow yourself to listen."

I have my children to save, her inner voice thrummed. *I can do this.*

Her father slowly faded into the shadowy green around her.

She stopped and took in her surroundings, *really* took in her surroundings. Noticing the orientation of the mountains, the type and density of the trees around her, the position of the sun in the sky. As before, she was in the valley between two mountains, and the sun was reaching for the tip of the farther, snow-covered one. *West*. She had no idea which direction camp was in, but she knew she hadn't crossed the river, so if she headed west she should reach it at some point.

Jay had told her stories of people wandering in circles for days using this thinking. Heading *almost* in the direction they wanted to go but not quite enough to ever get there. But she didn't have much else in her toolbox at the moment. She could at least reach the river. And from there, she would find her way to camp.

⸻

IT WAS SILLY, really, how easily Clara found the river once she held herself accountable. She reached it in under an hour, the rushing water like music to her ears. She stumbled forward, ready to kiss the dirt once her feet met the trail. But something caught her eye before she was able to. Something white and fluttering off to the right.

She didn't want to know, didn't want to see, but a lifetime of avoiding things hadn't yielded her much success. So she peeled back the layers. She took the steps to the right and saw it.

The owl, white feathers splattered with red, beak dug into a bloody mess, wings outstretched over its bounty.

Clara swooned, saw it in flashes. A black hiking boot, size 7, North Face hiking pants, torn Barbie-pink raincoat. Naomi.

She must have clawed her way out of the river and up into the trees. She must have been heading for camp.

Clara ran forward, making to shoo away the giant bird of prey, but the owl just considered her with its rust-spattered face and single eye. It flapped its wings once, twice, over the corpse and then stepped back, as though to give Clara a better view.

But she didn't want it. Naomi's face was gone, eaten off by animals. The owl, Clara realized. A flapping piece of flesh hung from its beak. Naomi's coat was torn open, as were her ribs. She was hollowed out. The sleeves of her coat were shredded, and Naomi's wrists sliced open, the wounds still leaking into the mud beneath. The iron tang of blood and the more acrid scents of bile and feces filled the air.

Clara fell to her knees, retching, though nothing came out since her stomach was empty. It just served to make her insides cramp up even more. She wiped her hand on the back of her sleeve and stood again after a few moments.

"Get away from her," she said to the owl, her voice rasping.

The owl watched her without moving, beak seeming to form a cruel impression of a smile.

"I said get the fuck away from her!" Clara screamed, leaning forward. The sound came from deep within her, voice like iron grinding against itself. The angry inner voice that had taunted her for the whole trip, but now it was under her control, no longer controlling her. Two birds above in the trees took to noisy flight at her outburst and flew away, but the owl remained.

She picked up a stick and tossed it with all her might. Finally, the predatory bird took a few self-preserving hops.

Then Clara saw it, the yellow plastic of the beacon still hooked to Naomi's belt. The red light flashed dimly, coated as it was in a thick layer of blood. Clara swallowed, took one step forward. Her fingers itched and stomach turned as she inched closer to the carnage that was once her friend.

Once in reaching distance, she lunged and grabbed the sticky beacon, sliding it off Naomi's waist with a sickening, slick sound and tucking it onto her own waistband. Beneath it, she saw the camp knife. Holding her breath, she unsnapped that as well and added it to her own belt loop.

The owl opened its beak and released a bone-chilling cry mere feet from Clara's face. The shriek of a tortured woman, loud and crisp in the winter forest. Clara covered her ears with her hands. The owl hopped toward her, surprisingly big up close. It came nearly up to her chest.

"Fuck." She stumbled backward, hitting a tree.

The owl screeched again, lunging forward, wings outstretched over Naomi's body.

Clara held up her hands. "Okay," she said, sidestepping the tree behind her. She looked over her friend's body; a lump welled in her throat, lodged there, closing off her breath. She tried to exhale. "Okay."

She took another step back. Naomi was gone. *Let the forest have her now,* Clara thought with a barely concealed sob. She put her hands to her face as the trees swam around her, dizzying through her tears.

She should bury the body, she thought, say some words. Do *something* other than leave her best friend out here, belly slit open like an anatomy lesson. But the owl shrieked again, batting at Clara with its expansive wings, and she had to turn away to shield her face from its talons.

Clara turned her back on her friend, her heart heavy within her. She'd held so much hope, and now she had to go tell her best friend's kids that their mother was dead.

A sob ripped out of her, not unlike the owl's predatory screech. She headed for the trail, but then a sound behind her made her stop.

CHAPTER THIRTY-ONE

Vancouver, BC
December 13, 2014

I have just returned from another meeting with Juliana's school team. And I need to write because otherwise I may cry. I am just so confused and frustrated. Nothing I do seems to help, and clearly the school's safety plans have fallen short as well. I'm afraid I may be losing Juliana more and more with each passing year. So often alone, and so often angry.

Donald and I have tried to be gentle and understanding, but as more time passes, I'm wondering how much I really do understand her.

I've been finding her, more and more, listening to sounds that aren't there, speaking to people I cannot see, even when I try to use my other senses. The power within Juliana is so strong, but she will not let me shape it, often screaming or running away when I bring out my lessons of the olde ways.

The school has decided they will not let her return after this suspension. She has incurred too many infractions, they said, and the severity of each is increasing. We must find somewhere "better suited to her needs and numerous diagnoses." On this point, I do find myself partially agreeing with them. We must find somewhere better suited to Juliana, and I've spoken to Donald; I think the best place for Juliana right now is with us. For the safety of herself, but also those around her. I do hope that other child recovers.

Taking charge of Juliana's instruction will be a difficult undertaking, but my own mother educated Marie and I all on her own. I am confident I can do it, at least the academic piece, but I worry about Juliana's other difficulties. If she is indeed hearing voices from another plane, I do not know if my own knowledge alone is enough to help her, even if she were to let me, which I am sure she will not.

CHAPTER THIRTY-TWO

GURGLE GURGLE.

It wasn't the owl's screech or the wind in the trees. It was a wet, surging sound. The sound of pressing a finger into the slime her kids used to make at the kitchen table. The sound of moving through wet, swampy mud.

Clara turned slowly. The owl stood on the far side of Naomi's body now, arms outstretched like a cemetery angel, eyes intent on the ground beside Naomi—the ground that began to shift.

Kernels of dirt churned against the blood-soaked mud, until the earth around the body appeared to be vibrating. Through the reddish-brown mess of it all, something emerged, pink and shining like a worm. Then another poked through beside the first, and another. With a sickening dread, Clara realized they were fingers scraping up toward the sky.

Naomi's blood, so freshly spilled against the ground, stained the fingers as eventually two whole hands pressed through into the air. Dark nails scraped at the dirt, searching for purchase. Wrists and elbows ascended and then a mass of hair, black and matted. The owl remained motionless behind this spectacle.

Clara's heart pounded in her ears, but all she could do was stare. Her breath was caught somewhere in her throat, a waiting explosion of unreleased scream.

The matted hair tipped up to reveal a familiar face, recognizable even under the layers of blood and mire. Juliana's mouth slid into a slow grin, bits of dirt clinging to her teeth and eyelashes. She coughed a few times until it became a laugh.

"Hello, Clara," she said, her voice like metal scraping against pebbles.

Clara took a step back. Juliana had emerged so close to Naomi she practically came up through the body. Thick clots and pieces of flesh clung to her skin, like a layer of post-birth vernix. "What—what are—" Clara stammered, her brain unable to connect to thought.

"I'm ba-ack," Juliana said, her grin not fading. She stretched her arms above her head and then pulled each one to her chest in turn, as though she'd just finished at the gym. She gazed up at the sky and then tilted her head to the side, giving her neck an audible crack.

"Just try to walk through me now, bitch," she said. "The forest has given me my real body back, thanks to your friend's sacrifice." She turned and pressed a finger to where Naomi's nose should have been, like a little "boop" you'd give a toddler, before returning her gaze to Clara. "I have been reborn. Now things can really get started."

Clara took another step back, horror building in her like vinegar poured over baking soda. Slow at first, but once the reaction starts . . .

"What have you done?"

Juliana was pulling clods of earth away from her to extract each of her legs. The owl that had stood behind her let out a shriek and took off into the trees. Juliana's eyes followed it.

"Ah, as the owl flies," she said thoughtfully and then returned her black gaze to Clara. "That's Great-Grandma. She'll get to them before I do. Before you too, for that matter."

Get to them. Get to the kids. That thought, entirely her own, released the valve and sent her speeding back through the trees, heedless of whether Juliana had fully emerged behind her or not. All she knew was that she had to get to the children and keep them safe.

Branches sliced at her cheeks as she sprinted toward the river.

CLARA'S HEAD SWAM. She was drowning, a winding river unraveling within her.

She stumbled up the trail beside the overflowing rapids. Water sloshed up and over her feet in a few places where the trail dipped, but she carried on, blinded by rage now instead of fear. The rage she always pressed down surfaced with a vengeance. Radiating like a sun, strong and chaotic, it had no real target. She was furious at Naomi for going along with her. Furious at her mother for letting her teenaged self take on the heaviest burden of blame for her father's death. Furious at Emilio for leaving and turning the kids against her. And furious at Juliana. For making her trust her. For leading her out here.

Her anger turned on the forest, too. The wet divots in the mud where the water ran thick. The moss-covered tree trunks that closed in around her. The dank air, laden with the scent of rot and death. This cruel and bewitching place that swallowed them whole and wouldn't let them go. That birthed killers back from the dead. And, most of all, she was furious at herself for letting things get to this point. But rather than dwell in that deep pool of guilt, she dug her teeth into the inside of her cheek and continued marching up the trail. Nearly to the waterfall now, she could hear it screaming around the next bend. Roaring at her as though it was the voice of the forest's demon, or perhaps her own.

But she would not let it devour her.

She balled her hands into fists as she rounded the bend, then she stopped short.

The waterfall had become a writhing mass of white water, swallowing the trail to the right completely. The chain that denoted where the trail climbed the cliff was fully obscured by the spray. To the right, trees tangled their limbs together and brambles and ferns clustered, a nearly impenetrable wall. But she needed to get beyond the falls and above them to make it back to camp. So it was either climb a cliff covered in raging water or dive through brambles and underbrush. And she'd already done that. She shivered in the waterfall's spray.

Clara exhaled through her nose, letting her anger warm her. Her hunger and her wounds and her worry about the children all fed it, turning weakness into strength. There would be no more getting lost. No more sinking ankle-deep into mud between the trees. She would face this obstacle head on.

Clara took off her gloves and grabbed the rusty chain with both hands, letting the overflowing waterfall wash over her arms. She braced her feet against the rocky wall and began to pull herself up, one step at a time. The waterfall bathed her from head to toe, soaking her all over again, but she didn't flinch away. It cleansed her of all the doubt and angst and hesitation she had grown to think of as her personality. She let it chill her to the bone and strip away the muck she'd acquired in her years married to Emilio. In the years stuck in a job she hated. The years she'd spent believing she'd killed her father when she was only seventeen. All of it fell behind her to the bottom of the incline.

Finally, she emerged over the top of the rocks, sparkling orange in the glow of the sunset.

CHAPTER THIRTY-THREE

CLARA STOOD ATOP the waterfall only a moment to gather her strength. She gazed at the prism of the sunset's glow in the mist and then steeled her jaw and stepped toward the darkness of the trees. A light caught her eye, flickering beyond the tree line. Could that be their camp? Maybe the kids had started a fire. But then it began to move toward her, growing brighter and brighter until it burst forth onto the rocks.

The girl, skirts aglow, stood in front of her. Her eyes danced, warm chestnut against the flames. Her brow creased. *They're getting ready*. Her voice echoed in Clara's head.

Not like Juliana's had at first, rasping through the trees on the wind, but really inside Clara's head. Like a thought but not her own. *You are in danger*.

Clara swallowed. "I know." She laughed bitterly. "That isn't news to me." She thought of the bears and the hole Maddy had stabbed in her side, and the burning women in the clearing. She thought of her friend splayed open like a piece of meat at a butcher's shop and

Juliana emerging through her torso. The forest spun around her. A buzzing built in her ears. "Who are you?"

I'm the one who got out. The one who got away. But now they're all trying to leave, and they need you. They need the children to bring themselves back. The forest is hungry.

"So I've heard," Clara replied. She coughed in the cold air, putting a hand to her side.

Do not let them have you. Keep the children safe. And beware my granddaughter, for she knows not the power she wields.

"Your granddaughter?"

My Juliana. The wind picked up around them, tree trunks leaning perilously.

"Your granddaughter is— But how do we get out of here?"

The forest answers to no one. The river will be your salvation. Let it flow. I will try to keep them from you. Trust yourself, Clara. To flow is not to follow.

"But I—" The girl began to turn away, but Clara couldn't let her go. She darted an arm through the flames that didn't burn and tried to grab the girl's arm. Her hand went right through, but where their limbs overlapped, a spark flew, electrified.

SHE WAS IN the cabin, but it wasn't the cabin as she'd seen it. The roof was intact, sunlight filtered through the windows, reflecting off the vase of flowers on the table. Two girls sat there, scooping spoonfuls of soup into their mouths and joking with each other. A woman tended the fire in the fireplace and pulled a knitted floral shawl tighter around herself as she passed the window. She turned back to the girls, her face creased more from worry than time.

Suddenly a bang and others were in the cabin too. Men, clumsy and angry. They overturned the table, sending soup flying against the far wall.

The girls screamed and thrashed in their grasp, kicking out wildly. The mother lifted a cast iron pan and brought it down on one of the men's heads. Then they were on her, seizing each of her limbs while one man slashed at her face with a fork from the table. The tines scraped a bloody mark across from her temple to her nose, straight through her eye. It only made her thrash harder. The men bound the women, dragged them to the woods to a clearing where trees had been trimmed into poles, piles of sticks and kindling laid at the base of each. There, they were tied up, doused in fuel. The men's laughter echoed through the forest, like metal scraping.

CLARA YANKED HER hand away as though stung, and found herself back in the forest facing the burning girl who had tears streaming down her face.

"But you got away," Clara whispered. "The third pyre was yours. The empty one."

A horrible, wrenching sound exploded from the darkness of the woods then, like the whine of machinery.

The girl gave the slightest of nods. *Go. Leave your pyres empty as well.*

She started for the falls but then turned back, eyeing Clara's backpack. *You have something that belongs to me.* Her eyes sparked as she approached Clara again. She reached a hand and placed it on the rucksack. *Give it to me. I am only an echo here, stuck forever in the path I traveled to escape. But if I have a piece of me, something tying me here, I can be a small bit more.*

"Eleanor Crawford," Clara said. "Juliana's grandmother. Of course." She pulled the journals from the pocket of the rucksack and handed them to Eleanor. As soon as the girl took hold of them, she began to age. She grew taller, wrinkles set into her face like river canyons eroded over time, and scars grew up across her skin like mountain ranges. The flames around her dampened but never fully dissipated. Eleanor looked down at herself, smoothing her hands over her dress, which had grown with her and become a floral frock. "I'll handle my family. You save yours."

And with that, she darted off between the trees, faster than Clara thought a woman of her age could move.

Clara followed into the shadowy forest. Immediately, things looked familiar, almost as though she were coming home. A few steps in, she saw Tilly's hammock, hanging limp and soaked from the earlier rains.

That grinding, machine sound wrenched the air again, and Clara threw her hands over her ears. Her heart thudded in her skull. The trees filtered out what was left of the sun's glow, so she had to squint in the dimness. Time was a skipping and shapeless thing, like salmon flashing in and out of view along the river. Clara could not let herself believe evening was once again already descending. In the absence of clear sight, her nose filled with scents of burned-out fires, wet tarps, and rotting leaves. She wanted to call out to the kids, to Eleanor, but something had clamped a claw around her lungs.

The grinding sound suddenly stopped and another took its place: the beating of wings. Clara looked up to see the owl swoop low and disappear into the branches above. *Fuck.*

Moving quickly now, Clara zigzagged across the ground, noting landmarks. That hammock, the fire ring, meaning the tent should be across the—

Clara walked headlong into something tall and hard. She stumbled back, seeing spots, and tried to reorient herself. There hadn't been a tree in the middle of their campsite. She must have gotten turned around.

But as her eyes adjusted, she could see that it wasn't a tree she'd walked into, but a tall pole lodged into the ground. Blinking, she noticed another just a few meters from the first. And another just beyond that. *What the fuck?* As she stood there, a rumbling shook the ground and she had to cover her ears against another shriek. Something erupted from the earth. At first, Clara was terrified it was Juliana coming from the dirt again, but as it moved further upward like a fast-growing tree, she saw it was another pole.

Clara put her hand against the pole closest to her. The freshly birthed wood was smooth and warm to the touch, almost alive. She flinched, thinking of the women she'd seen burned in the vision earlier, and shivered at the idea of what fate might await them if they didn't get out of this forest.

Finally she saw it: the tent. It stood a few feet behind these new additions to camp. She stumbled forward, barely able to breathe. What if they weren't inside?

No. She refused to believe that was a possibility. They had each other. They were resilient.

It occurred to her that she never thought of her kids that way before. Not when they were little, not after Emilio left, not on this trip. She'd thought of them as hungry, hurting, always needing her too much. Never resilient. She had resented them for it, she realized, for the parts of herself she'd cut out or ignored so she could meet their needs and keep them safe. But as she neared the tent, she heard their quiet voices in the darkness, and knew they were strong, so much stronger and more independent than she'd ever given them credit for. It wasn't up to her alone to get them out of here. They were a team. And she'd never been more grateful for them.

"I'm back," she said quietly before bending to grasp the tent zipper.

Before she could do it herself, the tent door unfolded outward and Maddy dove into her arms. "Mom! We thought you weren't coming back. We've been waiting, and—there were terrible noises. We thought you wouldn't come back." Her daughter sobbed into her arms.

"It's so good to see you." She inhaled Maddy's smell, still discernible even beneath the scents of campfire and sweat and damp. She peered into the tent. Thea was curled up, sleeping soundly, but with swollen eyes. She'd been crying.

"Mom," Tilly rasped from the corner of the tent, where she leaned with Aiden. Both of their faces were covered in a sheen of sweat, bags under their eyes. "You made it."

"Did you find . . .?" Aiden trailed off, eyes searching the dark behind her.

Clara swallowed and shook her head. "She's gone," she said, her voice breaking. Aiden's face crumpled as he stifled a sob. Tilly put an arm around him.

The smell in the tent was thick. Unwashed bodies and mold, but something else too. Something sour and sick smelling. Clara shuddered. It was the smell of rotting flesh. "We have to get out of here," she said, thinking of the poles outside. *Pyres*. Like the ones she'd seen by the cabin. "We have to get out of here *now*."

But Clara's legs gave out at that moment, and she found herself on the ground.

"Maddy. Get off her," Tilly's voice echoed from somewhere that seemed far away, and Maddy's arms released from around her neck. Clara tried to protest. That wasn't what had brought her down. It was the weight of exhaustion and hunger, the weight of their predicament, and the weight of Naomi's body, lying emptied and bloody in the underbrush.

"I'm fine," Clara said, trying to get to her knees. "Get your things. We're going. She'll be right behind me." Her mind went back to Juliana pulling clotted mud off her, testing her new legs, new muscles like an infant.

Tilly's hands, cold and clammy, pushed Clara's hair out of her face and pulled her into the tent. She was too exhausted to resist. Aiden crawled around to pull off her shoes. They were a pile of writhing bodies, snakes in a nest too small for them. They all peered into the darkness outside the tent.

Thea stirred, blinking. "Mama?" she asked, rubbing her eyes. Aiden pulled up next to her and wrapped his arms around her, and their bodies shook with silent sobs.

But Clara couldn't help them. Her own body began to shake, vibrate really, beyond her control. "What's happening?" Tilly asked, zipping up the door.

"I think," Clara said through her chattering teeth and clenching stomach, "I think it's exhaustion. I should . . . I should drink something. And eat." *And then we'll get the hell out of here.*

At the last word, her stomach somersaulted. She wanted food so badly, she would have eaten the leaves if she hadn't made it back. "Do you guys still have food?" The desperation in her voice was unmistakable. Her fingers contracted and released, claws grasping at invisible morsels.

"Of course," Maddy responded. "We rationed it. And planned for you to come back."

"Should we build a fire?" Tilly asked, and Clara could tell she was masking worry in her voice. "You're shivering so much."

Clara shook her head. She sucked down the pieces of dried fruit and nuts half-chewed until her throat clogged and she stifled a gag. Tilly passed her some water. Her stomach groaned and churned as it received the first solid food in days. Clara suppressed a wave of nausea, but grabbed another handful of trail mix and brought it to her mouth. She told herself to be careful, to not take too much—they still needed to ration—but it was the best food she had tasted in years, in her whole life.

She nearly cried with relief. The shaking in her legs gradually subsided, followed by a dull but tolerable ache. A patter of rain drops sounded against the side of the tent and began to intensify, the wind whipping them in great gusts.

She took in the motley group of children, all of them sitting around the edges of the tent, feet toward the middle, overlapping like a knot, twined in sleeping bags and blankets. They were grimy, hair matted and cheeks sallow, especially Tilly and Aiden, whose skin had taken on a sort of yellow sheen, exacerbated by the sickly green of the tent. Clara took another sip of water, relishing in the fullness of her stomach. Four pairs of expectant eyes waited. But this time, she felt ready.

"Aiden," she said, "how's your leg?"

He raised it from under one of the blankets, and peeled back the clean gauze on his calf. There, skin puckered red around a stitched seam. "I'm not going into pre-med for nothing," he said weakly, eyes red. She had to admit, it was an artful job, but the wound was swollen and angry. He needed a real doctor, not a high school student who had volunteered with EMS.

She gave a nod. "Can you walk on it?"

He swallowed, squared his shoulders. "I can."

"And Tilly?" She shifted her eyes to her darker-haired daughter.

"I'm—I can make it. Whatever we need to do, Mom, I can do it. I mean, we can't fucking stay here." She tried to muster her usual teenaged sass, but the swear fell flat and Clara noticed her shiver. "There were . . . noises. Outside. Did you see something when you came in? We didn't look. Weren't sure if it was safe."

"It's fine," Clara said, her jaw set. She would not imagine Tilly tied to a post and set on fire.

"What *is* going on here, anyway? What happened to my mom?" Thea asked, her voice small.

"There's no time to explain. How many head lamps do we have?" Clara asked as the wind picked up outside the tent.

"Explain," Tilly said, then shrugged. "Quickly."

"All right. Well, you were right. It's my patient, Juliana," Clara said, breathless.

"But she's dead," Tilly responded.

"Not anymore. She used Na—She found a way to come back. And now she wants to bring back her family. And we will not be here for it. How many headlamps do we have?"

"Do we really need to leave now?" Maddy pulled her blanket up to her chin while Aiden dug through their piles of blankets for the lights.

"This tent is zero protection," Tilly said. "Zero. If Mom says we're leaving, we're leaving." She gave Clara a determined look and then slithered out the tent opening, her leg dragging behind her. "What the fuck? It's snowing. And what the hell are those?" she asked as her eyes fell on the poles.

"You don't want to know," Clara said, scooting out after her. She helped Maddy and Thea out, and they huddled against Tilly on the ground.

Tilly pressed herself up to standing. Aiden crawled out last, his hand full of head lamps.

"There's only two headlamps and a lantern," he said and handed the lantern to Thea. "And I've got the food too."

"It's all right," Clara said. "I have one in my backpack."

It took Clara a moment to understand the kids' confused faces until she remembered they hadn't seen the pack before.

"Whose backpack is that, Mom?" Maddy asked.

Clara fumbled. "I . . . don't exactly know. I found it. I think it might be—"

"Found it?" Tilly echoed.

"Yes. I found it."

"But who did it belong to?" Tilly asked. "Where are they?"

"It doesn't matter. I think—" *they're dead*, she was about to say. But cut herself short. "There was no one around."

Tilly scoffed. "So it's Juliana's then. Dumped after she killed that dude."

"Matilda, that is not—"

"*Oh Claaaaara . . .*" The voice rode on the wind, weaving in and out of the trees.

The kids all froze, huddling closer to each other as though pulled by some unseen force.

"She probably found you by tracing her backpack," Tilly scoffed.

"If Mom were here—" Thea whimpered.

"But she's not," Aiden said in a whisper, then reached over and squeezed her hand after he saw her face crumple. "If Mom were here she'd want us to do whatever we could to survive. I'm here, Thea. You can do this. *We* can do this. We have to." Thea gave a nod.

Tilly leaned close to Clara. "The landslide—"

"We'll find a way to pass it. We have to," Clara insisted, pulling the other kids to their feet. "Get ready to run."

Tilly slid her hand into Clara's and whispered, "All right then. Let's do this."

CHAPTER THIRTY-FOUR

"*CLARAAAAAAA!*" JULIANA'S VOICE was closer, but thankfully didn't seem to be moving very fast. Clara hoped she was still finding her legs, not able to run, but she wasn't all that familiar with the process of being birthed from blood-soaked dirt.

She grabbed Maddy and Thea. "Go!" she called and pulled them in what she hoped was a path that would angle down toward the river, bypassing the rocky descent with the chain. And, more importantly, in a direction she hoped was *away* from Juliana. Aiden and Tilly were right behind them, leaning on each other for support. They whipped through the woods, her feet sliding and sloshing on the new snow, what must have already been four inches' worth. It piled into her boots, freezing her ankles. How could so much snow have fallen in such a short amount of time? Flakes of it lined her lashes, making it impossible to see in the dark. They ran blind and all she knew was that they were headed downhill. But Juliana kept pace, calling her name every few seconds in that rasping crypt voice. Clara wondered where Eleanor had disappeared to.

As though summoned, she caught a flicker of light to her left, a pale flame making its way through the woods on an interception course for Juliana. Thank goodness. They may make it out of this after all.

But then something swooped from above and clawed a chunk out of her cheek. She stumbled, losing her daughter's hands and flying forward. Her face stung and blood trickled down her neck. "Get down!" she screamed. The owl swooped again, this time only getting her arm. A voice thundered through the forest, almost coming from the ground itself and vibrating up through her bones.

We grow stronger. You will release us. I will peel the skin off your body. I will rip the flesh from your bones. I will feast on your entrails and burn your bones. I will bleed you dry, lap up every drop. I will devour you. The forest will absorb you. And you will birth us afresh.

Clara's head felt like it would explode, like a loudspeaker was rammed inside where her brain should have been, sound waves near to shattering her skull. Bile rose in her throat, her body rejecting every command she gave it, muscles twitching out of control. It wasn't Juliana—this was something more powerful, something older. And angrier.

The owl shrieked. Wings battered the side of her head. She raised her hands again to protect her face, to fend it off. Talons ripped through her jacket, sliced long, bloody streaks into her forearm. She cried out into the darkness, trying to locate the kids. Lantern light on a bloody patch of snow. Thea's face, eyes aflame. White feathers, snowflakes in the air.

Then it all stopped. The shrieking owl, the battering wings. A hand wrapped around Clara's bleeding forearm. A panicked grunt in the cold. Clara focused then on Thea, the broken lantern in one hand, the other hand trying to stem the thick, crimson fluid leaking through the jagged tears of Clara's jacket. On the snow at her feet, the gigantic owl lay, wings spread wide in lifeless flight.

Thea took a moment to catch her breath. "I hit it. I hit it with the lantern." She hiccuped then, and Clara wasn't sure if it was from the cold, the terror, or the idea of killing this beautiful creature.

"It wasn't just an owl," Clara said reassuringly. The owl's head lay motionless, its single, lifeless eye trained on Clara. Dizziness began to set in.

"Mom!" Her girls ran up with Aiden. The falling snow reflected the light from their two headlamps, twinkling like shooting stars.

"Shit," Aiden said. He moved behind her and she felt the backpack sway and pull as he dug out the first aid kit. "We don't have enough gauze for this. This is . . . this is beyond what our kits can handle. We've used so much already," he said, swallowing.

"Hang on," Tilly said, and Clara felt her digging around in the backpack. She handed Aiden a crumpled T-shirt, pulled from the depths of Juliana's pack. Clara hoped it wasn't too mildew-covered. "Let's wrap it as best we can and get the fuck out of here."

Aiden gave a nod and set to work wrapping a shirt around Clara's arm, not even bothering to have Clara take off her jacket. "Press it down. As hard as you can. Shit. I can see the bone. I don't know. I'm sorry, Clara."

"Thank you. It helps." She realized how much pressure she was putting on these kids. But it didn't matter, they had to get out. They'd already proven they were survivors. And so was she.

"Now we keep moving." She swayed a bit on her feet but then found a point of focus and steadied. Her arm pulsed in time with her heart, her fingertips growing cold and numb.

Tilly slipped on the snow, and Aiden caught her. "I won't leave you behind again," he said quietly.

Tilly nodded, her jaw set and gaze distant, but she whispered, "Friends to the end, no matter what."

Movement on the edges of Clara's vision made her turn. At first she thought it might just be a side effect of her blood loss, but then she saw it. There, through the trees, lumbered the old bear she'd seen near the cabin. One eye was trained on her, the other a murky white. The face jogged a memory loose, her vision of the old lady, frying pan in her hand dripping onto the ground below, and a large gash through one of her eyes.

The one-eyed owl, the one-eyed bear, the one-eyed woman. They were one and the same. Clara swallowed, her body tensed, still eyeing the bears. The smaller one trailed behind its mama. They were still far enough off that the others hadn't noticed yet, nothing more than a large shadow between the trees.

"Everyone okay? Let's keep going." She had been in these woods too long to assume that just because they'd beaten one owl, the forest would let them go easily.

They ran in silence, nothing but the sound of snow crunching underfoot and their breath, haggard and heavy. Clara let the children go first, so she could see them. Aiden and Tilly led the way, Tilly leaned on Aiden's shoulder, both limping as though in some macabre three-legged race. Then Maddy and Thea, one after the other, stumbling and stiff, running half asleep.

Clara tried to imagine how they could get out of here. They couldn't outrun Juliana forever. They'd left the tents. Left the sleeping bags. Aiden managed to grab the food, but they were still days from anywhere. She couldn't afford to think like that though. She had the beacon, useless as it might be. And they had each other. She wouldn't let herself be pulled down by doubt. They *would* make it, Clara told herself. Like a chant inside her head. Even the squeaking compressions of the snow seemed to say it.

We can make it. We can make it. We can make it.

But then Aiden and Tilly stopped short. So short Maddy ran into them, dazed. Clara followed the line of Tilly's headlamp to a shadow ahead of them. The bear's head was much larger up close, its one eye easily the size of a baseball. Snow covered its matted fur.

A cloud of steam puffed from the bear's nostrils, and a low growl filled the air like growing thunder.

"Mom," someone said in a small voice. Clara wasn't sure if it was her own child or one of Naomi's, but it didn't matter now. She was the only mom left. Clara positioned herself in front of the kids, a shield between these beasts and them. The larger bear exhaled another puff of steam that carried the scent of death. It took a step forward and Clara backed up a few feet, the kids stumbling back behind her.

The snow swirled around them, the wind sending it in spirals, stinging against their cheeks. She knew the conventional wisdom when confronting a black bear was to stay, make yourself as big and loud as possible to scare it away.

But Clara also knew these were no ordinary bears.

"The other way," she whispered. "Run."

They spun and sprinted back the way they came, the bear lumbering behind them, hot, putrid breath on Clara's back. It should have been able to catch them—every time she slipped, Clara imagined its strong jaws clamping around her—but it only kept pace with them. *We're being herded*, she thought, as the younger bear began to swerve back and forth around their flanks, nipping at their heels.

As the unnatural posts came into view again, speckled white with the driving snow, Clara knew exactly where they were being herded. Back to camp.

A fire was lit in the fire ring Maddy and Thea had built only a few days before, back when Naomi was alive and Clara thought they might actually survive. But now, at the sight of it, all of Clara's hope froze over. They would die here. They would burn here.

Piles of sticks and branches had been lain at the base of each post, pyres ready to be lit. Clara swallowed down a scream. Maddy's fingers clamped onto her good wrist, and Clara knew she had to be strong for the girls, for Aiden, for all of them.

A shadow flickered in front of the campfire, drawing Clara's eyes. Juliana stepped toward them, her body so covered in mud and blood one could barely tell she wore no clothes. Her hair hung down in clumps, running red rivulets over her shoulders and down her arms.

She grinned, her teeth matching the snow. "You thought sending that decrepit echo of a ghost after me would save you?" she asked. "But no. Too bad for you. She only strengthened me."

Juliana brought her hands from behind her back and showed the journal Clara had returned to Eleanor. "*Her* power is my power now, however little. She was always so weak, never really seeing the potential for growth. Content to snip flowers and brew potions to make people feel good. That's not real power. *Real* power is coming back from the dead. *Giving* life." She turned her grin on the kids then and snapped her fingers. "And taking it away."

Clara grit her teeth. "We can just walk through her," she said, trying to make herself believe it, even after all she'd seen. "I've done it before. She's just a ghost."

Like a flash, Juliana's arm whipped out and grabbed Maddy by the throat, her pale, bony fingers digging into the soft flesh there. Maddy cried out and thrashed against Juliana, her eyes going wide.

Clara screamed and lunged forward, but Juliana raised a hand and her body stopped suddenly, as though frozen in cement.

"I have my body back now. You can't walk through me. And I am more powerful than ever. The forest runs through my veins now, feeding me, giving me new life. Eleanor's last gift to me."

"Let her go!" Tilly screamed, but Juliana only squeezed Maddy harder. Tilly hesitated, looking sideways at Clara for guidance.

"I got this," Clara said. She thought of all she'd read in Eleanor's journal, thought of Eleanor herself and her peaceful demeanor. As in the cabin, she heard the trees' whispers, felt their roots growing beneath her, their power running up through her feet like a surge.

Slowly, Clara felt the hold on her weakening—or rather, she realized she had the strength to push against it. She pressed forward, as though in slow motion. She was getting closer to Juliana, so close now. She would tear Juliana apart. She would do whatever it took to save Maddy. She was close enough now to reach a hand out and grasp it around Juliana's wrist.

And that's when the trees began to move.

CHAPTER THIRTY-FIVE

Vancouver, BC
May 12, 2018

On my walk this morning, I found a dying heron. She lay half submerged in the marshy edge of the pond, neck and head stretching for dry land. There was little I could do to save the beautiful creature. My mother would have said it is an omen. She would probably be right.

I believe I have finally lost her for good. Juliana has left us before, for days at a time, returning gaunt and distracted. But now she has been gone for over a week, long enough that Donald has finally convinced me to file a missing person's report. I never wanted to involve the police before, always trusting that she would return peacefully on her own. But now, I think she is truly gone. I feel it in my bones.

I also know that I will not last much longer. Every year, my spirit crosses further into the afterlife, and my child Marie has been visiting me in my dreams, telling me comforting stories of what lies ahead for me. This time, when Juliana returns—if she does—I may not be here to receive her again. I know Donald will do his best to show her the love she deserves, but she is a difficult person to love, and always has been.

I only hope that she will find her own peace out there in the world.

⟶⟵

Vancouver, BC
June 20, 2018

She has returned! My eyes are filled with tears as I write. She has returned to me changed. Juliana knocked on our door early yesterday morning—Donald and I were still taking our coffee at the kitchen table. When she entered, she presented me with a bouquet of flowers and herbs, and she asked me if she could return to being my apprentice. It is hard for me to move around now, so the extra help in the greenhouse and around the house is of course needed. It has been a joy to have her around these past few days. She has even begun asking me more about my sister and grandmother. It has been so healing for me to speak aloud about these things that we all endured. I showed her the maps of where our dear old cottage lay. I even have an old photograph of Mother on the front stoop that Juliana took a particular interest to.

I am finally content, and I am sure I will see my daughter Marie in the afterlife soon, knowing that I may leave Juliana to carry on our line.

CHAPTER THIRTY-SIX

CLARA HEARD IT before she saw it. Behind the *pat-pat-pat* of something dripping onto snow, a faint creaking noise grew louder. Like a long-rusted door hinge groaning into action, but lower and earthier. The rumble built, she could feel it under her feet now, a kind of jerky vibration. It felt different from the smooth ebb and flow of the trees she had experienced moments before. This was something natural behaving unnaturally.

Juliana grinned that grin again and released both Clara and Maddy at once, letting Maddy crumple to the snowy ground at her feet. Clara dove forward and pulled a shaking, coughing Maddy into her lap, tears rushing down her cheeks.

Then she saw it, the roots pushing up through the snow, sinewy like snakes but rough with bark. The air filled with sparkles of ice dust and shed snow as the tree branches lowered, groaning, to link with the rising sinews, creating a kind of cage around them.

"You have no idea what it's like, feeling this singeing fire in your veins your whole life," Juliana said. "You all will be my salvation.

You always did want to save me, right Clara? They're growing stronger." Clara followed Juliana's gaze to the shadows beyond the firelight where the old woman and her daughter approached, their eyes flashing. Clara looked around for the bears, but they seemed to have vanished. "And once you burn, the trade will be complete. They'll return and I'll finally be free."

The specter of the old woman raised her hands and the roots creating their cage broke form and snaked around their wrists and arms instead.

"You're right," Clara said, desperate as the roots dragged her and her children across the snow and toward the poles. Her voice shook, the blisters on her back rubbing rough against the ground. "I have no idea what it feels like. But I know how it feels to want to save your family. You're doing the wrong thing by taking mine away. This isn't the way to restore balance. It's not the way to bring peace. You're just propagating the cycle!"

Juliana grunted a laugh. "Oh, Clara, Clara, Clara and your big, big heart." She shook her head. "I'm not trying to bring peace. Or restore balance. Or whatever fucked up shit my grandmother would have called it. I'm only trying to end *my* pain. No one ever cared about *my* suffering."

"*I* cared, Juliana. Don't you remember? I cared for you!"

Juliana shook her head, clicking her tongue. "Nope. No, no, no, Clara. You cared about yourself. Doing better at your job. Making yourself feel better for 'fixing' my situation. You didn't actually care about me. I was a tool you wanted to use."

"No. You're wrong." Clara thrashed against her bonds.

"Only my Great-Grandma cared. Only she and Auntie told me how. Which is more than Grandma El ever did."

The roots tightened and Clara saw her children—all four of them now—ripped off the ground and thrust against the poles, arms tightened behind them. The forest filled with their screams and Clara felt a violent, protective rage boiling within her, but there was no outlet for it. She was stuck fast, her torn and bloodied arms pressed rough against the pole behind her. She seethed, the children's screams only intensifying her rage.

"You feel it now, don't you?" Juliana asked, striding up to Clara's pyre. She sniffed the air beside Clara's cheek. "I can smell it. The fire inside you. You'd do anything to help the ones you love. You'd do *anything* to stop that burning, even if it meant tearing the world apart. Isn't that right?"

Clara shook her head, but Juliana's words cut her deep, seeing right through her.

"I don't know why my grandmother didn't feel it."

Blood dripped near Clara's feet and she saw it was dripping from Juliana's hands down into the snow. *Pat-pat-pat.* She couldn't possibly still be so covered in Naomi's blood that it dripped off her in those quantities. And besides, it would be coagulated by now. No, it looked like the blood was coming from Juliana herself, oozing from her pores and running down her face and limbs. Her skin was sallow and waxen. Clara had the impression that if she pressed into it, her finger would just keep going, as though pressing into a piece of Play-Doh the girls used to have when they were younger.

"Your grandmother tried to help you," Clara said. "She seemed like a good woman." Though Clara hadn't known her, she felt a sadness at the thought that Eleanor was gone for good.

Juliana scoffed. "She *denied* me." She tilted her head to the side, her eyes sparking in the moonlight. "Do you know the suffering I've been through? And all that woman did to help me was read me books and feed me tea. Pathetic waste of a witch, if you ask me. All the while, my blood was literally boiling in my veins. Do you know what that feels like?"

"I don't," Clara said, feeling her own blood escape the bandages, her arm growing colder with each pulse. She wondered if maybe she did know what it felt like though—that constant pressure to be what Emilio wanted, to be there for Maddy, to keep Tilly from straying. The constant pressure to do better at her job. To be good enough. Did she not feel a pain under her skin everyday as well? Tiny splinters in her heart? "It must have been awful," she whispered, tears in her eyes.

"I just wanted her to love me. To listen to me," Juliana said through gritted teeth. "Instead, she gave me flowers to eat and sang to me and braided my hair as though that would make me a normal girl."

"She *did* love you. So, so much." Clara thought about all the times she stood outside Tilly's slammed door, wanting to knock, wondering how to reach in. Always saying the wrong thing. Doing the wrong thing.

"She did not." Juliana opened Eleanor's journal, which she'd retrieved again, and flipped through the pages. "Listen to this: *If only she could be like the other children. If only she could make friends. If only she could be like my Marie.* 'My Marie,' she wrote, meaning my mother. Who died giving birth to me. You have no idea what it's like living under that shadow of blame for your own parent's death. After that, how could I ever be good enough? Not even trying to bring back her sister and mother could erase that kind of guilt."

Clara straightened up. She imagined she could see the faint form of her father just off behind Tilly's hammock. "Juliana, you know that was not your fault."

"Thank you, Dr. Gomez, but your psychoanalytical assurances would never change Eleanor's mind. And it doesn't matter now, since she'll be gone soon."

Soon. Not already, Clara realized with a flicker of hope.

Juliana held the journal out over the fire. "I can return her to just an echo. And then erase that as well."

"No!" Clara cried. "You won't . . . It won't make things better." She worked her wrists painfully against the bonds around her. The bark dug into her skin, chafing and leaving little room for escape. She kept snagging on the bone of her thumb. Stuck, stuck, stuck. "Juliana, please let us go. You've come back. Please spare us."

"This isn't about you, Clara."

With that, Juliana turned away and beckoned the old woman and her daughter closer. They both raised their arms and flames began to lick the edges of the pyres.

"No!" Clara screamed, trying to see all four of the children at once.

"Mom!" One of the kids screamed.

She was the one in charge. She had to save them. This was the weight of responsibility, the force grinding her down all along. But was it not also the force that moved her forward, like wind in a sail, speeding her along and giving her direction? If she gave into the weight of it, arranged her sails just right, could she use it to her advantage, rather than letting it capsize her? No sense in fighting against the forces of nature. It was all right there in front of her all along.

The men who hunted down the mother and girls in these woods, who burned them for being unnatural. *They* defied nature, those men. And they left that energy here, like a bloody boot print. Left it on the women who burned, the one who got away, and on down through their blood to Juliana, like an infection.

And the women left in the woods, Marie and her mother. After decades of being left to rot in the festering wound the men left behind, well, their desires became distorted and demented. They wanted to escape, to live again—who wouldn't, of course—and to seek revenge.

Clara knew about being left to fester and rot. About having to pick up the pieces of someone else's mess.

Juliana may be controlling the forest now, but she was pushing against it, bending it to her will, rather than letting it unfold as nature had intended. But maybe true nature was stronger than that. She thought about rivers diverting around obstacles. Diverting around whole fucking landslides.

She relaxed her hands, stopped pressing her wrists against the restraints. She took a deep breath and exhaled, then pulled her bad arm up and out of the hooked root in a swift motion.

She felt the pop up to her shoulder, her thumb dislocating and allowing her to slide her hand out. She let out a small cry, but none of the others seemed to notice, so intent they were on watching the flames grow higher around the children. Clara held in a sob and grasped at the knife on her waist with four numb fingers and no thumb.

She managed to grab it out and wrenched her body around so she could hack at the root holding her left hand. With each slam of the knife against it, the root tightened until it squeezed against her wrist and she could feel her pulse in her fingertips. She dropped the knife and began to pull at the root with her numb fingers and flopping thumb. It didn't give, holding tight as though the bonds were made of iron rather than wood.

Clara was seeing stars now, exhaustion and blood loss setting in. Her mind began to spin with crazy ideas, desperate thoughts. She had to get the tree to release her. She would not die here. Juliana had said something about gaining Eleanor's power of the forest by taking her journal.

Maybe some of that had rubbed off on her in the time she spent carrying the journal, Clara thought. Maybe that was why she'd started hearing the whispers in the pine needles and imagining the roots swelling underground.

She let out a long exhale and tried to find her calm. *Breathe in, breathe out*, she told herself in her best therapist voice. She tried to let go of the rage inside her and listen, really listen to what was around her. With one last desperate effort, Clara put her forehead against the root and inhaled deeply. "Please," she sobbed. "Please let me go. You need to rest. Go back underground and rest. You don't want to be doing this. Please, please let go and go back to your home."

At first, as the pressure in her wrist released, Clara thought she must be dreaming. But then it slid away from her with a *plop* and buried itself underground. Clara's heart leapt. She wiggled her wrist and ankles and, emboldened, stepped forward. She bent low to the ground and slid her hands beneath the snow, tears of pain and terror streaking through the dried blood and mud on her cheeks. She dug her fingers into the ground.

She breathed into the pines and firs around her, felt it like a flow, like rushing through water, speeding with the wind at her back. She felt the trees' own heartbeat, nutrients running root to tip. The ground began to warm under her touch, and she saw the bonds around the kids soften and loosen before collapsing into the flames below.

"No," Juliana said. "*No.*" The snow crunched and shifted as the roots retreated from around the children, sliding back into the ground, where they'd lain before Juliana and her aunt had pressed them to violence. "You haven't given it anything," Juliana hissed. "The forest shouldn't listen to you."

"I'm letting nature return to balance," Clara said. "A wise woman once told me that the forest answers to no one."

"Unless you make it," Juliana whispered.

The kids all fell to their knees amid the flames at their feet. Clara couldn't get up, couldn't move to pull them out but trusted them to come to her.

The roots continued to recede. Juliana hunched in the flickering fire light, her skin taking on a yellow sheen and sagging slightly. Purple divots formed around her eyes. "You have no idea what you're doing. No idea of what balance means," Juliana cried.

Clara looked over at the old, one-eyed woman. Her form flickered a few times, like an old movie, her teeth gritted.

The little girl beside her looked at Clara and gave a barely perceptible nod. The children converged on Clara, Thea and Maddy crying into her lap. Aiden helped Tilly, as she couldn't put any weight on her ankle anymore.

Clara put a hand out to Thea and Maddy. "Shh, shh, you're going to be okay."

When she looked up, Juliana was advancing on Aiden and Tilly with hobbling steps. Her own blood leaked from her eyes and nose now, her teeth stained red with it. Tilly grabbed Aiden's hand. "Mom?" she called.

"I think it's okay." Clara rode the wave of calm that followed after returning nature to its place. "They can't hurt us anymore. I think they're weakening."

"But the trees . . ."

"The forest is released from her contro—"

Before Clara finished, a black root snaked up from beneath the snow cover—small, not even an inch in diameter—and rammed through Aiden's chest.

It emerged, slick and dripping from his back. His face went slack, almost white as the snow, then his form fell, taking the murderous root with it.

Tilly's screams filled the night. Clara was motionless. Mind blank, jaw slack. Paralyzed once again by another bad decision.

"DO NOT UNDERESTIMATE ME!" Juliana's voice was thunder. Clara felt it deep within her, the thrumming bass shaking her insides. "You think because you borrowed some sort of power from my weak old grandmother that you released the forest from *me?* From *her?*" Juliana pointed to where her one-eyed great-grandmother stood.

The old woman advanced again and more roots snaked up through the snow, thin and sinewy, hovering in front of them, like tentacles ready to strike.

Juliana continued. "She has been a part of this forest for generations. One little party trick that you can't even control is nothing against her power."

Tilly lay hunched, still screaming, trying to wake up an Aiden who would never wake again. Thea stood stricken, tears streaming over her cheeks.

She'd lost everything. Maddy huddled on the ground, hands over her face.

Clara had failed them.

She looked up at Juliana. The black specter of grief surrounding her as it had at their first meeting. Growing, growing, nearly taking over, like a dark flame obliterating the forest behind her. Clara couldn't imagine so much pain.

"Loss doesn't have to define you, Juliana," Clara whispered, her voice wavering through her tears. "You are loved. Your grandmother loved you. I loved you."

The roots faltered, but recovered themselves, inching closer.

"I don't want to be alone anymore." Juliana took a step forward, raising her arms.

Clara nearly squeezed her eyes closed, ready to give in, ready for the end. But in the distance, she saw a flickering flame dancing against the trees. "Wait!" she cried, buying time. "Your grandmother. She's back. Ask her! Ask her if she felt the way you think she did."

"My grandmother is gone. I told you."

"So were you," Clara replied. "And here you are."

The bloody woman's eyes flicked over to the flames, the black specter of grief pulling back, condensing and swirling like smoke. Tentative. The old woman lowered her arms as well and looked at Juliana.

Eleanor. Her voice shook, frail and quiet like a dried leaf on a branch. *You did not tell me she was here, Juliana. Did you keep her from me? My daughter?*

"She isn't! She's just an echo! Eleanor is gone and, besides, she never wanted to help you anyway. *I* did. *I* made the sacrifices! Grandma wanted to leave you to rot."

The flames grew nearer, and girl Eleanor's form within became visible. She saw them and changed course, coming closer. Clara wasn't sure what kind of aid she could hope for now that Eleanor was reduced to her echo form again, but she was grateful if only for the distraction. Shaking, she gathered Maddy and Thea to their feet, and called to Tilly. Tilly's face was swollen and tear streaked, but she wore the mask of someone who had reached the limit of their tears.

"Get ready to run," she whispered.

Tilly glanced back to where Aiden's body lay. A growing circle of red spread out beneath him, melting the snow. "But—"

"He's gone, Tills," Clara said, putting a hand on her daughter's shoulder. A wave of sadness and exhaustion washed through her, and she didn't fight it, but rode it, letting the tears fall silent and wet across her cheeks.

Juliana's eyes remained trained on the flaming girl.

"Because of you, I'm all alone," her voice trickled through the trees like tears, icicles tinkling.

I told you before. You were never alone, the flaming girl responded. *I am always here for you. I always have been. Come with me. Come home.*

"But your mother? Your sister, Marie? You're going to let them stay here, endure this torture for eternity?"

Girl Eleanor turned to the old woman and the child. She took the other little girl's hand—her sister. *I've missed you, sister. Come with me. Come with me where we're meant to go.*

The younger girl nodded and left her hand in Eleanor's. She looked up at her mother, whose face remained unreadable.

"No!" Juliana said. "No! Don't leave me here. You're meant to come with *me*! I'm bringing you back"

Eleanor took Juliana's hand in her free one, and the blood began to wash away, revealing the haggard, exhausted woman beneath. Signs of rot dotted her forehead and arms. Clumps of hair fell from her head.

Our power flows like a river. I have guided my own boat on it, and tried to teach you to guide yours. But we do not fight the river's flow. We must let them rest. We cannot bring them back. Come with me, and I will show you. We must all rest now.

The roots that had been poised to attack Clara and the kids began to sag, limp and listless. Juliana's eyes filled with tears, but the one-eyed woman stepped forward.

No, Eleanor, her voice thundered. *There is no rest after what we've endured. There is no other ending to this story. We are coming back, my daughter.* The roots tensed once again.

Clara didn't wait another second. She grabbed two hands, ignoring the pain searing through her thumb, told Tilly to go, and they ran. Unnatural shrieks and groaning trees and tinkling ice crystals chased them through the snow, but she did not turn back.

"To the river," she whispered, and they ran through the darkness.

Only the cloud-streaked moon and the dim flames from far behind them guided their way.

CHAPTER THIRTY-SEVEN

THE RUMBLES AND screeches grew closer behind them as they ran. Clara turned back only once and saw the forest undulating in the silver light. They were coming.

"Faster," Clara demanded, her voice hoarse with the effort. "To the waterfall."

They reached the clearing. The storm had subsided and moonlight glinted off the freshly fallen snow. Clara felt echoes of a few days before, as though she could see a shadowy replay of Naomi going over the falls and disappearing below.

Then the image of her broken body flashed through Clara's consciousness. She swallowed it down, trying to focus on what was before her eyes. They could do this—they could escape. Follow the flow. That was what Eleanor had said. The river. It had to be the river.

"What now?" Maddy asked, shaking.

Clara eyed the edge of the rocks, the rapids roaring at them, screaming the answer. Doubts began to seep under her skin.

"Mom?" Tilly asked, waiting for Clara's instruction. She slid a hand into Clara's.

"We jump," Clara said.

"But my mom—" Thea began.

Clara shook her head. "I think your mom climbed out of the river and tried to—" Clara cut off. She didn't want to say *tried to come back to us* because those words wrenched something painful in her chest. "I think the river itself is safe."

"Safe?" Maddy asked, peering down at the whitewater with big eyes.

"Well, relatively," Clara said, with a glance over her shoulder.

"It's either chance the friendly rapids or stay here with the creepy witch bitches that just tried to burn us at the stake. I'm ready to jump," Tilly said.

"I don't think—" Thea started through her shivers. "We'll all die. The river killed my—My mom is dead because of this river. *Dead.*" The last word ended in a sob.

"No," Clara shook her head. "Your mom made it out downriver. I saw her footprints. She climbed out and made it back into the woods. But then—"

"If she hadn't, then maybe . . ." Thea trailed off, wiping her eyes with the back of her sleeve.

Clara nodded. "Maybe."

"We need to decide now." Maddy pointed back the way they'd come, where the trees writhed, twisting themselves together, the forest roiling like a sea. A tsunami of trees and roots edging ever closer.

From the turbid darkness, the girl in flames emerged. Juliana trailed behind, no longer bloody, just haggard and stumbling. She fell to her knees on the rocks, her bare arms bruised. Tears streamed across her pockmarked cheeks. She screamed in frustration and anguish, like an animal's cry piercing the night air. Clara felt it in her bones. The loss, the pain, the confusion and doubt. The regret of taking the wrong path. She knew it, like a familiar stray cat that always hovered around her back door. She and Juliana weren't so different, in a way. Always clinging to things in the past rather than making something of their future. Always feeling trapped in their own pain.

Behind her, as if on cue, the other two figures emerged from the woods like a tempest. The old lady spoke, her voice like an echo off the far mountains. *No one can leave until we're free.* The ground began to shake, pebbles near Clara's feet shifting and sliding over the edge of the falls.

It's time to rest, Mother, Eleanor said.

There is no rest for us, who have been burning for an eternity. Clara felt a heat emanating from the rocks at her feet. A strange light began to flicker across her vision, and she realized trees were bursting into flames. First one, then a handful, then it grew. *All will burn here today. Help us, Juliana. Help us.*

Juliana hunched further, hands on the rocks, skin slackening off her bones. She coughed, and blood spattered the rocks. "I just don't want to be alone," she whispered.

You won't be alone, the old lady boomed, and the fire beyond the tree line burst toward the sky in a great mushroom cloud that then began to morph and change direction, headed straight for Clara and the kids.

"Okay," Clara whispered. "We jump."

They linked hands, pain lancing through Clara's broken thumb, and plunged into the darkness over the falls.

THE FREE FALL over the edge of the falls was longer than she had anticipated. Her daughters' screams filled her ears, mingled with her own until it twanged like a too-tight guitar string. And then the smack of the water. Enough force to knock someone out, enough to knock all of their hands free. Untethered, Clara plunged beneath the waves, flailing, forgetting where she was, spinning in the darkness. She wanted to scream. But she was underwater. After all they'd been through, she had lost them again, lost herself.

Just when she thought she would never find her way in the churning water, her head broke through the surface of the churn.

"Matilda!" she cried out over the water's roar. "Madison! Thea!"

Darkness surrounded her, apart from the sparkle of moon against the white rapids. The current pushed her downstream at an alarming rate. The waterfall faded from view as the cold water enveloped her.

She struggled, reaching out for rocks or other debris with her good hand, desperate to stop herself and find the children. The current was too fast, like a driving force. She simply could not fight against it. So, eventually she didn't. She remembered the words Juliana's grandmother spoke about sailing her own boat down the current. She didn't fight it, just let it be. *Trust the river's flow.*

A calm descended over her. She no longer felt jostled, but delivered, transported. She was buoyant and free. Near her, a head popped to the surface, Maddy. She grasped her hand firmly. Another wave of relief. "Don't fight it," Clara yelled to her over the waves.

She scanned the surface of the water once more, waves writhing and diving over each other. Tilly and Thea clung to rocks downstream, battered by the force of the water. Clara guided Maddy there as best she could. "Let go!" she cried to the other two girls. Thea's eyes were wild with terror. She shook her head, wet curls swinging around her. Tilly made her way across a fallen tree to where Thea still clung, and they made the leap together.

The current brought them all to each other. Linking hands, they let the river deliver them from the forest. Clara had to hope it happened quickly. Her toes were numb. All of their lips were blue. The riverbanks sped by in a white blur of snow and ice as the sun rose on them.

By the time the river had pulled them past the edge of the forest and they flowed along to more populated areas, Clara was barely able to breathe. Each inhale felt like glass shards in her lungs. She was cold, so cold. They had all managed to stay together, clinging to each other's hands with numb fingers. Clara's mind churned slowly, barely processing the transition from wild to urban. Buildings began to slide by, and trees done up with their fall foliage. No snow at this elevation.

Further down, a walking path appeared along the riverside. Clara saw the early morning walkers out, rain jackets on and hoods up. She called out, but her voice came out like the squeak of a rusted wheel. Tilly stirred beside her and pointed. A couple, old enough to be Clara's parents. In matching blue jackets and rain boots. The woman held the leash of a border collie while the man carried some kind of ball throwing device. Tilly cried out, louder than Clara had managed. "Help!"

The border collie perked its ears and began to bark, pulling the flustered woman toward the riverbank. Just as they flowed past her, Clara saw her mouth widen in surprise. She called to her husband, who pulled out a phone. They ran alongside the river, trying to keep up with the four of them, but the current was too fast, too strong. Soon the couple was out of view.

But Clara would always remember them as her rescuers. As the couple slid out of view, the river widened and flattened, creating more rocky outcrops and banks for them to grab onto. They washed up on one such pebble-covered beach in the middle of the river and Clara helped drag the children up out of the water. An autumn wind blew against their sodden clothing, making them shiver even more than they had in the water.

Clara gathered them in her arms, huddling them all together to conserve warmth, and they sank down to the ground. She couldn't run for help because her legs were barely functioning, muscles twitching madly or not responding at all. She tried to talk, but the shivers wracking her body made it impossible. Instead, she squeezed the three girls tighter. *We made it,* her mind chanted. *We made it. We made it.* She could cry she was so relieved.

The next few hours seemed to happen in flashes, like the blinking red lights of the emergency vehicles. Crinkling silver blankets, small sips of water, stretchers, questions. Jay's face shimmered in and out of her view. Holding the beacon. Shaking it. Shaking his head. Had she already told him about Naomi? She felt dizzy. When they pried her frozen arms from around the girls to put each of them on a separate stretcher, she finally found her voice and screamed and thrashed until someone calmed her.

A day later—or less or more, she really didn't know—she sat in the hospital and marveled at the four white walls around her, the ceiling over her head, as she answered the questions of a young police officer. The woman had a short blond bob, a notebook, and kind eyes. The bed under Clara was soft. Artificial sounds and scents surrounded her. The *beep-beep* of the machine behind her left shoulder. The smell of antiseptic and bleach. Wheels creaking on a linoleum floor.

Somewhere, though, somewhere deep beneath all of that, she could still smell the sweetness of rotting leaves, still hear the rhythmic swish-swish of wings.

The police officer shook her head again and sucked her lips in between her teeth.

"It makes no sense. Why do you have claw slashes on your arms and burns on your back? And the wound in your side is consistent with a knife stab. I don't get it. Were you attacked by an animal, a weapon, or both? Who was out there in the woods with you?"

Clara thought back to what Juliana had said: *What happened to me wasn't just wildlife.*

"There were . . . animals, yes. And I fell, quite a few times." Flashes of writhing roots and rotting bodies flitted behind her eyes. "We were stuck in the storm."

"And we've still not been able to recover the bodies of," she checked her notebook, "Naomi and Aiden Daniels."

"The storm," Clara repeated, her chest clenching. The steady beep-beep of the heart rate monitor began to speed up, and a nurse in blue scrubs popped into the room.

"I think we'll need to break for today, Officer," he said.

"Where are the others who were with you?" the woman asked. But Clara swallowed back a sob and looked out the window. *Where are the others.* The stabs of guilt over not having gotten them all out pierced her more painfully than any of her physical wounds.

But at least they had made it, the four of them. They made it out of the woods. They survived.

CHAPTER THIRTY-EIGHT

CLARA STOOD IN her room, looking out the window over her armchair. Sunlight glinted off the row of cars in the rear parking lot, sending rainbows dancing against her walls. Tilly and Maddy would visit soon, like they did every Monday and Thursday for dinner. Tilly drove them on her own, with her newly acquired license she was so proud of. Clara knew Emilio monitored their progress on the app, both leaving and returning. But at least he let them come. Clara had prepared. She asked the nurse to bring dinner up to Clara's room and to move in a small table, so they could all eat together.

She stood when she heard the knock at the door, and the nurse, Leah popped her head in. Her eyes were large and little scared, as they were every time Leah had come to see Clara, and her long nails were a dark green rather than the bright purple of a few months ago. She stepped to the side and let Tilly and Maddy file into the crowded room. "You guys be good now," she whispered, with a surreptitious glance to Clara before closing the door behind them.

"When can you come home?" Tilly asked, dishing out the cafeteria food onto a plastic plate and passing it to Maddy. "We miss you, Mom."

Clara sighed. She wanted to come home so dearly, but she also had other things on her mind. She cocked her head to the side, listening to the voices. *Come. Come. Come back.*

"Mom?" Maddy jumped in after Tilly's question hung in the air for a few seconds.

"As soon as all the charges are cleared," Clara said, taking a bite of a stale bread roll.

"They can't keep you in here forever," Tilly said. "Even Dad is saying that. If Maddy *and* me *and* Thea all back up your story, why can't they believe that you're innocent?"

Innocent? Clara rolled the word over in her mind, recalling the feel of her hands against Naomi's body moments before she flew over the falls and was swallowed by the river below. Clara let out a laugh at the thought—*innocent!*—startling the girls.

Tilly's brows pinched together. "You okay, Mom?"

"Oh," Clara said. "I'll be fine soon enough. And I'll come home to you both. I promise. Once everything is put in order, I'll be home." She patted Tilly's knee and talk turned to other topics, like Tilly's college acceptances and Maddy's dance recital. The girls stayed longer than usual, wrapping their arms around Clara for long hugs. She loved the smell of their hair, the sound of their voices, the warmth they brought with them. Once they were gone, her room would be quiet and empty again, leaving too much space for the voices to fill up. When the door shut once again between them, the lock sliding into place, Clara's eyes filled with tears. She stared out through the barred window as she watched them get into Tilly's used car and drive away.

Moments later, Leah knocked again. "Ms. Gomez, there's a reporter here to speak with you. Are you up for that?"

Clara nodded. "Yes. I was expecting them. You can let them come right in."

The woman entered hesitantly, pushing her glasses up her nose with one hand while balancing a cell phone on the arm of her chair with the other. Before she turned the recorder on, Clara caught a glimpse of the lock screen photo; the reporter with a teen boy, possibly her son. The hint of a smile quirked on Clara's lips.

"Thank you for being willing to speak with me, Ms. Gomez."

"Please." Clara smiled, showing all of her teeth. "Call me Clara."

The reporter led with the obvious questions, no attempt at subtlety. "What happened in the woods on Broken Trail?"

Clara's tongue probed a hole her teeth had carved near her lip. "What happened to us wasn't just wildlife," she heard herself say.

Another voice filled the void before the reporter's next question: *I was your friend, Clara. Come back for us. Come back for us all.*

"Have you and your son ever been hiking?" Clara leaned forward, toward the other woman.

The reporter pushed her glasses back up her nose and gave an awkward laugh. "Um, not really." She cleared her throat. "Can you tell me anything about Naomi and Aiden? Your friend and her teenaged son who are still missing?"

Clara shook her head, more to clear it from the voices rather than to answer the question. She turned her gaze onto the reporter's green, eager eyes. They demanded an answer from her. She inhaled sharply and responded, "I hope you aren't expecting a survival story. Some of us didn't survive, you know. And those of us who did . . . well . . ."

ACKNOWLEDGMENTS

THIS BOOK IS a kaleidoscopic view of my worst fears, all mixed together and magnified. Considering that, one would think it would have been very difficult to write, but it was deceptively easy (as far as writing books goes!), thanks to my amazing support systems. I would not have been able to do this without you.

First off, I have to thank my mom, who showed me what strength was, and who has always supported my writing efforts without question. Also, thanks to my wonderful family for allowing me to disappear into fantasy lands for hours (okay, fine, *days*) at a time. And thanks to my BFFs Adrienne and Candace, who are fortunately nothing like Naomi.

I can't forget my Coven writing besties: Tanya Pell, Taylor Grothe, Rae Wilde, Jess Mitacek, and Thea Lyons, who supported me through so much more than tricky plot holes and bad syntax. And of course everyone else who read early versions: Poppi Multz, Mo Asher, Vesper Doom, Ellyn Franklyn and more.

I am so grateful for the fabulous editing of Elana Gibson and the long conversations in which she helped me puzzle through the most difficult plot points. And thank you to the team at CamCat Books who have been through so much these past two years and still manage to be supportive as hell.

And thanks to you, dear reader. I never truly believed that my words would be in the hands of a real live person who wandered into a bookstore or library and picked my book off the shelves. It is you most of all who has truly made my dream a reality!

ABOUT THE AUTHOR

AMANDA CASILE HAS been writing stories for as long as she can remember. Her mother still keeps a two-paged story about a lonely unicorn that Amanda penned in kindergarten and read for show and tell. *Broken Trail* is her debut horror novel. (And you won't find any unicorns in it.)

Amanda lives in suburbia with her normal husband, naughty cats, and nice kids. When not writing or spending time with her family, Amanda can be found wandering the woods looking for ghosts.